Holding On To Heaven
Love United Series # 1

Holding On To Heaven

By Melyssa Winchester

Copyright © 2013 Melyssa Winchester

Beautiful Home. Barney E Warren. 1911. Lyrics used by permission.

This book is dedicated to my girls, the ones who work tirelessly with and for their children yet still spare the time to encourage me to follow my dream.

PROLOGUE

Gabriel

Today is a day like no other before it. The preparations are made and the plan now in motion. Heaven is alive with hope at the prospect of what is to come. After careful planning by our Father, change was on the horizon.

"Gabriel, my son, come. Join me and watch as Heaven's greatest gift is unveiled to the world. Today is a day one will not soon forget. You must be a part of it."

I love my father a great deal. More than that, I have the utmost faith in him but there was a small part of me knowing what was to come, that still had my doubts.

"Are you sure she's ready for the magnitude of this endeavor Father? Would she not be better served having more time to prepare?"

"You doubt me Gabriel? Having witnessed what I can do, you fear what we are about to embark on?"

"You know by now that I have the utmost faith in your ability to lead us all sir. I only concern myself with her, as was your intent in giving me my orders was it not? If she is to be the saving grace for the humans and essentially the second coming of Heaven on Earth, should she not be prepared for any and all complications?"

"I would not be secure in sending her if I thought for a second that she wasn't ready. It is her time and she won't be alone. You will be there to guide her down the right path should she falter."

"My greatest achievement has always been the world, as you well know. In recent years, there has been a loss of faith. With her inception we will change that and bring about a better tomorrow for generations to come."

From the moment of my creation, Father told me of the magnificence of Earth and all that inhabited it. In recent years, it seems to be on a rapid decline. Dark forces had begun to descend leaving a great deal of chaos in their wake. After watching and working where we were permitted, it was now time for the bigger picture.

To take the light back from the darkness.

Serenity was such a deserving name for the angelic ball of light that is now set to make her descent upon the Earth. She will restore a sense of peace to a world gone mad and also to a group of Heavenly hosts that were slowly losing their faith.

I have a part to play in this moment as well, more than that of the casual observer. I am to be her guardian. To watch over her as she makes her entrance until the very moment she is called back home. Protecting her and showing her the way. I am tasked just as much as Serenity herself in saving what is left of the world. Not something I took lightly.

It's possible my hesitation was not regarding Serenity and the undertaking at all but centered around my own ability. Could I really follow through and do what Father asked of me? Am I strong enough to hold it all together if for some reason it fell apart?

"My son you must not let the seed of doubt reside within you. Just as I have the utmost faith in Serenity, I also have it in you. Everything you have experienced up until this moment has been to prepare you to take your rightful place by my side. You must not be swayed from that."

It should have come as no shock that he read my mind. All thoughts were visible to the Almighty. There could be no secrets, no thoughts better left hidden. He knew them all. The pride in his voice as he spoke to me from his heart straight to mine was crippling in its intensity.

All any child ever wants is their parent's approval and hearing it from him now, filled with a confidence I had never truly known empowered me. If he believed in me then I could do this. I would do this for him, my brothers and sisters but most of all for the world.

"I will forever cherish your never ending faith in me Father and I will not let you down. I will prove myself worthy."

It is my sacred duty as an agent of Heaven after all.

CHAPTER ONE

Serenity

As far back as I can remember I've heard voices. My earliest memory is the day I turned five. My grandma on my mom's side had passed away a week before. It was at her funeral, when my mom made her way to the casket, my little hand clasped tightly in her own that I heard it. Clear as day, the voice of my grandma, telling me things no five year old should have to hear.

"Serenity dear, do not let your mother fall apart. You must not let the demons take control of her."

I was five. What the hell did I know about demons and for that matter, how I was supposed to stop my mother from falling apart was beyond me. I'm still learning how to tie my own shoes for crying out loud. Stopping a grown adult from doing something they would most likely do anyway wasn't even on my radar.

With what I can only explain as childish naivety, I believed she hadn't really passed away. That she'd actually woken up and spoke the words to me aloud. So I answered her back.

"No Nana. You do it."

Well let me tell you, the last thing you want to do at a funeral is talk to the dead, or rather answer them. My mom wasted no time pulling me away from the casket going so far as to pull me completely from the room, all the while checking to make sure no one else heard my outburst.

"Serenity, what do you think you're doing?"

"Talking to Nana." I replied, as if talking to my dead grandmother was something I did naturally every day.

Oh come on, I was five, what did my mother expect? It wasn't as if at that point I had a lot of knowledge of death to fall back on.

That was my mother's first glimpse of my 'gift'. I'd like to sit here and tell you that it was her last but then I'd be lying.

From that point on it happened more frequently. It grew from being just family members that I could speak with to the most random people. Hospitals were my worst enemy. Between the sick and the dead, it seemed no one there ever knew when to shut up.

By the time I turned twelve my mom had been through enough with me. The excuses I gave didn't fly anymore and it was then that she brought me to the first doctor. She had to be thinking either I was crazy or that she was losing her mind. Neither option more appealing than the other so finding a cause became her life's mission.

We must have gone through six or seven doctors in the first few months alone, all of whom told her I was a perfectly well adjusted young girl with an over active imagination. My mother just wasn't buying it. I can't say I blame her given that I was the one living with the constant barrage of voices in my head. There was no way I could even dream of making up something that level of crazy.

By the time my thirteenth birthday rolled around, I was officially the patient of a psychiatric treatment center. The mission my mother was on finally paid off in that she found the one doctor in our small town of Summerview that believed something really was wrong with me. Maybe she didn't believe that I was crazy but at the very least, I wasn't adjusting the way I should be. So her method of handling it was advising my mother to have me committed.

Summerview Psychiatric Treatment Center became my home for the next two and a half years. As much as you would assume I hated my mom for putting me in a place like that, I actually found myself thankful she did. It was the one place where the voices couldn't get to me.

In my experience when someone is shown something they don't want to see, or rather what they can't handle seeing, the first inclination is to turn away from it. Well in my case it would seem that the minute I walked through the doors of the center, the voices proceeded to do that very thing with me. It's as if I was too crazy for even them to handle. So they left me alone.

It was the best two and a half years of my life.

While the real reason I was in the center remained under wraps it didn't stop the staff from coming up with an adequate diagnosis for what they believed my problem was. The most popular one being that I was schizophrenic. Apparently being able to hear and converse with the dead fell under the umbrella of that particular ailment. I didn't bother fighting the diagnosis. I figured the sooner they labeled me the sooner they'd leave me alone and find someone else to focus their attention on.

To everybody else I was just the girl who heard voices and it seemed to make my attempts at fitting in go that much smoother. It was in one particular group therapy meeting that I met her, the girl that would become my best friend.

Emma Daniels on the outside seemed like most of the kids I'd gone to school with before I'd been taken away. She seemed happy, well-adjusted and for a while I wondered if she was a figment of my imagination given that I couldn't see just what her problem was. We all had our reasons for being there but with Emma, I really couldn't see it. So of course not knowing ate away at me until I finally gave in and went looking for answers.

I know. I could have easily just asked her but what thirteen year old does that? Asking someone what their level of crazy is, well it just wasn't socially acceptable no matter where you happened to be at the time.

Breaking into the records office I found out she was manic depressive with suicidal tendencies. I have to say, I was shocked by given that she displayed no sign of depression in the times I'd been around her. Not even in group, when you were encouraged to talk about your illness, did she ever make one mention of it. It was then that I decided to get to know her. If I was being labeled incorrectly, I had to assume that she was as well. It just made sense to me that we should stick together. So that was exactly what we did. For the next two and a half years we were stuck together like glue.

It hasn't changed much since either.

The day my mother showed up to get me, about three months after my fifteenth birthday I wasn't ready to go. Having gone the entire time being more than just the girl who heard voices, I wasn't ready to accept the change. The doctors explained my progress to my mom though and after a few meetings with the staff, I'd been deemed healthy enough to leave. Provided of course that I remained on the medication I'd been taking since the day I'd been diagnosed.

I followed the rules when I got home but after a while, I gave up on taking the pills, opting instead for going it alone. If I had been able to go almost three years without hearing a voice, maybe now that I was home I really was cured and I'd be able to live a normal life. Or at least as normal a life as a person like me could actually live.

The normal didn't last long. By the time I turned sixteen the voices were back and it seemed even more powerful than before. I heard them so frequently I had a hard time telling where they began and I ended. We became one.

My mother told me once that there hadn't been a moment where she'd been able to get any peace from me. I'd followed her around everywhere. This is what I likened the voices to. At least with my mother she could shut the bathroom door to get away from me. With the voices there was no door. It was free reign even when I didn't want it to be.

Fast forward five years later and I'm about to start my second year of college. I moved out on my own, got a job and been living apart from my very over protective mother for almost two years. It hasn't been easy but I learned quickly to contain my responses to the voices and have even managed to create a relatively normal life for myself. At least that's how it appeared to someone standing on the outside looking in anyway.

There were only two people that knew the truth and one I didn't speak to anymore. The other is Emma. She remained at the center after I left until her release a year after my own. We managed to stay in touch through letters and phone calls once a week. She was never far from my thoughts. I opened up to her in ways that I hadn't been able to do with anyone else and she did much the same with me. We were closer than friends. We were sisters, bonded by our struggles.

When I went away to college I chose one that was close to her. If I had to go through this life with my so called gift then I was going to do it with the one person that understood it.

Our first week back after summer break I heard it for the first time. A new voice, one that in all of the years I'd been hearing them had never come to me before. This voice seemed different than the others. It's stronger; more distinct. He was able reach me even when I was sleeping which is something the other voices have been unable to do. He seemed to want to help me, listen to my thoughts and make sense of the things that up until that point I'd been unable to understand.

A few weeks after he made contact with me I finally broke my silence and told Emma. As much as I trusted her I always assumed there had to be a limit on her understanding and the last thing I wanted to do was alienate the one person that had been there for me.

Turns out, she must have grown a pretty thick skin when it came to my revelations because in telling her, she gave me an alternate way of looking at things.

"So this guy, he talks to you in your sleep?"

"Yeah he does...well no," I backtracked. "Sometimes he sings to me but most of the time he just talks."

"What does his voice sound like?"

"Ems, what kind of question is that? He sounds like a guy. I don't know how else to describe it."

"You tell me you hear a guy in your head and you don't expect me to ask questions like this?"

She had a point. I suppose to the casual observer this might actually sound pretty cool but for me it's become second nature. I didn't put much thought into the sound of the voice speaking to me, or the fact that I had voices speaking to me at all. It was just something that happened and that I dealt with. Emma wasn't like me though, she found it all fascinating.

"So what does he sound like? Is his voice all high pitched like that one kid on the radio or is it all low, sexy and mysterious?"

I knew she wouldn't stop until I told her. She may have issues but in every other way Emma is exactly like the rest of the teenage population. It all came back to how a person looked, spoke and smelled. It's female hormones at their finest.

"It's not high pitched at all. In fact it sounds pretty low key. It's very melodic, calming even. Whenever he talks to me I feel the most relaxed I've probably ever been. Like nothing can get to me. It almost feels dreamlike."

"Ha! I knew it. You like him."

Huh? How did she come to that conclusion?

"How the hell do you get that from what I just said?" I asked rolling my eyes.

10

I knew I wouldn't like her reasoning. I never did when she got this way.

"Oh Emma, he sounds so dreamlike. His voice is calming. He keeps me relaxed. It's so completely obvious that whoever this voice is, you like him."

"You're insane."

"No actually I'm depressed. You know this. You aren't denying it though which is interesting. It looks like my best friend finally has her first crush on a guy."

I didn't often admit this but sometimes I wish I could be more like Emma and see the world the way she does. How she could make fun of her own illness and shrug it off as if it wasn't a problem when given our past together we both knew it was. I eventually got to see the issues she faced when we roomed together during our stay in the center. It wasn't pretty.

Her romantic notions aside though she did help me take my mind off just who the voice was and what he really wanted with me, at least for a minute, which is exactly what I had been hoping for.

"I do not have a crush on the voice in my head Ems." I sighed. "Can we drop it now?"

"Sure but I just want to say one more thing first."

Rolling my eyes at her again, I motioned for her to say her piece.

"You said that he comes to you and keeps you calm right? That he has the ability to block out the other voices and that whenever he's around, you feel almost normal right?"

"Yeah I guess. What are you getting at?"

"What if it's not just a random voice? If he has the ability to cut down on the chatter in your head, maybe he's something more specific."

"More specific how Ems? What exactly do you think he is?"

"Maybe he's your guardian angel."

CHAPTER TWO

Gabriel

I have to hand it to the friend. She figured me out pretty quickly. Not that Serenity was buying any of it. Judging from the look on her face she believed anything but what had just been presented to her. In this case I was thankful for her disbelief because it allowed me to do my job that much easier.

During my time here I have to remain anonymous. I have to be a casual observer, only making my presence known when it is called for. With Serenity in no immediate danger I had to cloak myself. I could not allow her to find out exactly who or what I am. At least not until the time is right.

For the last twenty years I have observed her. I have been with her through the various hardships of her life, especially the ones that seemed to affect her most, like her father disappearing. I was there saving her when she'd been so lost in her own misery that she wanted to give up. Considering that it was against the laws of Heaven for her to pass on before her true time, I had done exactly as instructed.

When she was eight and she'd fallen off her bike, ending up in the hospital for a week, I'd been there. It was actually supposed to be a more serious incident but I intervened. It was what I had been placed here for. Nothing could stand in the way of what she has been placed on Earth to do even though throughout the years she had no idea just what that is.

Serenity knew she was different yet still considered herself imperfectly human. She had no idea of the magnitude of her power and just what she would eventually mean to the world. It is my job as her guardian to make sure that until the time is right, she never would.

What I'd managed to learn about her over the years watching is that she is probably the most uncoordinated person roaming the planet. If I didn't have eyes on her every second, she was bound to walk into things, fall over her own feet and just like with the bike accident years before, find herself in situations that would prove to be dire if not for heavenly intervention. Sometimes just with the time it took me to blink; she would find herself in a situation where her life was at stake.

The difference for me in this mission as opposed to the others I had been through is easy to discern. Even though she was a constant risk to herself, she always managed do it in a way where it looked fun. It truly is never a dull moment with her and I enjoyed the time spent focusing on her as much as I did because it meant there was less time to be bored.

Considering her origins, I had gone into the assignment with expectations of a relatively easy watch job but that had been blown out of the water less than five years into it. Serenity Richards needed more supervision to stay alive then most babies did and they were known to be helpless.

The day her mother put her in the center, things had gotten murky for me. I was disallowed entrance. Whoever owned the house over the decades since its inception had barred it against the supernatural. Angels; Demons; Spirits and all other creepy crawly things that went bump in the night were not allowed anywhere near the residents on the inside.

It was during that two and a half year period that I lost track of her, unable to reach her by any method I tried. It caused great worry within me given how easily she found herself in peril. Father, having sensed my overwhelming concern lined up a human host so that I could gain entrance the traditional way but I found that even with the best attempts at fitting in, that hadn't worked either. I'd still been ejected.

So for two and a half years I remained dormant in my care of her. She'd been completely alone other than the human companionship she found with the human girl I now watched her with. Securing Fathers consent, combined with thought implanting, she soon became the perfect watcher of Heaven's most precious gift. Emma is a most blissfully unaware guardian.

A relationship that had held up even after Serenity was released. So now not only was she being guarded by me, she also had a friend, one of the strictly human variety that wanted to see her alive and well. It was the perfect partnership and one that I am more than grateful for. I wasn't called to her side nearly as much since Emma became such a big part of it.

I struggled with the decision to make myself known to her when I appeared three weeks prior. By my father's own admission I was to remain detached from her, allowing her to make her own choices and live her life with minimal interference from above. I found that hard to handle though as time carried on, growing bored with the constant silence that surrounded me. It was then, as the voices became more powerful for her that my decision was made.

I could have easily revealed myself to her in my true form but the goal was not to frighten her, nor was I trying to break the rules Father had set down from the beginning. So I came to her in a way that she would most identify with and also the one that would land me in the least amount of trouble. I became just another spirit in her head, one that would be substantially more important than the ones before.

As it would turn out, the risk paid off. Serenity had not seemed at all rattled at hearing yet another voice in her mind especially given that I had come to her while her body had been in complete rest. Something I knew bordered on the impossible.

*****

"Serenity..."

"She's not available at the moment can I take a message?"

Her attempt at humor is not lost on me. It is obvious that she is more than a little accustomed with the barrage of voices at all hours so hearing mine was no surprise. She'd even conditioned her own mind for the inevitability of it.

So what did I do? I played along with her.

"Yes I would. Can you tell her that I'd very much like to speak with her? That it is of grave importance that I do."

I watched as she moved around on her bed, pulling herself into a sitting position. Raking her hands through her hair as she made herself comfortable, I heard the sound of a sigh escape her lips.

"You're kidding me right? I thought this was the one time I could escape you guys. Isn't there a rule somewhere not to harass during hours designated for sleep?"

"I'm afraid there is no such rule. Though not everyone can speak to you when you are in what you call the hours of designated sleep. That is something only a select few of us are able to accomplish."

"That's just great. So I'm available for chat twenty four seven. What do you want?"

"I wanted to check in on you. I want to make sure you're alright."

"Well genius, up until about five minutes ago I was perfect. Things couldn't be better. I was having THE BEST dream and was actually sleeping soundly for the first time in weeks. Then this irritating guy had to come and rip it all away from me."

I couldn't help it, I laughed at her contempt for what I'd done. It seemed that humans reacted much the same as angels when they were unhappy. They reverted to sarcasm instantly as a form of defense.

"Tell me; now that you're awake do you hear any other voices?"

Judging by the look on her face as I asked the question it was obvious I'd given her something she hadn't been expecting. I was aware with the time I spent observing her, listening in to her body's frequency that there wasn't much time in the waking hours that she is left without them. Sitting where she was now though it seemed she is experiencing her first moment of absolute peace since her time in the center.

"Actually now that you mention it, I don't hear anyone but you."

"Then my mission has been tested and is complete."

"What the heck does that mean? How are you doing this? Better yet, who are you and what do you want with me?"

"All your questions will be answered in time. All will become apparent. For now though just think of me as someone that wants to help you."

"Yeah because waking a person up from a dead sleep is totally helpful."

"Given that you can no longer hear the voices while I am here speaking with you I'd say that it was most helpful in comparison with what you have been dealing with thus far."

"Fine, you win. Can I go back to sleep now?"

"Yes pretty girl, you may go back to sleep. Thank you for speaking with me. I hope to speak with you again soon."

I pulled myself out of her mind but not before hearing her speak again.

"What did he just call me?"

*****

It had been much the same the first time I had come to her soothing her with my singing. I had no idea at first what possessed me to do it but once started, I found it almost addictive. It was something that not only soothed her to sleep most nights but also calmed the roughest parts within me. She hadn't exactly taken to it at first though.

The ease at which she could become annoyed was unmatched by any human before her. What most would just blindly accept she could not. I found her mind and its inner workings to be the most interesting part of her. I could never know on any given night what her reception would be for me.

That first time she had not gone easy on me and I enjoyed every second of it.

*****

**"There is a land of delight, where the angels dwell,
Beautiful home, beautiful home.
The joy that is waiting, no tongue can tell
Beautiful home above.
There's a joy which eternally fills my heart,
Beautiful home, beautiful home."**

"Ugh, you're kidding me right?"

"I am unsure what you believe me to be kidding about pretty girl. There are few things I get to enjoy in life, singing happens to be one of them."

"So that means you have to serenade me? With a song about Heaven, in the middle of the freaking night. I mean really, does that seem normal to you?"

"It is a song about Heaven, of that you are correct. A place so beautiful that human eyes cannot handle the mere sight of it."

16

"Ugh." She groaned loudly. "I kind of figured that much out myself thanks."

"Does it not please you to hear me this way?"

Her reaction to my singing startled me. Whenever I sang in the past it had been met with a much better reception. An angel's voice was akin to that of God himself, simple yet powerful at the same time. All of which Serenity did not seem to feel, which confused me greatly.

"It's not that," she stated. "I just wasn't expecting to hear singing as I was trying to sleep. I usually like the quiet."

"Tell me something... Have you heard voices in the duration of my singing to you?"

"No."

"Then what is the harm?"

"I apologize. There is most definitely no harm being done. I was only over here trying to sleep. No bother. Please continue where you left off."

"While I may not understand most human responses, I do understand your use of sarcasm. If my singing to you is causing you distress then I can stop."

"Okay smarty pants. If I ask you to stop, are you going to get your panties in a knot?"

"Serenity, I am unable to wear panties."

As the laughter fell from her lips she immediately slapped her hand over her mouth to silence it. The sight of her, attempting to hide the most basic of human expressions made me smile. It was nice knowing that I could make her laugh.

"I'd be worried about you if you did."

*****

After that first time my visits became second nature to her, whether I was there to talk or sing. It had become something so expected that soon she enjoyed falling asleep to the sound of my voice, serenading her with songs of hope that were heaven sent. I enjoyed that reaction most of all. As the frequency of the visits grew, I found myself enjoying the effect on her, most of all watching her face, completely at peace as she slept. I wanted that peace to remain within her forever.

17

While my primary goal had been to watch over her, protecting the very life force within her, that reaction was quickly rising up the list in terms of importance for me. I lived for it.

For the next three weeks following the first, I came to her every night. First telling myself that I was doing it for her, believing the more I visited the better off it was in the long term. It was from there that I proceeded to tell myself that I did it as much for me as for her. I rather enjoyed the way I felt when in her company.

I was beginning to walk the fine line with the rules but I found myself caring less and less as time wore on. It is something I just wasn't willing to give up, even though I knew the more time spent together the more she would begin to question just who I was and what my intent was in spending the time with her. Something I could not get into quite yet.

While she may not believe what Emma was telling her, I knew it was only a matter of time before she her mind started working and the questions began. The greater purpose for her life was going to come up, and it was going to come up soon there was no way around it.

Until then though, I resolved myself to enjoy my time with her and not focus on what is to come.

I couldn't possibly be breaking the rules in doing it that way could I?

CHAPTER THREE

Serenity

Emma's words stayed with me all week, especially in the times when his voice would come. It was as if in those times when we were alone together, I found myself wondering if there was anything to the crazy idea my best friend brought up.

He seemed more than a little concerned with my well-being, making a point of asking each and every time we spoke, which sometimes was more than just the times I wanted to sleep. More than that he seemed interested in my day, who I met and what I thought of the classes and teachers I was interacting with. Something no spirit before him had ever done.

I tried not to let Emma's randomness play into our time together but it was hard not to with the way the conversation often went. What started out as me being on guard believing this voice to be just like the others was quickly turning into the opposite. I found myself actually enjoying the time we spent together.

Is it possible Emma was right and I am falling for the voice inside of my head? I've never considered myself to be crazy even with being institutionalized but if I was developing a crush then maybe it was something I had to take the time and revisit.

What did he want with me? I already figured out that he wasn't like the normal spirits. He could do things that it had been proven the others could not. The way he spoke to me on the nights when he wasn't singing made me believe that he was much older than I'd originally believed. Either that or he had seen and been through enough experiences that had aged him considerably. Something that really wasn't that unheard of given the way life could be.

With each passing day, the visits between us happening more often, the more the amount of questions I had kept growing. Whenever I asked him anything about himself though, or what exactly he was doing inside of my head when I was pretty sure there were more entertaining people he could be haunting, he always gave me the same response.

All will be told in its right time.

Unfortunately for him, that wasn't an answer I could just blindly accept. So after each visit I would piece together random facts he let slip, determined to put them together and figure out just what he was so hesitant to tell me. So far though he hadn't given me much to go on other than the fact that he wanted to silence the voices and make sure I remained safe. That only gave more credit to Emma's angel theory, something I most definitely could not wrap my mind around. It even went a step further though as he made sure at the end of one of our visits that I knew I could call on him at any time by just focusing on his voice and its sound.

I wanted to tell him that it would be a whole lot easier to call for him if he would just give me his name but I chickened out. It was strange that he hadn't wanted to introduce himself though. It's not often that I didn't learn of a spirits name. It was just another thing that set him apart from the others.

So this is where I am now, alone in my room, Emma having gone out for the third night in a row. Sitting on the bed, eagerly awaiting his presence, determined that this time, I wouldn't let him off so easily and I'd get the answers I wanted. Maybe not everything could be explained right now but didn't I at least deserve to know who I was talking to?

Truth be told, I didn't have a lot of experience with guys and even less when it was just the voice of a guy reverberating in my mind. It wasn't that I wasn't interested in them, because well, I am human after all but given the amount of time I got to enjoy complete silence in my brain, taking the time and getting to know someone past just the obvious was the furthest thing from it.

On one of the rare occasions when my mom attempted to get close to me, she explained that she was disappointed that I hadn't turned out more like her. Apparently I am the mirror image of my father, well if he had been female anyway.

According to her when I was born I'd had her hair coloring but by the time I turned seven, it changed completely until it was my father's shade of brown. Add to that my eyes changing from the dark shade of blue they had been at birth to the hazel color that remained every day since and it was no surprise she was so disappointed.

My skin was fair, to the point that even through my teens I had very rarely gotten acne. This was just another thing to add to the list of things that annoyed my mother to no end. It seemed according to her that the older I became, the more I turned into the very image of the man that had walked out on us years before. It made any real attempts at building a relationship with my mother practically impossible from that point on.

So I knew that I was decent enough looking, even if it is only because of my father.

Because of the way I looked, there had been guys in my life, especially over the last five years that had shown some form of interest in me. It seemed though that once they got past the shallowness of the physical they faltered before getting to know the parts of me buried underneath. It was pretty well documented that I wasn't exactly all there. People didn't go out of their way to mock me but when they thought I couldn't hear them, well that's when their real feelings became known.

There had been one guy though, that I had been able to form an attachment with. I hadn't seen him in just over two years but he made an impact none the less.

Mom moved us about a year after I was released from the center and he'd been my next door neighbor. He didn't seem to mind that sometimes I seemed to be talking to myself when no one else was around or that I actually preferred being on my own to being in a large crowd. No, he accepted me as I am. He reminded me of the male version of Emma except less boy crazy.

Graham Hudson is the one guy in the last ten years to treat me like I was normal. I wasn't sure where he was these days given that when I'd gone away to college we hadn't kept in touch but I hoped that wherever he was, he's happy. He deserves that much. If it hadn't been for him during those first couple of years back in the real world, dealing with the voices, I don't know where I would have ended up.

I owed him.

"Serenity..."

With a quick glance at the clock on my nightstand I realized that just like the times before, he was right on schedule.

"No. You don't get to do this. If you're going to keep coming to me every night then we better get some stuff out of the way right now."

"I'm unsure of what you mean."

"Who are you and don't you dare give me that line that you will reveal it all at the right time. Right now is the right time."

"I am Gabriel."

Well that wasn't hard at all. I should have taken this approach sooner. Maybe I would know a whole lot more than just his name and that he wanted to protect me by now.

"Hello Gabe."

He laughed at the shortening of his name and I found myself liking the sound. He hadn't really laughed much since he started talking to me, so when he did, I took the time to enjoy it. Though in his defense, if he was a spirit, there weren't exactly a lot of things to laugh about. I had to figure wandering the world aimlessly would get pretty depressing after a while.

"Hello Serenity."

Since I'd gotten him to open up I figured I might as well go for broke and ask him what he was doing inside of my head. Maybe this time I'd actually get a better response. Who knew getting upset with a spirit could give you such great results?

"Why do you visit me so often?"

"It is what I enjoy doing."

I wasn't exactly sure what to do with that so I just continued. "Could you be more specific?"

"I've been watching over you for some time now. You struggle with the sheer magnitude of your gift and I want to do everything in my power to alleviate that pain for you."

"Why do that for me?"

I didn't hear him for a while and I started to think I'd pushed him too far and he'd vanished. Just the thought of him leaving made my stomach queasy. I didn't want him to go. I couldn't explain why but ever since he'd shown up and started talking with me, I didn't feel like the freak I am. In fact for the first time since I had been cursed with this horrible ability, I was starting to see why people called it a gift.

Gabriel had a calming effect on me and while I couldn't explain how or why it affected me so much, I enjoyed it. I wasn't quite ready to be rid of it just yet.

"You do not see it Serenity but you are very special. That is why I want to protect you and why I come to you every night. I'm taking a tremendous risk being around you this way but for some reason I cannot ascertain, I need to be here."

For the second time in the conversation he rendered me speechless. As I racked my brain trying to come up with something to say, other than admitting that I felt the same, he spoke again and I resigned myself to the fact that if he kept this up I'd be living the rest of my days mute.

"I know you have many questions for me and I promise you that when the time is right I will answer every one of them but right now it is not that time. I have said as much as I can without going against the very reason I'm here. I'm very sorry."

The door opened then, light spilling in from the hallway and landing right in my line of vision causing me to pull the blanket up in front of my eyes to block it. Focusing all of my energy on the voice of the guy in my head and blocking out Emma and her amazing ability to pick the worst possible time to interrupt, I tried to reach out to him before he disappeared.

Call it daddy issues, call it whatever you want but I wasn't ready to say goodbye to him.

"Please don't leave. I have so much I want to say..."

After a few minutes of radio silence I realized that whatever gift I had to speak with spirits obviously wasn't working both ways now. They could contact me whenever they felt like it but I was powerless when doing the same. That just depressed the hell out of me. I wasn't ready to say goodnight to him, not with everything that had just been said. I wanted more time. I wanted to let him know he wasn't alone.

Finally resigning myself to the fact that I wouldn't hear from him anymore tonight, I turned over in the bed, mumbling a goodnight to Emma before curling myself into a ball, finally releasing the sigh that I'd been holding. When I finally finished mentally berating myself for not answering him when I'd had the chance, I closed my eyes tightly, fully prepared to let sleep claim me for another night. It was then I heard it, faint to the point of a whisper yet somehow very clear.

"I will never leave you Serenity. I am always with you."

CHAPTER FOUR

Gabriel

It's official.

I'm breaking every conceivable rule in maintaining contact with Serenity at least to the degree that I have taken it to. It hadn't come as a shock when I had been called home. It seems he is getting a bird's eye view at my attempt to become closer to my charge and I could only imagine that he didn't like it one bit.

I am to be a casual observer here, only involving myself in dire situations. He had drilled that into my head so many times that I knew it by heart. I also knew that being tasked with being a guardian angel for a girl that was troubled and haunted by her gift meant that sometimes the rules needed to be broken. If Serenity was indeed the answer to our prayers for a better world then shouldn't that mean keeping her happy trumped everything else? At least until the time came where it no longer mattered and she had taken her rightful place?

It is in moments such as this that my lingering doubts about what was right made the most sense. Maybe Heaven needed an upgrade after all. The way things were being run right now left something to be desired.

"What do you hope to accomplish in going about things the way you have been my son?"

"Do you really want to know or did you just call me home to tell me that you are unhappy with my methods?"

"You dare speak to me this way after I gave you a chance? When I could have easily chosen Michael or Raphael who are more qualified?"

I was reminded of the conversation we shared before I began my assignment. How proud he was, more than pleased at giving me my first real chance to shine in as many centuries. It was completely different than the way he is now and I found myself feeling sick at the drastic change that occurred.

Even with things changing around me daily where Serenity is concerned, I still very much want to please him. I wanted to make him proud and strengthen his belief that in choosing me he had made the right decision. Hearing anything to the contrary was just too upsetting. By his own words though he brought up an interesting question.

Why even choose me at all if he believed my siblings to be that much better than me?

"Father, I don't mean any degree of disrespect but you did ask me what I was hoping to accomplish and I feel the answer is quite clear if you just see what I've actually been doing."

"What is it that is supposed to be clear to me? Are you speaking of something other than the growing feelings for your charge?"

So this is what this meeting is about. The seer of all things had been able to see how I was beginning to feel about Serenity. Another rule that I was breaking. It all made sense now.

"Father, one has nothing to do with the other. I am building trust with her. That is what you requested of me is it not? Other than showing her my true form there really is no other alternative to get the result we require. She has no idea of the power that burns within her. She believes herself to be simply a flawed human specimen. The thing I most wanted to correct. If when the time is right you want her to remain on the side of righteousness, then you must let me do this my way, otherwise you will send her into this blind and she will balk and run."

"You seem to have given this much thought Gabriel." he replied, his tone no longer angry, which gave me hope that he might be willing to hear me out.

"It's all I've been doing for the last twenty years while I watched her. I want this to succeed as much as you do. You must never doubt that but in order for it to happen you must allow me some room to move."

"And this has nothing to do with what you feel for her?"

"No. What I may feel for her is separate entirely from the task at hand and I will treat it as such in the remainder of my time there."

"You must remain detached Gabriel. If you allow your personal feelings to distract you then all of us fail and this will be for naught."

"I can't stay away from her Father, not if you expect me to do my job and do it effectively. You must not ask that of me."

"You are to spend some time apart from her then, to prove to me that you are not being led by human emotions due to your time on the planet. That you are in fact doing what is best for the undertaking. There will be no argument on this. You must do as I say or I will send Michael in your place."

Everyone believes Heaven to be this glorious place that when you pass on and enter the gates, is all happiness, peace and overwhelming calm but it is so much more than that. This mission my father had taken me on had opened my eyes to just how political everything is. It really is like Earth in a lot of ways, though you wouldn't find many that were willing to admit it.

I have never been the first pick in terms of Heaven's children. In fact if I'm really honest about it, I'm like what the humans call the black sheep. I am the one that has doubts, voices opinions and isn't happy just towing the line for my father and the rest of my family. I want more; expect more and will settle for nothing less than all of the answers at any given time.

It is this attitude that I believe is the reason behind me being chosen for this undertaking. Out of all of the Heavenly Hosts, I was the one most like Serenity herself, at least in her human form and because of that when the time called for it, I would be the best person to call on because I would understand her almost better than she did herself.

Michael has always been the favorite, at least since Lucifer was cast out and forged his own much darker path. He is the go to guy in situations like the one I now find myself in because he doesn't let the human way of being become him. He is stronger than I am in a lot of ways, especially in his ability to not let anything, human or otherwise possess him.

Father threatening to bring him in to guard Serenity was the more logical choice but I couldn't let it happen. I had to do this and unlike what I had told my father it had everything to do with the way I was beginning to feel for her. A realization I knew that no matter how strongly I tried to hide it, Father would find out.

I had been there through every event, large or small in her life. I am invested in ways I couldn't even begin to describe. The truth of the matter is if I was sent back home unable to complete what my father desired of me, I would go back half the angel I was when all of this began. In spending as much as I have been watching her, I have come to understand her and sympathize with her.

It's a proven fact that angels do not feel. This is why Father created the world the way he had. He wanted to create in his image real feeling, growth through emotions and actions. Humans existed to be what angels could never be. It is even worse for Archangels as we are meant to be warriors for our father. We are the light and the strength in an otherwise dark and dangerous existence. For centuries upon centuries we have been taught to be better than our human counterparts. Unfortunately, I didn't fit the mold. I don't think I ever would.

As much as I wanted to please Father I knew what he was asking of me was impossible. Given how closely I guarded her over the years, to the point of becoming close to her even without her knowledge, it would be impossible to walk away.

There is only one way I could handle this.

I would do as Father asked even though it would pain me to do so. I would cease all visitations with Serenity in an effort to prove I am the right person for the job. I would do it just this once because the alternative just wasn't an option I was willing to go along with. I would stay away from her so that I did not risk being sent away from her forever.

Once my obligation was filled and I had proven my worth in the undertaking, I would go back to her and I would make sure I'd never be taken from her again.

Serenity

I can't believe I'd been so stupid. That when I heard his voice that night three days ago I really believed he'd meant what he said. I didn't like admitting it but I had become so accustomed to the nightly visitation whether he was speaking or serenading me that I had fallen hook, line and sinker for a few sweet words.

28

I am an analytical person by nature. I never let my heart make decisions for me nor did I just follow along with blind faith. I dealt in cold hard facts and physical proof. It's the way I have always been and something I didn't believe I needed to change.

It started when my father walked out on us and practically disappeared. I was young and believed that his leaving had in some way been my fault. I hadn't been what he expected so he bailed out before I managed to get even more attached. As time went on it became less about blaming myself and more about not trusting anyone to really stay around when they said they would. Dad told me he would never leave me and well you can see how well that turned out.

If I didn't allow attachments and I didn't take every word from people as gospel then no one could hurt me. For as long as I can remember it's served me well. So why with Gabriel had I just taken him at his word?

I knew why. It's because I was that girl.

You know the one. The girl that goes out with a guy and then reading too much into the situation goes home each night and waits by the phone, her heart breaking in two with each day that passes with no word. Gabriel was a voice in my head for crying out loud and he already had the ability to control my responses. He had the ability to break me and he wasn't even real.

I have reached new heights. I am no longer just a freak but the most pathetic of ones.

"I will never leave you Serenity. I am always with you."

For the last three days those words haunted me. Making sleep completely impossible and making my waking hours even harder to handle. I moved from class to class like a zombie, all the while carrying a smidgen of hope that tonight would be the night he would come back to me. He would tell me that he stayed away for some life or death reason and that he wanted nothing more than to be with me the entire time.

My course work was suffering with me already having to take an incomplete on an assignment that just a couple of months before I would have completed and handed in well before the due date. I was late for work most every day since the radio silence and the few people I did enjoy talking to were beginning to see me for who I was and turning their backs on me.

With the way things were going, I was going to blink and be in my pajamas watching some sappy romantic movie and bingeing on ice cream surrounded by a room full of cats. Though if that happened then at least I'd be considered normal for the first time in my life. So there was that.

God, I'm pathetic. Emma was right. I'd fallen for the voice in my head and judging by the nose dive my thoughts were taking, I had it bad. Maybe it really was time to revisit the whole crazy theory, because if this wasn't the epitome of crazy, I didn't know what was.

"Serenity..."

Oh god, it was worse than I thought. Now I'm hearing things.

"You must guard yourself, darkness is coming."

"Please make sure Mark knows I didn't sleep with that guy."

"Why did I have to die in my underwear? Do you have any idea how embarrassing walking around in your tighty whities really is?"

"Why must children these days wear their pants around their ankles?"

Standing in the hallway about halfway to my next class the flood of voices took a hold of me, each one more ridiculous sounding then the next, forcing me to listen to their pleas, looking for any acknowledgement that they were indeed being heard. When closing my eyes tightly and pushing random thoughts through my brain didn't seem to stop it, I turned back the way I'd come, prepared to run them out.

If they were determined to take over my mind then there was no way in hell I was going to lose it in front of a hallway now full of students. I was already considered a loner. I really wasn't looking to add more labels to it.

As I began walking I heard it again, the one person that had the ability to stop the other voices so that I could focus. The low rumble broke through and immediately my heart rate which up until that point had been beating into overdrive began to steady.

"Focus on my voice Angelo Ragazza; I'm here with you now."

I did as he said and focused solely on the sound of his voice not allowing any of the others to force their way through. As upset as I was that he was showing up now, after leaving me hanging it was overridden by my overwhelming need to calm myself so that I

30

could make it to class on time. Having a mental breakdown on the way to a psychology class while ironic was just not something I was willing to do.

"Can you hear me if I speak to you like this?"

"Yes. I am able to hear your thoughts."

The magnitude of what he just admitted was not lost on me. It meant that for the last three days if he really could read my mind and meant what he said, he knew exactly what his leaving had done to me. The mental and emotional breakdown it had evoked and the responses to all of them as they flooded my nervous system.

If he could hear me then that meant he knew exactly what I wanted to tell him days before. He knew how I felt. He knew everything.

"Who the hell are you? Who have I been talking to for the past month?"

"As I have already told you, you have been speaking to me. Gabriel."

I have no idea what upset me more, the fact that he was so matter of fact in his answer or that it held a smart ass undertone to it. Either way I didn't like it. The time for going easy and letting him reveal things in his own time were over. If he wasn't going to tell me what I wanted to know then he might as well never bother coming back. My hurt slowly began turning into anger and I held onto it for dear life. I needed to feel something other than the sheer agony I'd been feeling for the past seventy two hours.

Shit.

He knew what I was going to do because he could hear my every single freaking thought.

"What does Angelo ragazza mean?"

"It means angel girl but that is not what you really want to know."

"Well aren't you the observant one today? Would you like a cookie for being so smart?"

"I am always observant. It is as much a part of who I am as using sarcasm when you're upset is for you."

Damn, he had me there. He didn't need to be able to read my mind to know that I'm angry with him. Or that I am disappointed in him and even a little with myself. I had spent this long not creating attachment with other people because of the torturous nature of my so called gift and what happened in my past and what did I do right from the first time he spoke to me? I'd gotten attached.

"Where have you been? What happened to always being with me? Or were you just lying when you said that?"

"I want to tell you everything but right now isn't the time."

"You know what, spare me Gabriel. You're just saying the same stupid line you always do. I'm starting to think it's the only words you know how to say."

"I am sorry that you feel that way but that is not the case."

"I waited for you for three days; I missed you but did that matter to you? Does it matter to you now? No, because if it did, then you'd tell me the truth. So how about you just do us both a favor and continue doing exactly what you've been doing and leave me the hell alone."

I knew how I sounded and it just made me even more annoyed with myself. I had gotten myself attached to the voice in my head to such a degree that now I sounded like an irate girlfriend. I was no better than some of the other girls on campus with the way I carried on. I needed to get myself together and I needed to do it quick.

Turning back toward my class I began walking, focusing my mind on any random memory I could think of to block him from being able to respond to me. I meant what I said; I didn't want to hear it anymore. I was already having a hard enough time dealing with my life. The last thing I needed was for him to speak again and fill me with more excuses.

I had been given more than my share of those for this lifetime. He could save it.

Making my way into the classroom and taking a seat as far in the back as I could manage, I opened my textbook and immediately began reading. I could only hope that I would get through this one class without a spirit deciding I was its new BFF. It was time I focused on what was really important, my classes, my work and my future. No more pining away for a spirit that played mind games.

I listened as the professor began his lecture, putting pen to paper and taking notes the more he carried on. It was then that I heard it, faint as usual, the sound instantly putting my body and mind at ease. The pitch low yet melodic as he spoke the words that shot straight into my heart, leaving his mark.

"I was fulfilling an obligation to my father. I do not understand what it is to lie and despite the way that it appears I never left you. I have been with you the entire time."

CHAPTER FIVE

Serenity

"Psychology is an academic and applied discipline that involves the study of mental functions and behaviors in a scientific capacity. It has the immediate goal of understanding groups and individuals by establishing general principles and through researching specific cases. By all accounts it ultimately aims to be a benefit to..."

Hearing a sound and looking up, the professors' voice fading out, I watched as two students made their way into the room, the door slamming again behind them. It took me a minute to realize who was standing at the front of the room. It's not often that my best friend went unnoticed but this time she had because it hadn't clicked in.

"It is so nice of you to honor us with your presence Ms. Daniels. Class starts promptly at 2:15."

"I know Professor French but I actually have a reason for being late this time."

"I assume it has something to do with the young man standing to your right?" he asked with a raise of his brow. Strong powers of observation ran through that one, I could tell.

"Yes sir. The Dean requested that since Ryan here has this class same as I do, that I show him the way."

"Oh yes! You're the transfer student I was informed about. Ryan McGregor, is that correct?"

"Yes sir."

"Well take your seats, both of you and Ms. Daniels; make sure that you're here earlier tomorrow. It would be ideal if you were on time if not a little earlier. I would hate to have to write you up for your tardiness."

Emma immediately began making her way to the back, turning only once to motion for Ryan to follow before eventually making her way all the way back to where I was seated. I lowered my head as she reached me, her late entry causing all attention in the room to turn in my direction. The last thing I wanted to deal with given the way my day had already started.

Pointing to the empty seat on my left, Emma threw her body into the seat behind me, the grin on her face as she did alerting me to the fact that the wheels in her brain were turning. She was planning something and I wasn't entirely sure I wanted to know what. If it had anything to do with being social to the new guy, then I was most definitely out. I had more than enough guy troubles just with the one in my head. I didn't need to business with any more.

"So, what did we miss?" Emma whispered with a small tap of her pen on my shoulder.

"Not much really. He was just breaking down one of aspects we'll be studying for the next few weeks."

"So I could have just stayed in bed then?" the new guy interjected, causing me to look over at him. Meeting his eyes, I had no other choice but to take him in. Where I had only gotten a small glimpse when he'd been standing at the front of the class and then as he had taken the walk of lame on his way to his seat, now I was being confronted with the entire package.

From what I had seen at the front, he was tall but not unusually so. Given the size of the rest of the guys in the room he was about average. His hair was on the darker side of brown, almost bordering on black and it was side parted resting just a little above his shoulders. It reminded me of the singer in a band I liked. It was a look that in that last couple of years, I'd seen a lot more guys emulating.

The side of his face showed three individual piercings in his ear, which then led me to the rings that curled around the left and right side of his bottom lips. Snake bites, that's what they were called. Something that had been popular with a lot of the guys in Green Haven before I moved.

Not wanting to spend too much time focusing on his mouth I looked up and I was met again with the clearest set of blue eyes I've ever seen. If it hadn't been for the sliver of black that seemed to border them I wouldn't really be sure they were blue at all. They almost looked cloudy white.

When he cleared his throat I pulled back from my dissection and immediately turned away. The last thing I needed was to be caught ogling a guy I didn't even know.

"Ryan McGregor" he spoke then, bringing his hand out in front of him and despite my best attempt not to look, I found my eyes drawn to it. If his face had gotten to me than looking at the smoothness of his skin threw me completely off balance. As I stared at his hand, still in front of him, obviously waiting for acknowledgment, I saw what looked like the end of a tattoo peeking out just under the sleeve of his shirt.

Yeah, he's totally got to be a musician.

"Well look here, I think I've died and gone to Heaven."

Mentally shaking myself in an attempt to block out the unwanted voice, I placed my hand into his, shaking it, ignoring the tingle that began the instant our hands met. It was only when I looked down at my arm that I saw how far reaching the reaction had been. The faintest traces of goose bumps were beginning to form.

"Serenity Richards."

"It's very nice to meet you Serenity."

Pulling my hand out from his I turned my focus back on the professor, who was still in the midst of his speech. Which meant that tuning him out to overthink what had just happened would work just fine.

I couldn't explain my reaction to Ryan and to be honest it bothered me and not just because I was limited in my social abilities. No this was something different and I didn't like the way it made me feel. Other than the times when the voices in my head overloaded me, I was always able to remain in control of my emotions and more than that, my reactions in any given situation. I didn't seem able to do that with Ryan and it freaked me out. Just what the hell is going on with me?

Emma tapped me again, this time sliding a paper up and over my shoulder until it fell on the middle of my desk. Putting my reaction to Ryan out of my head I picked it up and opened it as quietly as I could manage. Without even reading it I knew what it would say. I suddenly began to feel like I was back in middle school again. Two girls whispering about the new boy in class.

Given what was written on the paper, it wasn't that much of a stretch. Only Emma could get away with writing something like this.

Is he cute or what?!!!!

I smiled to myself as I gauged the level of her excitement based on the amount of exclamations on the page, covering my mouth with my hand as I felt a small laugh break through. Yes, I most definitely felt like I was back in middle school.

"Hmm."

I looked up and found Ryan looking at me, a smirk on his face.

"What?" I whispered, folding the note over in my hands while my eyes remained locked on his.

"Oh it's nothing. I'm just really glad I didn't stay home today." He turned away then, his attention falling back on the front of the room, leaving me alone to ponder just what he meant.

Did he just flirt with me?

Unfolding the paper again, I wrote back determined to play along with her if it meant not focusing on the guy that was far too close for my comfort.

Yeah I guess. Have fun with him.

Passing the note back, I followed instructions as the professor asked us to turn to a spot in the course book. Leaning in as close as possible I began reading, forcing my eyes to stay where they were and not turn towards the strange new guy next to me. With the way the goose bumps were now covering my arms I knew there was something off about him. Something I wasn't sure I wanted to find out.

Whatever the pull was, I couldn't react to it. Better that I leave this guy and his rock star looks to Emma. She was much better equipped to deal with him and the strange bodily reactions he managed to evoke. Though I had to admit I was more than a little curious as to why my hand still managed to tingle minutes after we touched.

Just who is Ryan McGregor and why is my body almost under attack in reaction to him?

Gabriel

Serenity was right to question her immediate reaction to the new student. I could feel it as well but couldn't quite make out exactly what it was about him. As it is right now, watching the two of them interact, I felt most unsettled. There was most definitely something off about this Ryan McGregor but until I had more time to investigate, I knew I couldn't voice my concerns. Not to Father and most definitely not to Serenity.

When she cut me off earlier, not giving me time to explain the way I wanted to, it bothered me in a way I was unaccustomed to. I am not programmed the way humans were, to feel things yet that is exactly what happened. Maybe it was as Father said and it is just an after effect of being surrounded with them for so long. Whatever the reason, I did not enjoy it.

I am such a benefit to Heaven because of my ability to not make attachments. Yes I questioned things and I pushed boundaries but I was always able to remain detached no matter the situation I found myself in. With Serenity though it was entirely different. I am finding it difficult not to react.

Could it be her power? Could that be what seemed to call to me, changing me, making me appear almost human?

Her energy is powerful. More powerful than anything I had ever had the opportunity to come into contact with. At least anything of the human variety. Being around it for a prolonged period of time the way I had been could be changing me, causing me to adapt more to her way of life then my own.

Whatever the reason I knew that it was only a matter of time before it affected the job I was sent here to do. It was already presenting that way and the last thing I needed is for it to become worse and result in being sent away permanently. If it is her power than anyone sent down in my place would be put in the same position.

No, I couldn't let whatever was happening with me interfere with the job at hand. Father is right. I had to keep my head and focus on the end result. Given that she didn't want to hear from me anymore, I had my out. I could remain in the background safely now and not risk becoming more attached then I already was to her. I could protect us both that way. It is what I needed to do.

It just wasn't something I wanted to do. Not with the fire burning within me watching her struggle not to react to Ryan

McGregor. I had to get out in front of this soon otherwise I knew I couldn't be held responsible for my actions. I would slip up and that is something I cannot afford.

I could not allow myself to become human.

"You must not let her become closer with Ryan or you will lose her forever. Focus on the burning, it is trying to tell you everything you need to know. Embrace the fire brother."

CHAPTER SIX

Serenity

When I got back to the dorm later that night, finally able to enjoy a couple of nights off work, I made a plan to use the time to catch up on the course work I'd been putting off and catching some much needed sleep. Having a backup plan to the nightly routine I shared with Gabriel would get me through this. It just had to.

As I made my way into the room I was shocked to find Emma home, lounging on her bed, the smile on her face a dead giveaway that she wanted to talk.

She hadn't been home like this for the past two weeks, opting instead to stay with other random girls she knew from other classes, in order to give Gabe and I alone time, or at least that's the reasoning she gave when I'd asked her about it a week before. Despite the fact that Gabriel was in my head and we had all the privacy we needed didn't seem to play into her plan.

"Hey" I said, tossing my bag down onto the floor. "I wasn't expecting to see you tonight. Isn't Thi Beta throwing a party?"

"Yeah I think so but honestly Ser it's been forever since we really hung out. I think we need to catch up. I miss you."

I can't really recall a time where I'd been missed by anyone. When I started being able to hear the dead, my mother pulled away from me, putting all of her attention into finding out what was wrong with me and fixing it. I was more a problem in need of a fix then a daughter. I don't think she missed me at all the entire time I'd been put away in the center. She was probably enjoying the time away from the crazy. Other than my grandparents when I was younger, I'd just never been more than an afterthought.

I guess I should have been upset about it but honestly, I'm alright. I understood where my mother was coming from. Who in their right mind signed up for a daughter with mental problems when they found out they were having a baby? It's just not something you're ready for or willing to accept, at least not right away. So I didn't really think I missed out on much. Plus I was a solitary kind of person anyway. Attachments never usually ended well.

Hearing Emma tell me that she missed me though, it got to me because I missed her too. Sure she acted immature sometimes, more like a tween girl then the twenty year old that she is but I wouldn't change her for the world. She came into my life when I needed someone and even knowing my level of crazy, she never left. That meant something to me. Scratch that, it meant everything to me.

"I miss you too Ems. So since you're giving up a raging party for me, what did you want to do?"

"Binge on ice cream and pick apart sappy movies?"

"So the usual then?" I asked laughing. This is what I missed. Just staying in, not worrying about voices; classes; work or guys and just goofing off with my very best friend. This is my definition of perfection.

"Exactly." she stated. "So I have to ask..."

"Hmm?"

"Gabriel, what happened there? I mean you seemed happier than I've ever seen you for the last few weeks and then all of a sudden it was like we'd gone back in time to the center and you were lost again. Do I need to find him and kick his ass?"

Emma kicking anyone's ass is laughable. She's lucky if she is a hundred pounds soaking wet but the fact that she would even suggest it meant a lot. I didn't realize that I had changed that much since we started speaking but judging from the concerned look on her face, I had.

"No, ass kicking not needed. You were right the other day but it's crazy so I'm just letting it go."

"I was right about what exactly?"

"You said that it sounded like I had a crush on the guy and well I guess I did, hell I think it was more than that for a little while but like I said, it's crazy. I can't be falling for a random voice in my head. For all I know he's some dead guy or someone so sick they're close enough to death that I can hear them. What could really come of something like that?"

"You do realize that you're the only one that thinks you're crazy right? People might not understand you but honestly Ser; you're the only one who uses the c word. It's all just you."

"Are you being serious right now?"

"Of course I'm being serious. You're a medium Serenity. That is an actual thing, which you would know if you spent half as much time researching as you do believing you're crazy."

She did make a good point. Other than when I was younger wondering what my gift is and reading a little about it, I hadn't really looked deeper. I just accepted what I read and moved on from it, all the while being programmed by my mother to believe there really was something wrong with me. As much as I want to say I'm not affected by the way she was back then and even the way she is now, it seemed I was turning out more like her then I ever intended to. The crazy really was in my head.

"Okay fine, let's say you're right and the fact that I can communicate with the dead doesn't make me crazy, doesn't falling for one of them do it?"

"I don't think so. I mean you're different. You aren't really like the rest of the girls around here, or even me so maybe your dating method is different too. Or I'm just as crazy as you believe you are and I'm enabling you. You know, either way."

"That's definitely got to be it. We've both gone mad."

We both broke out into a fit of laughter, neither one of us showing any signs of stopping until the phone began to ring; breaking into the moment and bringing us back to reality.

"That's going to be for you." I said immediately motioning to the phone. It wasn't often people called the room for me but it was a consistent thing for Emma. People seemed to just gravitate towards her and I couldn't exactly blame them. I'd done the very same thing years before and had never looked back.

"Nah, this time I think it might be for you."

The finality of the way she said it, as if she knew something I didn't made me wonder just what she had gone and done. As much as I loved Emma, the last thing I needed was for her to be going behind my back and starting things I wasn't prepared to finish. She knew I didn't handle that well.

"What did you do?"

She put her hands up in the air in surrender as the phone continued to ring behind her. "Promise you won't kill me?"

"Again, I ask. What did you do?"

"I sort of gave that new guy in our psychology class our number. I mean Serenity; the guy couldn't keep his eyes off you the entire class. I figured I'd help him out."

"By giving him my number?"

"Our number but yes. Now are you going to answer it or not?"

It would have been so easy to just get up off her bed and walk away, not even bothering to dignify her question with an answer but I couldn't do that. At least not with Emma. This was just the way she is. I can't believe I hadn't seen it coming. It hadn't been the first time she tried to play matchmaker. She was doing it with the best of intentions but I'll be damned if it isn't the most annoying thing in the world.

Reaching across her, I grabbed the phone off the cradle on her nightstand and pushed the talk button. Might as well get this over with. If I didn't answer it, Emma would just badger me about it until I did, or until I called him back, something I just wasn't going to do.

"Hello?"

"Yeah...umm...is Serenity there?"

Well Emma had been right, it had been for me and judging from the stutter he displayed right from the jump, I had to figure he is just as put off doing this as I am answering.

"This is her."

"Oh! Hey! It's Ryan, you know...umm...from class."

I couldn't help it. I was finding the nervousness in his voice, with the slight stutter kind of entertaining. Maybe it wasn't the nicest thing to do but I didn't care. It was hilarious and honestly, a little cute.

"Yeah I know who you are Ryan. What can I do for you?"

"Well you know I'm new and I'm two weeks behind. I was hoping that if you could spare the time, you could help me catch up in some of the classes we have in common."

Before I had the chance to answer, I felt Emma's hand on my sleeve, yanking on it. Looking up at her she mouthed words at me and as hard as I tried to figure them out, I didn't understand a bit of it.

"I said...what's he saying?" she whispered motioning to the phone.

"I think he just asked me out." I mouthed back careful not to let Ryan hear me.

Emma laughed. Sometimes I swear I needed an interpreter to be able to understand her. It was amazing how the two of us, as different we as are could be as close as we were.

She grabbed the phone from my hands and immediately began speaking. Another talent she had that I was envious of. How easy it is for her to talk to people. Something that judging by the fact that I had just left the guy hanging, I sucked at.

"Hey Ryan, its Emma. Serenity says she'd love to get together with you. Just text her the details of when and where and she'll be there."

Holding the phone back out in front of her, she pushed it closer in my direction. Apparently now that she accepted for me, I was allowed to speak again. Rolling my eyes, I grabbed the phone and put it back to my ear.

"Sorry about that. She just grabbed the phone out of my hands."

"No problem. Was she right though, I mean would you like to get together? You'd be doing the world a great favor by helping out one of your fellow students. You might even end up with your name on a park bench someday."

Unable to contain it, I laughed out loud and immediately sucked in my breath as I realized what I'd done. Man was I pathetic or what, even laughing at an obvious joke felt foreign to me.

"I doubt that but sure we can get together and go over what you might need extra help with."

"Yes!" he shouted his excitement evident. "Thank you. You really are a life saver Serenity."

I made sure he had my cell number so that we'd be able to set up a good time for both of us to get together and I ended the call. When I put the phone back on the nightstand, I threw myself back in my spot on Emma's bed and felt her eyes on me. When I looked up I saw her trying to contain the laughter that was hiding behind the huge grin on her face.

"Oh god, what are you so happy about?"

"My little girl is growing up!"

I was seriously debating whether or not to go back to our earlier conversation and take back the not killing her part now. As

44

hard as it was to believe for Emma, it was even harder for me to grasp. The fact that for the first time since befriending my next door neighbor years before, I had set up plans with a guy. It wasn't just any guy either, it's the rock star looking guy, one of the last people I would have ever thought would be interested in someone like me.

"Yeah, yeah, yeah. I'm all grown up and wearing my big girl panties finally. Can we just get on with our girls night now?"

All conversation of Ryan and what may or may not turn into my first real date in years ceased and we got down to the business of pulling apart the movies we found the most entertaining.

It was the first night in a while where the spirits were leaving me alone and I hadn't needed Gabriel and his voice to do it. Maybe backing away from him earlier was the right thing after all. Not only was my mind at ease without him but I also had a prospective date with a good looking and very real guy to look forward to.

Maybe I really could be a normal girl after all.

CHAPTER SEVEN

Gabriel

I couldn't allow this. It is more than enough that the guy had to be in her class with her, able to spend time with her, walking; talking; laughing and whatever else humans enjoyed doing when they spent time in each other's company. He didn't need to take her on a date. That exceeded the levels of what I could tolerate.

Jealousy.

That is what they called what I was feeling. I hated it. No, hate wasn't even a strong enough word for what I felt for this. I loathed it. I am beginning to understand better than anyone just why Father had made it so that angels didn't feel because this was causing me more than just a little bit of discomfort. It was throwing me off completely. I was practically seething after Serenity had gotten off the phone with him and it was showing no signs of simmering down in the moments after.

It is not lost on me that the reason any of this was able to happen at all is because I had done as Father asked of me and stayed away from her. She had every right to be upset given my earlier statement about never leaving her. I never left her but because I didn't speak with her she really had no way of knowing different. Then there was the way she had accused me of lying to her, something I had no familiarity with. I had heard of it of course, but I am unable to do it. She didn't know that and unless I told her everything, there was no way I could prove it to her. Just another thing to add to the list of things about this entire situation that irritated me.

I had done the unthinkable. There was no way around it. I had begun to fall for my charge. If I had trouble realizing it before it was so painfully obvious now that it may as well have had a big neon sign glowing above it. I am experiencing a great deal of conflicting emotions regarding this, none of which I knew how to cope with. I am literally braving a new world.

Not speaking with her made what I believed to be the place where my heart resided ache. I was jealous at the mere thought of another man being anywhere near her. Knowing she was upset with me left me feeling as if I had been on the receiving end of a firing squad aimed directly at my stomach.

How did humans deal with this kind of thing on a consistent basis? I am now beginning to understand the art of one pulling their hair out in times of extreme duress. I just wanted it all to stop.

You know how you can make it stop.

It is true. I did know how to make all of this end but it is a choice I am unwilling to make. Even knowing that there was now another guy on the scene, one that could be there for her and protect her, I just couldn't bring myself to take the step back and ask Father to replace me. It was completely bleeding over into the undertaking and I didn't even care.

For the first time in my life I was experiencing what it felt like to be selfish and I found that I liked it. I would not leave her. Not even when the time came for her to take her rightful place.

In Heaven we all have one angelic being that is made specifically for us. It is the better half of us. A combination of the parts of us that we couldn't be and the parts we most desired. We would all meet our counterparts when the timing was right and with as much time that had passed since my creation I still had yet to come across mine.

Michael had found his, Raphael as well, shortly after him and if what I noticed before I had been sent on the mission was any indication, Uriel wouldn't be very far behind.

Serenity was mine. I knew it as easily as I knew my own name and purpose. That is why I was going through all of these changes because I am adapting to the form she was presented to me in. If this had been happening in Heaven it would have been much simpler but because it was happening on Earth, it had to present itself in the purest of human forms.

By now Father had to know what was happening, there could be no way of hiding it especially when it was of this magnitude. I knew it was only a matter of time before he called me home and pulled me away from Serenity all together, all in the name of the mission he wanted to see reach its end.

47

As much as I feared his wrath when the time came for me to go home, it wasn't enough to stop me from taking the next step. I had to follow through with this. I was almost powerless against it even though I was one of Heaven's most powerful beings.

I knew then what I had to do. It was the only way.

I had to leave her for a period of time. Given that we hadn't spoken since earlier that day, I was sure she wouldn't even notice I was gone given how quickly I could move through space and time. I didn't want to leave her unguarded but I was just going to have to trust that nothing would happen in my short time away. This is for her anyway. I am going to give her the one thing she wanted from the very beginning.

I am finally going to let her see me.

Serenity

2:34 AM

Sleeping had become pointless.

I had been trying since midnight to fall asleep and failing miserably. Emma had passed out sometime towards the end of the third movie in our critique marathon and I'd just lain on her bed watching in silence. When I finally moved over to my own bed, falling comfortably into the memory foam mattress, I'd thought sleep would be swift. I'd been wrong.

I sensed the occasional restless spirit making their way around the room and the odd time they would say something to me but it ended quickly once they realized I was in no mood to answer them. So while earlier in the night had been pretty quiet, here I was now, cold, alone and unsure of what to do to change it.

My thoughts kept going back to my earlier talk with Gabriel and how I had ended things. That wasn't me. What I had said and done had been a knee jerk reaction to being left alone. Being abandoned, even in the smallest form just wasn't something I dealt with very well. It always reminded me of the way my father had just gotten up and disappeared from my life. It evoked memories in me I'd rather not face.

I was used to not being on the radar for most people, I had come to terms with it a long time ago but I thought things had been different with him. Had he really meant it when he said that he

48

hadn't really left me? That he had been there with me even if he had been silent?

My heart wanted to believe him but my head wasn't having any part of it. For as long as I had been alive people have lied to me, left me and let me down. I had a hard time believing that Gabriel could be any different. Sure he was a voice in my head, one that had spent a lot of hours with me, preventing spirits from getting to me but at the end of the day did that make him any less like the other people that had created so much damage in my life? I was having a hard time believing that it did even though my heart wanted me to.

Then there's this thing with Ryan. Some random new guy shows up in my class and by the end of the night we sort of have a date? I mean where did that come from? The girl that up until now had only had two people in her life she would even consider her friends had suddenly come out of her shell long enough to begin something with a third?

Sad reality is I'm actually looking forward to seeing him and being normal for a change. My entire life all I have ever wanted was to just be a normal girl. The one that gets dressed up goes on dates and genuinely had a good time as much as possible. Who actually enjoys her life. I craved that for as long as I can remember and now here I am, right on the cusp of achieving it and I'm finding myself excited at the possibilities. Maybe I didn't have to be the freak that heard voices for the rest of my life. Maybe I could be Serenity, the girl who can speak to the dead and still go out and party her ass off.

Yeah, I know, wishful thinking.

Just suck it up and call to him. You can end all of this right now if you just give in and ask for help.

Yes he could help. He is the only one that could put the on switch in my brain into a permanent off position but I couldn't do that. Not after the things I'd said. There had been truth behind my words at least a little bit. I couldn't be this attached to just a voice, it wasn't healthy. I needed the break from him just as much as I was sure he needed it from me. I had become so dependent on him to calm me that I'd forgotten how to manage it on my own.

I needed to learn how to do that again. I was the only real defense I had. Even if what he said was true and he was there with me always, I couldn't keep using him to make myself feel better. It wasn't right.

So going against everything my mind wanted me to do, I did what my heart wanted.

Closing my eyes, I focused on the way I felt when we were together and I called out to him. It's time to find out if Gabriel really is true to his word. I lay back down in the bed and did the only thing I could.

I waited.

CHAPTER EIGHT

Gabriel

It has been years since I have been back to this place. As I take in the scenery around me I realize that in all of that time it hasn't really changed much. While the seasons seemed to change with each passing year like clockwork, nothing else had.

I have always enjoyed this time of year. Of all the incarnations that the world takes on by far this one is the most beautiful in its simplicity. There was a rustic feel upon entry here. Things were very basic, homely even and the more I take in of my surroundings I realize that I have missed it.

Even as I stand in place watching, leaves make their descent from the trees, slowly floating in space until they reach their inevitable final resting place on the lightly frosted greenery below. There is a sharpness in the air that secretly makes me yearn for the modern convention of a fireplace. The weather cold but not so frosty that it requires anything more than a lined jacket.

Houses line the street, in order that seems to go on for miles. Each plot of land filled with trees both in front and back, some of which holding tire swings from earlier generations of children having grown up and moved on. If I hadn't already had the most splendid and beautifully crafted home, this would be what I would imagine the perfect home to be. It was quiet, but not so much so that it seemed abandoned. It really is a vision to behold.

The last time I found myself here had been to take a human form. Back then it had been imperative that I do so and Father had gone ahead and found me the perfect one. Now, two years later, I was back again for a repeat performance. Only this time, it was different in that the subject in question was going to give me his permission so I could enter his body whereas before he had been young enough to manipulate.

I always saw this time of year as a change. It is the ending to something that had begun earlier in the year. It is the time where the weather changed from warm to cool, the green of the grass becoming white with frost that would turn into snow, the leaves changing colors from the brightest greens to the shadier reds and browns. It fit perfectly given what I was here to accomplish. I was here for a change of my own.

To become someone else, something else.

Graham Hudson embodied every quality that I could ever need and want in a vessel. He was strong, able bodied and more importantly he was warm and giving. His heart is strong. He reached out to those in need and did whatever he could to help, in an effort to make things better. He didn't lead his life the way most humans did, choosing instead to lead with his kind heart and leave the rationality of his mind in the background. If an Angel could walk the earth as a human and not be one of the fallen, then Graham was the one.

He was also the first boy that Serenity had ever really loved. Whether or not either of them was aware of it, I had known because I had lived it.

When an Angel takes a vessel, it is true that we override them but when I joined with Graham the first time I had done things differently. The core parts of him that had made him the perfect human host I wanted to keep. I didn't want to override his natural temperament with my own. It hadn't seemed fair. It was unheard of to do things the way I had back then but that was me. I was different, much like the boy I had taken over.

His caring nature with Serenity, the patience he showed her during their time living in such close proximity to each other had all been him. Where I could have gotten involved I hadn't. Choosing instead to remain in the background and let things naturally play out.

Which is exactly what I planned on doing again this time. I am hoping that what had been started over two years ago would remain and I would be able to connect with Serenity in a way through Graham that is as natural as possible. I didn't want it to be a forced experience. Finding out that he hadn't left the neighborhood was a bonus in my favor because it meant that at least unconsciously he is still allowing himself to remember that time in his life.

I would reach out to him much the same way as I had with Serenity, through the mind and then if that went according to plan I would explain myself and ask for admittance. There could be no one else. Graham was the one. Yes, it is more than a little selfish, me doing it this way but I really have no other alternative. I cannot tell her the truth. Not until the time is right. Everything has to be aligned perfectly.

I spotted him, walking down the empty street, dodging the sparsely placed rain puddles on the sidewalk, his hands gripping his jacket in an effort to fend off the chill that had taken over the air, as he made his way back to his family home. The bag on his back only solidified my belief that this was his primary residence. He was a student here, remaining in Green Haven when all of his friends had carved their own paths elsewhere.

Graham had aged generously. His height well over six feet tall, his shoulders broad and thick. His hair showed that it had retained its light coloring and was just long enough that you could make out the split ends peeking out under the edges of the winter hat he wore. Positioning myself on the side of the street where he walked I noticed that his face showed slight creases, the sign of hard times and even harder work. Whatever the reason for him staying in this place, it is obvious he had been working tirelessly throughout.

Following him as he made his way into the house I knew that the time had come for me to put my plan into motion. Knowing exactly what I had to do to make it happen made me hesitate just slightly.

I was about to use my power to manipulate a human, something that for my brothers would be as easy as batting an eye but for me caused a great level of distress. I didn't enjoy having to do things this way but given the alternative I knew that I had to see it through and deal with the consequences later.

Taking great care, I chose the perfect image of Serenity, the way she had looked back when Graham had known her and using my power pushed the image into his mind.

Graham had only fond memories of his time with Serenity and I was banking on that being his response to the random image implant now.

The smile I witnessed causing his entire mouth to lift, strengthened my precarious position. I had been right in my judgment call. He did indeed remember her fondly. That would most definitely make things move that much smoother when the time came.

"Serenity..."

Her name fell from his lips the last syllable coming out higher pitched then the rest, almost as if in question. He was remembering her but also questioning the randomness of the vision. As I read his mind I watched the questions flash through in quick succession. Yes this was going to much easier than I thought.

"I wonder what ever happened with her."

I saw my opportunity and I ran with it. I had the answers he sought. It was time that I gave them to him.

"She moved to Stephenville and went to college. She's planning on becoming a doctor."

Graham spun around then, hearing my voice and immediately believing someone to be in the room with him. Typical human reaction to those that have never heard voices before. I had to take every step from here on out with extreme care. The last thing I wanted to do was spook him before I even got to the heart of the matter.

"Very funny. Who said that?"

"If you want that then you must move back."

Surprisingly he did as I asked and seconds later I shot out a burst of power, making the light that was hanging in the room explode, bathing the kitchen where we now stood in darkness.

Humans were interesting in this regard. Most of them could never handle seeing an angel in their true form. The myth that in seeing it was too much and burned their retinas was false but it did leave them with an overpowering sick feeling, which sometimes resulted in the expulsion of their stomach contents. Since Graham had once been my host, he was immune to those affects, something I was grateful for.

I made my presence known, bathing the room in the brightest of light. To him I would only be a large bright orb but I was there in my form, my wings in full length span.

"Who—What are you?" he stammered, trying to make his mind come to terms with what his eyes were witnessing. Another typical human reaction and one I had been expecting.

"I am Gabriel."

"Gabriel? That's it? You're leaving a little bit out don't you think?"

"You would be correct in your observation. What do you think I am?"

"A figment of my very over tired imagination?"

"I assure you I am not. I am very real."

"Prove it."

Overriding his thoughts I began implanting his mind with memories from his childhood, one after the other until he put his hands up in the air in an attempt to get me to stop. There was no one other than people present in the visions that knew about them so it was the easiest way I could think of to make him see that I am very real.

"Okay, so you're real. What are you exactly?"

"I am an angel. An archangel in fact."

I sensed his mind running a mile a minute and it was solidified as a nervous laugh escaped his lips.

"Right. Okay. So what does an angel want with me?"

"You will not remember this as it happened when you were much younger but we have met before. Something that was erased from your memory when our time together concluded."

He pulled the chair out and threw himself down into it, his eyes locked on the floor beneath him afraid to look in my direction. He was becoming overwhelmed by what was taking place and I understood it. It is not every day that one of the heavenly hosts visited you. I was actually expecting more of a reaction from him then I was getting.

He is most definitely not a typical human.

"You didn't answer the question." he said looking up in my direction again, using his hand to block the light that was shining directly at him.

"I am here because I need your help."

"Why me? If you're an angel then what can I possibly do for you that you can't just do yourself?"

Graham Hudson was a bright human. Whatever he had been told of Heaven in his childhood or from the time after I had used him as my vessel had been enough for him to know that we were all powerful and all knowing. I really had underestimated him.

"Your help is required for something that I cannot touch in my true form. It requires you and you alone."

"And what would that be? If you can't tell, I'm not exactly living the high life here. Unless you need me to fix something for you I don't think I'm going to be of much use."

One of the greatest abilities that I had in my arsenal was the ability to sense deceit. With a combination of tone of voice and our ability to read minds and the inner workings of the human body we were able to determine when someone wasn't being their most truthful.

This is not the case with Graham. He was telling me the truth. He did not believe himself to be anything special when in actuality he couldn't be further from the truth. He was the only one that could do this with me, which made him very special.

"You, Graham Hudson, student of the arts at Green Haven Community College, protector of his family and primary caregiver for an ailing mother are of more use to me than you can ever imagine."

He seemed taken aback at my admission. I knew of his life now. There was no walls I needed to break through with him. He was an open book to me.

"Okay fine, I'll bite. What do you need me to do?"

"This isn't for me. This is for someone you care about. They need you which in turn means that I also need you."

"I don't understand."

"Serenity Richards."

"What about her?"

"She needs you but we cannot proceed any further until you agree to help me in the manner I require."

"I haven't seen or heard from Serenity in over two years. Why would she need me? Last I knew she moved away with her mother and was living her life happily someplace else."

"You would be correct in your assumption but she is not living her life as happily as you seem to imagine. You know of her gift. Not the full magnitude of it but you have seen it. You know from experience that living with it the way she has been has never been easy on her."

Realization settled in across his features. He knew exactly what I was speaking of though he hadn't wanted to admit it to himself.

"How am I supposed to help her? I already told you, I haven't seen or heard from her in years."

"You are to help her by being exactly who you have always been with her. By allowing me one simple thing, you could be the very thing that saves her life and the lives of those attached to her."

I am being purposely vague but there is only so much information I am permitted to share with the young man. As it is, he knew more than even Serenity herself and I was dangerously close to breaking all of the rules to get what I wanted.

"What is this one simple thing you're talking about?"

"In order for me to help her adequately, I need a vessel. A human host if you will. With as much power as I have, I can do anything I need to in this form but I cannot be of any more help to her this way. I need to become human."

Shaking his head I listened as he laughed, obviously unable to wrap his mind around what was being said and what I am asking of him. Given the range of things that had been happening to me as of late, I could sympathize more than ever before. If I was completely human I would think I was crazy too.

"You want to use my body to become human so you can save Serenity?"

"In a manner of speaking yes but you would be the one saving her."

"How the hell am I supposed to do that? She probably doesn't even remember me."

"She remembers you fondly."

"Okay then, let's say that she does, how the hell am I supposed to save her?"

This was the moment of truth. I could very well tell him the real reason I needed him and what he would be a part of, or I could just give him the bare essentials and hope that he would agree and we could move forward. Giving my answer some thought I decided on giving him a little bit of both. I couldn't deceive him for my own gain, at least not entirely.

"By making her believe."

CHAPTER NINE

Serenity

Today is the day.

True to his word Ryan texted me in the morning, setting up a time to get together, for later that day, when classes were done. I wasn't sure if it was a residual reaction to the lack of sleep I'd gotten the night before or if it was something else but I actually found myself excited, even going so far as to will time to speed itself up in anticipation.

After calling for Gabriel the night before, I needed a distraction. I don't know what I'd been thinking but it was obvious he hadn't meant a word of what he'd told me only the day before. He was just like all the others that had come and gone in my life. Unreliable and the worst kind of liar.

While I should have been happier knowing I'd been right, I wasn't. It actually hurt. Despite my trust issues I really had put my faith in the mysterious voice that for weeks now had never let me down. I am the biggest kind of fool.

Making my way into biology and taking my regular seat I recalled the way Emma reacted when I told her everything earlier this morning.

*****

"Did you really expect him to show up Ser? I mean he is a guy. They are known for being thoughtless douche bags."

"Gabe was different. He's not the typical guy remember?"

"Of course! How could I forget? He's the angelic voice inside your head. How could I be so thoughtless and forget that."

"Wow Ems, tell me how you really feel."

"Well since you asked so nicely, fine, I will. I think you're being extremely hard on the guy. Just a voice in your head or not, you have no idea what he has going on when he's not with you.

Maybe he was in the middle of something he couldn't get away from right when you happened to call."

"Is this more of your guardian angel theory? Because you know how I feel about that."

"Yeah, yeah I know. You think it's a bunch of bullshit. Which I think is crazy really. I mean you can talk to dead people and somehow I'm the crazy one for thinking one of your voices might be an angel?"

Emma had a point. I have this ability that everyone seemed to think was some kind of gift and yet I really did think what she was saying was too farfetched to be real.

"Fine, you're right. He could be an angel but that still doesn't explain why he would lie to me."

"You're going to make me spell it out for you aren't you?"

"Of course, you know how much I love doing that. Your sarcastic ability is sexy."

Rolling her eyes in response she continued. "Even the best person on the planet, living or dead can't be with someone every second. It's just not possible. So instead of beating yourself and him up over this, why not accept him for being who or what he is. Someone that makes mistakes. Kind of like someone else I know."

*****

Emma seemed firmly planted in her belief that I was being too hard on Gabriel. Putting him up on some pedestal just so that I could bitch when he didn't live up to the hype. In a way she's right. I suppose in calling him the night before I had hoped that he would screw up because then it would justify what I already believed.

"Holy shit, you're in this class too?"

Looking up, my eyes instantly locked on the clearest set of eyes I'd ever seen.

"Looks like it. I guess I know what you're going to need to be caught up in."

He smiled and I watched as it made its way all the way up to his eyes. They seemed almost brighter in comparison to the way they'd looked a minute before, making him even more perfect it seemed. Could Ryan really be as flawless as he appeared?

"Uggh."

"That's a promising sound given that the class hasn't even started yet."

He laughed and again the light seemed to glow in his eyes, making my insides turn to mush.

"I was going to ask you something but no matter how I say it, it's going to sound like a line."

I immediately knew what he was going to ask. Given our current conversation there was only one thing that could be asked that would sound like a pickup line.

"Hey sexy, what's your major?" I asked with a wink, immediately laughing at the cheesiness of it all. I had no idea what had gotten into me but whatever it was, I kind of liked it. It was the first time in forever I was having a normal conversation like a regular girl. It is oddly exhilarating.

"Yeah that's the one. You nailed it. Though if I'd said it, it would have been a little different."

He had my attention now. I found myself eager to hear how he would have asked me. "How so?"

Leaning in as close as he could, his lips a mere breath away from mine, he began to speak, his breath landing on my lips and spreading right into my cheeks.

"So beautiful, what do you want to be when you grow up?"

From his breath on my face, heating me from the outside in, to the deep baritone of his voice I was done. Completely and utterly done. I realize I was inexperienced with all things guy but just from those few words my body was prepared to attach itself to his and not let go.

Before I had a chance to respond he moved back and had seated himself comfortably back in his seat. I knew it belonged to a classmate of mine, but the moment he took the seat I hoped he wouldn't be asked to move. I was like a woman possessed. I wanted to keep him near me and I had no idea where it was coming from. This wasn't like me at all.

"Well isn't he a delicious morsel of a man! The things I would let him do to me!"

Oh shit! This could not be happening now. Not when things had been going so well and I felt more normal then I had in years. Silently I pleaded for the spirit to screw off and leave me alone before I ended up making a fool of myself.

"You could just eat off that chest! Whatever that smell is, it's heavenly."

"Go away!" I seethed. My irritation clearly evident.

"What was that?" Ryan asked, his voice like a beacon, calling my attention straight to it and away from the problematic spirits I found myself saddled with.

He heard me. Shit, now I had to do damage control.

"Huh?" I questioned, hopefully succeeding in my attempt at playing dumb.

"You said something. I thought maybe you said it to me."

Smiling weakly, I kept up with my plan. "I didn't say anything, maybe you just wanted me to."

"Touché." he responded with a smile. "You just might be right about that."

He winked then, causing my breath to catch. If I hadn't gotten the hint before now, there was no longer any doubt. He is definitely flirting with me.

The minute he looked away, I allowed myself the chance to exhale. The professor chose that moment walk into the classroom and as I prepared myself to focus on the lesson, Ryan leaned over to me, his lips so close I could feel his breath on my ear.

"It's okay," he whispered quietly. "I hear them too."

Gabriel

As I waited for Grahams answer I began to feel it. The pull within me. I am being summoned back home. Father obviously knew what I was up to and is pulling me home to lecture me. My wings began receding back in, causing me a sharp immeasurable pain as they did. I had maybe a minute, two at best before I vanished from the room entirely and away from the one human that could help me.

"What's happening to you man, you're fading in and out."

I knew what he was seeing. It is reminiscent of what a television viewer sees when their channel begins freezing. I was cutting in and out for Graham. He had to know that my time was drawing to an end. Which meant that I now had a timetable for his answer. I couldn't sit around and talk him through it anymore. He

61

had to decide here and now, before I vanished because I had no idea if I would be able to return.

"Will you do it, will you help Serenity?"

He seemed to think it over, his eyes facing the table and his mouth frozen in a straight thin line. The lines in his forehead were creased, obviously giving the matter his utmost attention.

"I'm afraid I don't have much time Graham. So before I vanish, will you be my vessel to help Serenity?"

As the lower portions of my body began to transport away, he looked up from the table, his face giving away nothing, he spoke, giving me the answer I so desperately needed.

"Yes"

The pull overwhelmed me and before I knew it I felt myself in flight. Before I had the time to adjust to Grahams answer and how I was going to explain all of it to Father I landed rather harshly on the ground. I was officially home.

Time to face the music.

CHAPTER TEN

Gabriel

"Just what is it that you are hoping to accomplish with that little show down there?"

There are these moments where I would swear we were a normal human family. The way my father spoke to me, especially lately made me feel like nothing more than a petulant child that needed to be placed across his knee. When we had been created we were done in such a way that even though we all knew he was our father, we were treated as equal to him. I was beginning to seriously doubt the validity of his earlier statement. I felt like anything but his equal.

"I am hoping to do exactly what you think. What is the point of even asking the question when you already know the answer?"

Sighing in defeat I watched as he took a few steps away from me, his hand resting across his chin.

"You are aware of the reason I ask these questions Gabriel. Yes I know that you're aware that I know what you're doing but your true intent, what forces you to move forward, I cannot be sure of. So in asking you the questions that I do, I am hoping to discern the answer."

I wasn't sure what he wanted me to say to that. He knew what I was planning and I am pretty sure he knew the reason why. What else was there to say? Did he really just want me to admit what he already knew?

"You doubt me my son but my ability to sense the inevitable has never led me wrong thus far. I knew it the last time we spoke to one another and I am even more sure of it now. You are in love with this girl are you not?"

Still unsure of my own voice I could only nod in agreement. For now that was going to have to be enough for him.

"I should have informed you of this before you began the undertaking but your assumptions are correct. She is indeed your chosen one. She is meant to be your mate. At least when the time is right."

There it was. The very reason I am changing in such a drastic way. I am indeed adapting to her current form, becoming human. It didn't matter that she was something much more than human, that she is the destined one. All that mattered is that something had taken place between us and given that she was in human form when it happened, it meant that I had to adapt. There could be no turning back.

What that also meant is that Father had been right and that it is going to do nothing but damage the undertaking and Serenity's true calling. My love for her would blind us both if not carefully monitored.

"How long have you known what she is to me?"

There wasn't even a breath of hesitation before he answered which spoke volumes to me. This hadn't been something he learned along with me, no he had known before.

"I've known for some time now son. Since before the undertaking began."

"Why didn't you tell me?" As I heard my own voice I realized that the emotional side of me was breaking through as it cracked just slightly. There was an ache I couldn't describe in my chest just knowing that he had known and hadn't thought to share it with me. Yes we were definitely a lot more like humans then I first believed.

"You were not told because it was not of import. My son, this is Heaven. We do not operate the same way as the humans do. I could not anticipate that it would affect you in this way. I held back the knowledge because everything that happens as you well know has to happen of its own accord. My telling you would have done nothing but damage that and maybe even put you on a darker path then what was originally intended. That is a risk I am not willing to take."

As he spoke of my destiny, it hit me that he was the only one that knew exactly how it would all play out. He knew how the undertaking would end. What would become of Serenity and even what would become of me. So as I stood there, taking him in, the man that I loved like a human loved their parent, I wondered if he had intervened already to change the outcome to something more in his favor.

64

"I have not altered your destiny Gabriel. Even with the power I wield, I would never dream of taking that step. Which is the reason you are here with me now. We need to discuss what happens next. Exactly what your plan is."

Did I admit that I hadn't given it much thought past getting Graham to agree to be my vessel? Would he accept that or would he try to force one of his plans onto me in hopes of rectifying a situation that didn't have his desired results?

"You are aware that the last time I used Graham Hudson I was able to make the long lasting connection between him and Serenity. I plan to use that to my advantage to guide her into her rightful place. More than that I wanted a way to build her trust in me again as your wise attempt at keeping us apart damaged what I built considerably. The only way I am able to do that is with a human host."

"I realize that I may have done more harm than good in that regard and for that I am sorry. I have no objections to your use of the vessel. I only ask that you tread lightly. There is a dark entity surrounding Serenity and until I am able to ascertain exactly who or what that is, anyone that comes into contact with her in a combative way may be in danger."

I was stunned. I had not been expecting him to agree to what I wanted to do. In fact I expected to be pulled as far away from Serenity and the undertaking as possible given the way I'd gone against him.

"How are you unable to place the entity?"

"That my son is a question that I do not have an answer to. I am unaware of anything, real or even imagined that I couldn't place. The fact that I am unable to do something so trivial disturbs me to no end. It cannot mean anything good."

"I can track it. I felt it myself. It surrounds the young man Ryan McGregor but it seems that in regards to it my power has been nullified."

"Michael has agreed to help me with this, leaving you with only one solitary focus. You are to continue on as her guardian and handle that in whatever manner you must in order to keep her safe and alive until such time as she is needed. "

"Yes Father."

"I believe that I pulled you away at a most inopportune time. So go, get back to what you need to do and I will update you when your brothers and I know more."

Serenity

Throughout the course of the day I learned that Ryan shared three classes with me. As strange as it is, talking to a relative stranger the way that I am, I enjoyed the time we shared together. Even if we didn't talk throughout the course of the class, just having him there seemed to have a calming effect on me. Nothing makes a day go faster than having someone to share it with.

For so long now, that person had been always been Emma but our majors seemed to push us in opposite directions so the option of passing the days with her were few and far between. Even though it hadn't been my intent, it was amazing how easily Ryan seemed to fit into the empty space Emma left behind and how accepting I seemed to be of it.

"So now that we're done for the day, you're going to entertain the new guy and grab coffee with him right?"

Remembering that I wasn't alone, content as always to move from class to class lost in my own thoughts I turned my attention back to the guy walking beside me.

"Of course. I wouldn't want to leave him alone to fend for himself. Who knows what sort of trouble he might get into if left to his own devices."

As I smiled, he laughed causing me to break out with a laugh of my own. Where only the day before I felt awkward and put off around him, I was now feeling light and completely at ease. It was shocking the difference a day could make.

"My thoughts exactly. So what's your poison?"

"Sugar with a sprinkle of coffee on top."

As we made our way across the quad, past groups of other students hanging around on the grass, some studying, others throwing a football around, he moved closer to me, until his hand was just barely brushing against mine as we walked.

I didn't want to read too much into the interaction but the effect that even that small brush of his hand had on me made that practically impossible to do. I had already come to terms with the fact that he was flirting with me but I hadn't given much thought to anything more beyond that. I had been content just enjoying the back and forth of our constant conversations.

As his hand brushed against mine again the tingling I felt earlier when his lips had been near my ear came back in full force. I had only experienced this sensation one time before and it had been years ago. Feeling it now left me anxious and worse, with nowhere to place it.

"Was it something I said?"

"Huh?" I asked, again focusing my attention back on him, noticing that he'd stopped walking and his eyes were fixed on me, his expression unreadable.

"You told me your coffee preference and I responded and then nothing. I hope what I said wasn't out of line."

Well shit. How am I supposed to admit to him that I hadn't even heard his response? That I had been so affected by his hand brushing against mine that I'd become lost in it? There is no way he would understand it. He'd probably just think I was a freak.

"No, it was nothing like that. You didn't offend me at all."

"Where were you just now?"

"I don't know what you mean. I was here. Why, where were you?" I countered with an awkward laugh.

He his eyebrows raised in question, obviously not believing me for a second. I was going to have to work better with my deflecting and evading skills since it is painfully obvious by the expression on his face that I completely sucked at both.

"Serenity, you don't have to lie to me. If you weren't paying attention it's okay."

His voice was calm, smooth even. Like he really meant what he was saying.

"You're right. I'm sorry. I spaced out for a minute there."

"Does that happen a lot?"

"More than I want to admit, yeah. I really am sorry."

We just stood there, people moving in all directions around us, neither of us even attempting to go with the flow. I prepared myself to move in the direction of the coffee bar when he took me by surprise taking my hand in his, turning and moving in the opposite direction.

"What are you doing?"

"I don't think I'm in the mood for coffee anymore."

What am I supposed to say to that? Had I freaked him out so much that he was now taking me back so he could inevitably ditch me, without the guilt of leaving me stranded somewhere alone? Had I really messed this up so quickly?

Was I that much of a loser?

"Will you stop looking at me like that please." he stated, in a way more an order then a request. "I figured we could just sit over there under that lonely old tree and talk. If that's okay with you of course."

I allowed myself to let out the breath I didn't even realize I'd been holding and followed him, my hand still firmly placed in his, straight to the destination he was directing us to. He really wasn't planning on ditching me. Maybe there was hope for me after all.

As he seated himself, his back completely lined up with the trunk of the tree, he pulled me down with him, his hand never once leaving mine.

"What did you want to talk about?"

"I have to ask you something but I don't want to freak you out."

He obviously had no idea who I was and what my tolerance level is for things that might potentially freak me out. Something he'd quickly learn the more time he spent with me.

"Ask me anything, I promise I won't freak."

After a minute or two in silence, watching as he seemed to be carrying on an internal conversation with himself, I began to give up hope. If he was struggling this much with what he wanted to ask, maybe it was better off that he didn't. I didn't want to admit it but he was beginning to worry me, that off feeling from the day before making itself known again.

"How long have you heard them?"

"Them?"

"The voices."

"I'm not sure what you mean."

"You know exactly what I mean Serenity. You heard that voice earlier today in Biology the same way I did. Even though it was being crude at the time. So tell me, how long?"

I had no idea how I looked in that moment but if my mouth had been hanging open wide, I wouldn't have been at all surprised.

When he had made the comment earlier, I knew what he was getting at but I hadn't really believed that he may have heard them too. There is no way he could have known that what the spirit said had been crude unless he heard it himself.

"Since I was five, but it's progressed a lot since then. It's been this exact way since I was ten."

"I was six when I heard the first voice in my head. I remember thinking it was so cool, I could have an imaginary friend that wasn't really imaginary. I thought I hit the jackpot." he said laughing softly at the memory.

I couldn't believe my ears.

I really wasn't the only one that was dealing with this so called gift. There were more people out there, actual people that were just like me. Even though Emma seemed to understand, she just really couldn't get it.

"My grandmother talked to me when I was five. Which wouldn't really have been a big deal except we were at her funeral. Probably not the best time to be carrying on a conversation."

He smiled just a little and squeezed the hand that still rested in his. "You want to hear something silly?"

"Sure."

"When I was eight, after my mom figured out that I wasn't quite right in the head, I prayed and considering the way my mom is, praying was unheard of."

"What did you pray for?"

"I prayed that someone that was going through this would find me. That I wouldn't have to be alone. I was so tired of being the weird kid that talked to dead people."

"Did anything ever come of it?"

He nodded his head and his eyes instantly went to his lap, where our hands lay, still linked together, bonded. After studying them for a time, he looked up at me again and I felt my heart stop the minute he spoke.

"Yeah something did actually."

"What?"

"You."

CHAPTER ELEVEN

Gabriel

When I popped back in on Graham only minutes later, in the exact spot I vanished and been met with him diving halfway across his kitchen in fear of me, I realized that what had only been a few minutes for me had instead been much longer for him.

After having the surprisingly good conversation with Father, I am more than ready to get the show on the road where Graham is concerned. I just had to make sure that in any future instances, I prepared the host for my arrival. Damaging the vessel before entry just wasn't going to work.

"Jesus man, you sure know how to scare a guy." he stated, beginning to compose himself.

"It's quite common to use the word Jesus in cases such as these but for the record, if you knew my father, you'd realize it is quite offensive, so please refrain in the future."

"You're kidding right?"

"No I assure you I am not. I don't joke about matters such as name calling. Taking the Lords name in vain is a serious offense."

"You haven't really spent much time around people have you?"

"That is not of import."

"I'd say it is. I mean, if you think me saying Jesus is bad, then you need to hear some other people. It's actually a pretty common thing down here, especially with the people I work with."

While the topic of conversation had really been of no interest me, he had finally come up with something I knew needed to be addressed. His work situation. If this is going to work and he was going to my vessel, that meant his entire life was about to change. Graham would have to leave his sick mother and the job he had taken to support her, not to mention the classes at the community college he'd been taking to follow me back to where Serenity resided.

"I feel that I need to make you aware of things before this goes any further. This job you speak of, the college experience you are now engaged in, will have to come to an end."

"I know."

"You know?"

"Yeah, I mean what do you think I've been doing for the last three hours since you vanished into thin air?"

"I have no idea, I was not tracking you during that time."

"Geez. Now I see why you need my help. You're way too formal for your own good man. You need to relax. Not to mention you need to think more like a human and less like an Angel. It's weird and if you're gonna be me, you gotta knock it off."

"I do not think you are in a position to tell me, the more powerful out of the two of us what I should be doing."

"In this case, I am man, so get used to it. You're gonna make me sound like a robot. She's gonna be able to see right through it."

With the mention of Serenity I stopped. I am of the belief that Graham was indeed trying to fight against what is going to happen now that he had agreed, but in fact he was thinking about her, something I hadn't done. Maybe I needed to do as he said after all. Even ignoring the obvious meant that I was still more angel then human and he was right, it was going to be painfully obvious.

"When you left up out of here earlier, I put the pieces together. Everything that wasn't making sense to me. Hell, I even went on the internet and looked you up."

"The internet?"

"Yeah, you know, the place most people hang out when they sit down at a computer. Anyway, I went looking for information. As it turns out, you're a pretty big deal in terms of angels and Heaven and all that nonsense."

"You must show me this internet you speak of. I am really on it?"

"Yeah man, you are but that's not the point. I'm trying to say that I figured if you wanted me to help Serenity the way you claimed then I am going to have to uproot my life. So I asked for some time off with work and I went out and grabbed transfer paperwork for school. It's all filled out and ready to go but I thought with you being an angel and all, you might be able to make it go a little faster."

"You will appear there in two days, which should give me more than enough time to become acclimated to the human condition. I can make this paperwork you speak of move that quickly. I've got a schedule of her classes and I can let you know when and where she works. It will all be fairly simple."

"Damn, you've really planned this out huh?"

"Yes. It is of the utmost importance that I do."

"How does it work?"

"It's actually quite easy. I will become a part of you but I will only make myself apparent when you are not needed. I want this to be as authentic as possible. You care for Serenity and you have always been her protector, even before I used you as a child. She will feel familiar with you and I can get to her through you when it is needed. Nothing more, nothing less. I am not looking to deceive either of you."

He seemed confused by what I said which made me wonder if this was also because of something he had read about me on this internet concoction he mentioned earlier.

"You seem confused."

"Well honestly, I am a little bit." he stated simply, running his hands through his hair, now free of the winter hat that had adorned it only a few short hours before. "I thought being a vessel meant not having any control of myself. Being totally taken over by you."

"In normal cases that is indeed what takes place. So it would seem your reading has paid off in that regard. I am just not your average angel, nor are you the most average of humans despite your belief to the contrary."

"So you're leaving me in control of what happens?"

"That is the plan yes. You care deeply, you are tender hearted yet strong when the mood calls for it. You would be in a much better position to help me if I left you to do it instead of controlling it all through you. As I said, I want this to be authentic."

Taking his silence as a sign, giving him some much needed time to go over everything I'd laid on him up until this point, I again went over the conversation with Father.

He knew how important Serenity was to me and was more than okay with me continuing on even though it is a potential risk to his undertaking. Not only that but he was going to have Michael run point from Heaven to guard from the darkness that seems to have made itself apparent. That same darkness I felt when Serenity had been in contact with the Ryan guy at school. Could it be the boy himself that held the answers to what the darkness was, or is he just a meaningless distraction?

More than that, could I really trust Graham to handle the darkness when the time came? Or would I have to control him in order to defeat it? Should I warn him before we became one? I felt as though I owed him that much yet at the same time didn't want to needlessly worry him and risk him backing out.

It all came down to me wanting to do the right thing for Serenity. To prove to her that I was real and not just something she imagined and that I am better than the people that had hurt her before. Bringing Graham back into her life, knowing what he meant to her, would definitely put me in her good graces. There had been a void in her life and I knew that Graham would be the one to fill it.

"Earth to Gabriel, you there man?"

Realizing that in waiting for him to come to terms with everything we were about to do, I had gotten lost in my own vantage point, I looked up, again focusing on the human before me.

"Yes I assure you I am here. Why do you ask?"

"Because I asked you a question and you were too busy staring a hole in my kitchen cupboards to give me an answer."

"What is it you said?"

"Well I said I was okay with all of it and when could we start."

Sensing his eagerness to get on with the plan and knowing it had everything to do with seeing Serenity again, I smiled at him. It is just further proof that I had chosen wisely. There would be no one better suited for this task then Graham Hudson. Before we could get on with it though, there was one thing I needed to do.

"All in due time. There is something I must do first, but once that is complete we can begin. In the meantime, make sure all your affairs are in order. I am unable to tell you a time you will be back here again so you must prepare as much as possible now."

CHAPTER TWELVE

Serenity

I can't believe this is happening to me.

What started out as an innocent getting to know you conversation the day before, where incidentally we'd spoken about the most intimate part of ourselves, is today quickly becoming so much more and I'm in shock. This is not something I've ever done before. I didn't get close to people, especially relative strangers. I had done it though, with Ryan McGregor of all people.

The conversation from yesterday had been very real. He was like me and even went so far as to believe I was the answer to the prayers he made as a young child. A little heavy for a first date but something I wasn't fazed by. Maybe it's because I've been different my entire life that it seemed sweet to me. Either way, what was done could not be undone.

*****

"You think I'm the answer to your prayers?"

Blushing pink he lowered his head, playing with the ends of his hair nervously. "I know how that sounds and I swear I'm not crazy."

"I don't think that's so crazy."

"You don't?"

"No, I mean we can hear and communicate with dead people. You praying for someone that was the same way so you wouldn't have to be alone seems pretty normal. Pretty sure that's what the psych answer would be too."

"I really don't wanna know what our professor would think of us." he commented before laughing. "Can you imagine how quickly he would have us locked in white coats?"

At the mention of strait jackets I bowed my head, my body freezing in place. Given that I had been at the center for over two years with people that at times needed that very thing in order to

74

protect themselves, I wasn't sure how I felt about him turning it into a joke. It is so much more then something to poke fun at.

"What did I say?"

"Nothing. It was n—nothing."

The look on his face told me that he didn't believe me, which really shouldn't have surprised me. I sucked at all things remotely social and hiding the truth I was even worse with.

"Tell me Serenity."

"I've been there." I said, those three words already more than my throat could manage.

"You've been where?"

"In a place where those white coats you're laughing about are used."

I watched as my words registered on his face and his eyes became clouded over, going from their clear almost translucent blue color to a shaded grey. His lips curved down and I knew instantly what he was experiencing. I made him feel guilty.

"I had no idea. I'm sorry."

"It's okay. I mean it was a long time ago now but hearing anything remotely close to the way things were in my time there, still bothers me ya know?"

He nodded, squeezing my hand gently. "I get it. I'm sorry I didn't think before I spoke."

Choosing to brush it off, not wanting this one comment to ruin what had so far been a really great time, I shrugged. "No harm done. Though you're right. We'd be locked up instantly if we ever told him. He doesn't seem like the type of guy to be open minded."

The tense air around us lifted and just as easily as it had before, the conversation began to flow again, making me more than a little happy that Emma had accepted the date for me. It was turning out a lot better than I had ever imagined.

*****

When he walked me back to the dorm the night before, he suggested doing something like this and I laughed it off. I'd become so accustomed to people shying away from me, that spending time with people was a rarity. Let alone time alone with a guy. That was practically unheard of.

Yet here I am, sitting in the middle of the quad, a red and blue checkered blanket spread out underneath me, Ryan across from me, the only thing separating us the picnic basket he insisted on bringing to make the experience that much more normal.

Being here with him now, it was just as comfortable as it had been the day before, almost as if it is where I belonged. Knowing that I was no longer alone in my supposed disability made things that much easier. I didn't have to worry about how I might be perceived because if I did hear a voice, Ryan would too and he wouldn't judge me. In fact he flat out admitted he'd help me through it. It sure made it easier to be me, though being here with a guy, one I found beyond the normal realm of attractive made the ability to breathe a struggle.

Well at least you know there's at least one thing about you that's normal.

"Penny for your thoughts." He said, breaking through again. Something he seemed to do effortlessly.

"Not worth that much, trust me."

"Somehow I doubt that. Try me."

Did I dare tell him what was I thinking? Could I really open myself up that much and risk further exposure? I'd rather open up to people about my ability with the dead then admit I'm a hormonally challenged female. That seemed far worse in comparison.

I decided to tell him but water down the magnitude of it. "It's really nothing. I just realized that I've never really done anything like this before and well I like it."

"Do you mean the picnic or being like this with a guy?" he asked.

"Both I guess."

"Well Serenity Richards, if it helps at all, you're the first girl I've done something like this with too. I was afraid to do it with anyone before. Afraid they would see the freak side of me and run."

There it is again. Every time I admitted even the slightest bit of information about myself and the way my life had been before now, he was right there with his own sad story. We really were too much alike for our own good. Both living in secret. Hiding away from the rest of the world. All because we were afraid they

76

couldn't or wouldn't accept us as we were. It was horrible but somehow beautiful at the same time. We weren't alone anymore.

"Why did you want to do this anyway? It really doesn't seem like your thing."

He laughed then, my stomach as per its usual doing somersaults at the sound.

"Did you just make a generalization based on my appearance?"

"Maybe," I said, blushing. "I wasn't trying to but honestly, that's not even the most important thing anymore."

"Then what pre tell is?" he asked with a smirk.

"It seems someone actually paid attention in Psych this morning. This is big. Like breaking news big."

"I always pay attention in class." he said rolling his eyes, the smirk still planted across his lips. "I have no idea what you're talking about."

"Yeah, that's right," I said laughing. "You do pay attention. Usually it's to Suzy Abramson though."

"Is that jealousy I hear?"

"Eww! No. What you're hearing is me being repulsed just mentioning it."

"Well let me tell you a little secret. You only think I'm staring at Suzy and in a way I suppose I am but it's not intentional."

"Oh really, then what exactly is it that you're doing McGregor?"

He went silent and I swear I saw red coloring rise in his cheeks again. Blinking to make sure my eyes weren't playing tricks on me I studied him. He really was blushing. What the hell did a guy like this have to blush about?

"Watching you Richards. Happy now?"

Well shit.

I hadn't been expecting him to say something like that. Sure, I had been known to do the same thing in each of the classes we shared, almost as if I was drawn to him somehow but I hadn't really thought that a guy like him would ever do the same to me. I mean has he actually seen himself? That is just crazy.

"You're such a liar."

"Well in most cases I'd agree with you, but not this time. I'm not lying about this. I'd like to be lying about it because then I wouldn't seem like such a weirdo but I feel drawn to you. It makes focusing on much else difficult."

Had I heard that right? Is he really experiencing the very same thing I am? What were the chances? Surely it was just wishful thinking.

"Okay enough. I don't exactly know how to swim so I can't navigate through the sea of bullshit I'm hearing right now."

"Ouch." he said, holding a hand to his heart, a pained expression on his face. "That hurt pretty girl."

Pretty girl.

There had only been one other person to call me that and I really didn't want to think about him now. It had been bad enough that he'd come to me the night before in some sort of connection attempt. The last thing I wanted to do is think about him while I was here with Ryan. It seemed wrong, unfair even.

I had done my best to overlook what happened the night before but with Ryan's own words reminding me it was hard not to go back and remember it in painfully graphic detail. My analytical brain wanting nothing more than to sit here and pull it apart the way I hadn't gotten to before.

*****

"Serenity..."

"I'm not doing this Gabe. Go away."

"I know that you do not believe me and that you believe I lied to you. I want to be able to change your mind and make you see that I didn't but I know right now that I cannot. That it will take time. I just wanted to tell you that I'm here. That I'm not leaving you even though you've decided you want nothing more."

"I know now. Are you finished? I've had a long day and I'd really like to get some sleep."

"Of course, but Serenity..."

"Yes Gabriel?"

"I will prove myself to you. I will fix this. If you can't believe anything else I say, believe that."

*****

True to his word he vanished and I had been able to sleep through the night without any interruptions from the dearly departed. As much as I didn't want to believe anything he said to me, it was hard to deny the fact that having him back and coming around again had kept everything that went bump in the night for me at bay. Something I'd definitely been missing.

Could I really believe in him and his ability to fix this? I mean I didn't even have any idea who or what he really was. He had already kept his distance when he specifically told me otherwise on more than one occasion.

"You're doing it again."

"Jesus, I'm sorry Ryan."

"I feel like there's something going on with you besides the voices. I know you don't exactly know me but you can trust me. I mean if you wanted to tell me what's going on."

He's right. I didn't exactly know him but maybe it would help to tell someone else about Gabriel. Someone other than Emma who couldn't offer anything more than a go get him attitude, something that didn't do me a lick of good. Maybe telling Ryan, his experience with voices and all, would open the door to another way of seeing things. At the very least I could get it out of my own head and let it be someone else's problem for a while.

Could I really talk about Gabriel though? Especially with another guy?

Sighing and leaning myself back on the blanket I looked up to the sky. I had done this before, more times than I could count. Looking to the sky for answers, something that would point me in the right direction. This time was no different. Though there were still no answers to be had.

"There's this voice."

"Okay, what about it?"

"He started talking to me about a month ago, maybe a little more. Every night at the same time and even sometimes during the day, when the other spirits become too much, he would come to me. Talk to me, god, he even sang to me a few times."

"A spirit actually sang to you?"

"Yeah."

"That sounds pretty awesome. So what is it about this voice that's got you spacing out so much?"

It was do or die time.

"Umm, he said some things to me before, things that I found out weren't exactly true. I pretty much told him to go away. I didn't want him around anymore and well, he listened for a couple days but he came back last night."

I watched as he absorbed everything I was telling him. His eyebrows rose, though his facial expression gave nothing away as to how he was taking it. Hopefully he wouldn't think I was being silly.

"Do you know why he visited you so often like that?"

"He said it was to watch over me and make sure I was alright. Funny thing is, whenever he was around the other spirits couldn't get within ten feet of me. It was as if he blocked them all."

"Wow, I didn't even think that was possible."

Now this is where he surprised me. If I'm completely honest, even before Gabriel had come back the night before the voices had been blocked from speaking to me and I figured that Ryan had been the reason for it. I mean I knew he wasn't like Gabriel but it was almost as if I was so immersed in spending time with him that he had the same effect. I had been hoping it hadn't been just me but apparently it was.

"You've never had the voices blocked, even for a few minutes?" I managed to choke out, somehow losing my nerve given that I seemed to have a relief system he hadn't found yet.

"Well no, at least not before two days ago but even then they aren't completely blocked from me just muffled for a while."

"They're muffled for you?"

"Yeah. Look I'm not crazy I swear Serenity but since the minute I met you, everything seems to be dulled that way. I mean like right now. Sitting here with you, talking about the voices I would expect someone, anyone to make an appearance, yet there hasn't been anything. As for this voice you're hearing that completely blocks it, I mean I seriously don't know what to make of it."

"Now you know how I feel." I spit out, not focusing on the tone of my voice or how I appeared. He was having the same effect on me as I am on him and for the life of me, I had no idea why.

If Ryan and I silenced each other's voices then maybe Gabriel wasn't needed after all. Maybe I didn't need to know everything about him the way I wanted to before. Maybe I could just enjoy this with Ryan and finally be able to enjoy life again.

"It's not a spirit." he said, his voice barely a decibel above a whisper, to the point that I'd almost not heard him at all.

"What did you say?"

"It's not a spirit, at least not a dead one."

"What do you mean, it has to be. What else is there to hear?"

"You said he sang to you right?"

I nodded wondering where he was going with his train of thought and thankful I didn't have to wait too long to find out.

"What spirit do you know of that can sing? I've never had it happen and I've had tons of female and male spirits talk to me over the years. Add that in with the fact that he completely blocks other spirits from getting to you, something that even though we're muffled around each other I can't even do and well I just think he's not a spirit."

I was afraid to ask but I had to know so I blurted it out. "So if he's not a spirit then what is he?"

Ryan looked up and his eyes locked on mine, the lightness of them darker than usual, his expression almost grave. If I hadn't already felt so comfortable around him seeing him this way now would most definitely frighten me.

"Angel."

"Oh God, not you too." I mumbled rolling my eyes. Not only was Emma doing her best to try and make me believe that Gabriel is indeed my guardian angel, now apparently Ryan wanted me to believe the same thing. What had gotten into everyone lately?

"Okay I know it sounds crazy but just hear me out alright. All I ask is that you keep an open mind."

"Sure, I mean it can't be anything worse than Emma tried telling me."

"What did Emma tell you?"

"Why she believed Gabriel is different."

"Wait! Did you just say his name is Gabriel?"

As he asked it occurred to me that when I had been explaining the voice to him I hadn't mentioned a name. Judging by the surprised look on his face, it was apparent that he hadn't been expecting it to be the name that it was. I nodded and just sat back to wait for him to continue.

81

"Okay, well a guardian angel is believed to be a spirit that is sworn to protect a person in their greatest time of need. Stronger than your average spirit, they have been known to have abilities that are practically unheard of, which really does go along with everything you've already told me. Now that I know his name though I'm thinking maybe I was wrong."

Oh good. Finally the idea of angels could be dropped. Sure spirits were real, especially the ones left roaming the earth because well, Ryan and I dealt with that daily but angels, I just couldn't wrap my mind around.

"Exactly. I told Emma she was crazy for even thinking it and given my own problems I mean that's saying something."

I watched as he moved across the blanket until he was directly in front of me, our eyes still locked on one another, his expression serious. Taking my hand into his, he began to speak again.

"She's not crazy Serenity. When you were in high school did you ever take a mythology course, or hell, a world religions one?"

"Yeah. Religion was an elective and since I didn't do so well with Phys Ed, I took it. What does that have to do with anything?"

I was finding it hard to concentrate on much of anything with him rubbing his fingers across my bare knuckles the way he was. I'm not sure what his intent had been moving this close but if he had meant it in a calming way, it is a complete failure. He is driving me crazy.

"There is a strong belief system in most religions that regards angels as the most holy of God's army. Look I know you don't believe it but please tell me at some point you went over this. Gabriel, along with Michael, Raphael and Uriel are known as Archangels. God's Warriors."

I now understood what he was getting at and I immediately felt sick. Ryan wasn't crazy, no more crazy then Emma was for mentioning it. They were right. There was an angel in mythology named Gabriel though what his role had been I couldn't remember. It had been years since I'd even thought of the class.

Could it be true? Is Gabriel really an angel, or more specifically, an archangel? Is that why he had been so vague yet at the same time standing by his truth that he would never leave me? I didn't want to believe any of this but it was getting harder by the second to deny.

"Holy crap."

"Exactly."

"Well what the hell am I supposed to do with that? There's an angel coming to me every night and talking to me. I'm even more of a freak now."

Moving his body and leaning back, pulling me back into his chest, he gently began rubbing my arms. I knew it was meant to calm me but I was reactive when it came to his touch so I just listened as the blood boiled under my skin.

"You are not a freak Serenity. You have the ability of Clair-audience. You can hear and speak with higher beings."

"No, see that's not right. I'm a medium. I can communicate with the dead. That's it."

"Well pretty girl, I know you don't want to admit it but you're much more than just a medium. Here!" He stopped suddenly. "I can prove it. Try something with me."

"Okay sure…"

"Can you hear me right now. If you can hear me, focus your mind and answer me back the same way."

Yes I could hear him but this is also something that I knew I could do already. I had talked to Gabriel more than once this way, less than two days before. Hearing Ryan in my head though freaked me out. It was one thing to have a spirit you could communicate with but another person like me? Just what the hell am I and how could I ever think I'd be normal?

"I can hear you."

"Well that settles that then." He replied, this time speaking out loud and taking me back out of my mind, something I was more than thankful for.

"What does this mean for me? Why do I have to be the one that can do all of this Ryan? Why can't I just be normal?"

He continued rubbing my arms and I was thankful for the distraction. I didn't want to think about any of this anymore so focusing my mind on the way my body felt every time he moved his hands up and down my arm kept the breakdown at bay.

"It means you have more gifts then you thought. You can talk to angels Serenity. I know it's scary and you want to be normal but you're not. You know what else you aren't?"

"No but I'm sure you're gonna tell me."

"Alone. You're not alone. Not anymore."

Before I had a chance to react to his words I felt his lips brush against mine and in that moment my mind, complete with all of the fear and anxiety I had been experiencing faded away. All I could feel is the way his slightly dry lips felt as they grazed mine.

I never wanted it to end.

CHAPTER THIRTEEN

Graham

I'm not sure what made me more nervous. Leaving my mother to practically fend for herself even with the nurses there three times a week; going away to a new college or seeing Serenity again. Maybe all three were equally as nerve wracking. Either way I was feeling it more and more the closer I came to this new place I would call home.

I had been driving for hours, watching each passing road sign on the highway, so hyper sensitive was I to missing my off ramp. I wasn't even entirely sure the anxiety I was feeling was all mine. It could very well have been coming from the angel that inhabited my body.

Gabriel told me in great detail before the two of us joined of the time before that he had been with me. I hadn't exactly been young when it happened but given the way I used to party and drink it was really no surprise I couldn't remember a lick of it. Though according to Gabe that is also something he had hidden well within my brain. I wasn't supposed to remember. Maybe in remembering what it had been like back then, I could get a handle on how to deal with it now.

I was on my own. Gabriel could offer no advice on how to make this situation easier. I had to rely on blind faith that once I reached my destination, started classes and gotten into the swing of things, including meeting Serenity again that whatever I was feeling now would fade. So for the next hour as I drove along, that's exactly what I focused my mind on. The proverbial light at the end of the tunnel.

I pulled the car into the motel parking lot and as I put it in park I took in my surroundings. I would only be here for the night and then it would be off to the dorms first thing in the morning. I had to make the best of the situation but looking around now I realized that might be a lot harder than I'd anticipated. This place looked like it had seen better days.

"Gabriel, your bright idea of starting this at night sucks."

I was sure he could hear me, but I wasn't looking for a response. Three of the four doors that were in my line of vision were either half hanging off their hinges, had bullet holes or just looked like they were in desperate need of a paint job. If I hadn't been beat from driving I would have gladly pulled out and found somewhere much more appropriate but as it was, I just couldn't take any more solitary time behind the wheel. I was going to go crazy and not in the fun way.

After securing my key and paying for the night, I made my way to my room, eying the door as I went inside, wondering what had happened to it before I'd gotten there that had caused the obvious dents and grooves that didn't belong. I went in and immediately threw my body down on the bed, closing my eyes and thinking about anything that would take my mind off the shit hole I now found myself in.

"There's no place like home Toto."

Thinking about the state of the motel made me wonder just what it was about this town that Serenity found so appealing that she'd gone away to college here. If this place is any indication it was no doubt that Gabriel had come to me for help with her. This place was a mess.

Thinking about her, brought up the memory of the first time I saw her. I still had a hard time believing that it was almost five years ago. To me it still felt like yesterday, that's how much of an impression it made on me.

*****

I' watched as the moving truck sat there, a woman about the same age as my own mom coming back and forth every few minutes grabbing things and going back towards the house. I couldn't tell you why I kept looking given that I wasn't exactly in the mood to pick up someone twice my age but I did. It was only after a few trips back and forth that I saw her. Off to the right side there was an oak tree and there she was, sitting all alone underneath.

She was too far away for me to tell what she was looking at but from where I stood now, she looked to be about my age. It was only when my mother spoke to me a minute or two later, my eyes still locked on the new girl that I decided what I had to do next.

"New people moving into the Forester house huh? Anyone interesting?"

"Nah not really, looks like a girl and her mom."

"A girl huh? Well what the heck are you doing standing here then?"

My mom is always trying to get me to meet new people. She hated the guys I hung out with at school and I swear she hated their girlfriends even more. So a new girl in the neighborhood was like Christmas for her. Now there would be a girl that she could cross the street and get to know and try and hook me up with.

She did bring up a good point though. The right thing to do would be to go across, introduce myself and offer to show her around. It was what any good neighbor would do.

Or at least that's what I told myself to make the short walk over.

Whether my mother was the reason I was doing it, or I was just listening to some voice in my head pushing me in that direction didn't matter. It was just something I had to do.

The closer I got to her, I realized that she was actually lounging back against the tree and she was tapping away on her phone. Now that I knew she wasn't entirely on her own out here under the tree I felt like an intruder. The last thing I wanted to do was meet her for the first time and piss her off.

"Do you always stare at random girls when they aren't paying attention or is this a special treat just for me?"

I wanted to slap myself. While I had been worried about bothering her by saying a simple hello she'd caught me staring and was going to call me on it. I had to admire it though, given my general size, people didn't usually go out of their way to talk to me the way this girl did. It was obvious I didn't even rate on her fear radar.

"Nope, I just save that for new girls that sit under trees."

"Good to know. So umm did you need something?" she asked, her voice less clear then it had been only a second before. From self-assured to awkward. This was a change I hadn't expected.

"My mom saw the moving truck and suggested I come over and introduce myself. Well introduce my family I guess. I can't really be sure. Anyway, here I am."

"Nice to meet you 'here I am'. I'm Serenity. My mom, the lady that refuses to let the moving men help her carry stuff inside, is Rachel."

Again she spoke without a hint of awkwardness making me wonder if I'd just imagined the earlier slip. I was already perplexed by this girl and I hadn't known her but two minutes total.

"My name is actually Graham."

"You got a last name 'my name is Graham'?"

"Hudson. Graham Hudson."

"Well nice to meet you Hudson." she said as she began to shift from her position, preparing to stand.

I wished there was something I could say that would stop her since I knew what was about to come next. I wasn't quite ready for this conversation to be over.

"So is that your boyfriend you were texting?" I shot out, preparing myself for the mental beat down I'd give myself later over the stupidity of the question. Though given that I'd heard her talking on the phone as I'd walked up, it wasn't entire invalid.

"Umm, no. That wasn't my...umm...boyfriend."

There's the awkwardness again, almost as if she was hiding something and I'd somehow outed it when I'd come across her. She most definitely hadn't been expecting me to ask that.

"You just like talking to yourself then?"

"Something like that." she shot back, her voice icy. *"Look, it's been fun but I really should go help my mom before she injures herself."*

I watched as she practically ran from me toward the truck where again her mother was carrying another load out, ready to bring it into the house. I wasn't entirely sure what I said but whatever it was, I obviously upset her, something I hadn't been attempting to do. What had only been a joke had now become so much more than that.

Realizing that it was probably my cue to leave and head back home, I turned to go but not before calling out to her one last time.

"I'll see you at school Serenity."

*****

I learned what she had been hiding from me that day but it had taken a lot of time getting to know her before she would open up. When she finally did, she'd been expecting me to be shocked. I guess I should have been but if anything all it did was explain the real mystery of the girl next door. It was as if in telling me she'd answered all the questions I hadn't even realized I had.

When my mom made her off handed comment that day about going to meet the girl next door, I hadn't held much stock in it but years later, knowing the lasting affect that very same girl had on me, I knew it is something I might spend the rest of my life thanking her for.

It's that very same girl that brought me to this town now. It is her safety and helping Gabriel keep her protected that drove me and as I lay on the bed, surrounded in warmth from the memories I knew that I am right where I need to be. More than that, I was right where I wanted to be. All anxiety over whether or not seeing her again would be a good thing seemed to be waning.

In fact I couldn't wait for the morning because this time, I wasn't planning on letting her get away.

CHAPTER FOURTEEN

Serenity

"Wait, back up, you two what?" Emma asked, jumping from the bed as if it was on fire. She was practically on top of me before I had a chance to blink my eyes.

"I told you Ems. He kissed me and well, I sort of kissed him back."

From the minute I got home and found Emma lounging on her bed I knew this was where the conversation would lead. She had warned me before that she wanted to know everything that happened on our pseudo-date in the quad and as much as I would have rather kept it to myself, I knew that I wouldn't. Given my lack of experience in all things guy related, I would have to tell her just so that I could get some understanding of exactly what he might have been thinking.

Sure, she wasn't a guy but she'd gone out with enough of them over the years that she had the uncanny ability of being able to read their mind. It was really quite fascinating, the knowledge she'd managed to assemble in just a few years' time. She is the encyclopedia of guy. No doubt about it.

"Okay let me get this straight. You talk to Gabriel for months practically. At least every single night and you get nowhere with him until one day he just up and leaves you. You meet Ryan and three days later you're kissing him? What the hell happened to you?"

"What's that supposed to mean?" I asked, spinning around and facing her. If she was going to insinuate that I was turning into some kind of slut the least she could do was actually say the words.

She held up her hands in surrender, sensing by my tone that I was offended by what she was trying to say. It also didn't help that hearing Gabriel in the same breath as Ryan did something funny to my insides. Like it shouldn't be happening.

"Ser, you know I don't mean anything by it. I just—well I'm having a hard time understanding how things happened this fast. This is not you."

"Don't you think I know that? I don't do guys, at least not since—well you know."

"Graham."

"Thanks for putting that out there, as always you're so helpful. Yes Graham."

"Well you can't not say his name ever again Ser, I mean he is a pretty big part of your past. Hell, when you moved away, he is the person that kept you alive."

She was right about that. When my mother decided to move me, thinking that a change of pace was just what the doctor ordered, I left Emma behind. From the day I met her she had been my rock. That was at least until I let Graham get close enough to fill the void. Spending time with him the way I did back then had kept me sane when otherwise I felt like I was losing my mind. He knew everything about me and yet still somehow stood by me. It was nice, but it's also something that given the way I felt about him I wasn't entirely ready to talk about. Even with two years passing.

"Well right now he's irrelevant. This isn't about him. I didn't kiss Graham. I kissed Ryan."

"Right, so back to that then. How was it? Is he a good kisser? Because I mean he looks like he would be, not that I've ever thought about whatitwouldbeliketokisshimor"

"Emma, breathe." I said, cutting her off before she could go any further. "You're talking so fast your words are running together. Yes, he's a good kisser but I don't see how you can look at someone and just assume that. Though I don't really have much to go on. It was nice."

"Well you did kiss Graham that one time."

There it is. His name coming up again. Of course it was bound to given that he was the only guy I'd experienced much of anything with since the day they let me out. That didn't mean I had to enjoy talking about it though.

About six months before I'd left and come here for school, I kissed Graham. I would have loved to say that my first kiss was the things fairy tales were made of but that would be the farthest thing from the truth. Mainly because I kissed my best friend and he hadn't known anything about the way I felt about him. Or that I wanted to kiss him for a while before it happened. He hadn't been expecting it which in the end made it very anti fairy-tale.

"Can we please stop talking about Graham." I stated with a sigh.

Right now with Graham being as far away as he is, he really had no place in the conversation. What had happened with him had been ages ago and there was no sense rehashing everything now. Not when I am already overly preoccupied with the other two men in my life.

"Fine, don't talk about the only male experience you ever had before now. See if I care."

"See if I care? Really Ems? That is the best you could come up with?" I asked, sticking my tongue out at her, completing the transformation from adult to child just the way she intended, causing both of us to break out in laughter.

"So what happened after he kissed you, did things get weird?"

"I'm not exactly sure what to make of what happened afterward."

I didn't want to admit it to her but what happened after the kiss is kind of the real reason I am back in the room so soon before my next class. It happened to be one that he didn't share with me and given everything that happened, escaping to my room for the remainder seemed like the smartest thing to do.

As much as I think he didn't want to come across differently after the kiss, he really had no control over it. It started when he pulled away from me, his expression pained. I'd been reading a lot into him, making assumptions and letting my paranoia get the best of me. I didn't want to do that every time something happened between us but that expression, it threw my mind into overdrive.

I could believe that pulling away caused him pain because he didn't want to stop which is the positive response or it could be that he had done something he instantly began to regret, the negative response.

I really wanted to believe that he enjoyed it as much as I did but my experience told me differently. In just the same way as there had been that awkwardness afterward with Graham, it was replaying itself out all over Ryan's face.

92

Dammit.

As much as I didn't want to think about Graham, it always kept on coming back to him. Especially given the way events had gone today. It made me remember that day years before, the memory flooding my subconscious, forcing me to look at it even though doing so might be painful.

We'd gotten so close. I had finally broken down and told him about the voices in my head and though he could have run, he didn't. He'd stayed and even went so far as to look up what it might be and ways to cope with it so that I didn't have to suffer anymore. Which only made the bond between us, at least on my end, that much stronger. Days spent hanging out together, either at his house or my own turned into weeks where he worked his magic and had gotten me to leave the house. For movies first and then more towards the end the occasional party. He was just that good at being my best friend. He could have probably talked me into doing something illegal and I'd have gone along with it. Such was the pull of Graham Hudson.

It was after one of these parties that I stepped out of my comfort zone. Way far out given that I didn't have the faintest idea most days how to talk to people, let alone make a move on one. I was feeling strong though and taking the risk had seemed like the right thing to do.

So as he walked me home from one of his buddies' houses one night, making sure in the Graham way that I made it home safely, I saw my chance.

*****

"Can I ask you something?"

"Depends on whose asking. Is it the Serenity that drank those three beers thinking I didn't notice, or is it the Serenity that told me she never drank?"

"Ugh really Hudson, you're gonna be like that?" I asked with a giggle, shoving my hands into his shoulder in an attempt to knock him over.

"Hell yeah I'm gonna be like that Richards. You'd just get pissed if I wasn't."

"True." I slurred out, smile still planted firmly on my face.

"What did you want to ask me?"

"Why don't you have a girlfriend?"

The words tumbled off my lips and I prayed they came out right. It had been bothering me for a while, the amount of time he spent with me when he could obviously be out having more fun with other girls, ones that didn't actually have any mental issues.

"Uh, don't really want one I guess." he replied awkwardly. "Why do you ask?"

I stopped myself then. If we were going to have this conversation then I wanted to complete it, not start, reach my house and have it end. I didn't know when I would ever have the nerve to bring this up again so I wanted to deal with it now.

"Just wondered I guess."

"You just wondered about my relationship status? Yeah, because that's not weird at all." Noticing that I stopped he motioned in the way of our houses. It was obvious that as much as I wanted to have the conversation, he didn't.

"Well I am weird."

"No you're not Serenity. We've been over this like a million times now. You're not a freak or weird, or whatever. You're different."

Whenever he called me different it always made my heart beat faster and I always found it harder to breathe, as if hearing the words cut off all air flow to my brain causing me to go numb. Another reason I wanted to go through with this. Living with the way he made me feel was driving me crazy.

"You could have your pick of like, any girl at that party and yet here you are walking my drunk ass home. You spend most Friday nights, which I hear are date nights, at home with me watching movies when you could be out at a party and actually having a good time. Guess I just wondered why that is. Why you would torture yourself that way."

There. I'd said it, putting it all out on the table. The very things I questioned every time we were together. I guess I always believed he deserved better than wasting a life buried away in a house with me doing something as trivial as movie watching when he had a whole life in front of him.

His life shouldn't have to stop because I had issues leaving the house.

"It's not torture." He stated as he walked back the few steps to where I stood, resting his hands on my shoulders. Looking me directly in my overly glazed eyes he spoke again. "I'm doing exactly what I want to be doing, with exactly who I want to do it with. No torture involved. Okay?"

"I really should get you home, you look like you could fall over any second. I really shouldn't have let you--"

Pushing my lips to his, cutting off his train of thought, no longer wanting to hear his voice, I allowed myself the one thing I had been craving, knowing that this was my one and only chance to do it without fear being a factor. As I allowed myself to enjoy the feel of his lips on mine, I realized that it was even more amazing then I'd imagined it.

The sensation caused sparks to go off within my brain, making it even fuzzier then the alcohol had done earlier in the night. I was about to pull away when he responded in kind, his lips moving over mine, his tongue snaking out just a little to lick across my bottom lip, awakening a burning sensation in my body I had never felt before. A feeling so foreign yet so inviting I was powerless to resist it.

Desire.

As our lips moved together, the kiss about to deepen, he pulled away, backing up quickly. His hands instantly going to his lips, to the very place mine had just been. His eyes were locked on the ground as if afraid to look up and see mine. I wasn't sure what to make of it. I felt him respond, hell my body was still overheating from the experience yet here he was backing away.

*****

There is no doubt that the kiss had been powerful for me, for so many reasons. It had been my first real kiss. It had been the one and only time that I'd taken a chance on something I'd been feeling and given the way he pulled away and insisted again that he get me home before I passed out slammed the door on me ever wanting to do it again. So I hadn't.

Graham pushed me away that night for a reason he never did get to explain to me and I had just sucked up the pain and hurt I felt and moved on with my life. I made a promise that night that no matter how close I came to being in a situation like that one again, I wouldn't act on my impulses and I hadn't. Not in the years that passed have I ever been near a situation quite like that one.

Until Ryan.

"Serenity! Earth to Serenity."

Emma. Shit. I'd gotten so caught up in my own thoughts I'd completely forgotten that she was here and we'd been talking.

"Sorry Ems. Just thinking about what happened today." I said, lying through my teeth.

"What did happen? What did he do and why are you back in the room alone and not off making out with him somewhere?"

"I don't want to be off making out with him Emma."

"Fine but you don't want to be here either. So what the hell happened?"

"He pushed me away after Ems. He got up, stammered off something about needing to be somewhere and he left. Well he said sorry and then he left."

I could tell by the look on her face she was shocked. That she hadn't been expecting that to be the way it had played itself out. She had been hoping for a much better ending and I didn't blame her because I had been too.

"That son of a bitch. The next time I see him I'm totally going to rip him apart."

"Ems don't. Look, it's alright. I thought he wanted to kiss me and that he was as into as I was, but he wasn't. He regrets it. It's okay."

"No Ser, it's not okay. Good guys don't do that when they kiss a girl. They don't get up and leave."

"Well maybe they don't for most girls because those girls are worth it. I guess I'm just not."

Ryan

Son of a bitch.

When I took this assignment, it seemed so pretty damn cut and dry. Go to Earth, find the girl and befriend her. In doing so I would be preparing her for her destiny of which to this point she was blissfully unaware. It was even made easier by the fact that she is a medium. She is able to hear and speak with the dead, something we have in common. It would make bonding that much simpler.

Despite claims to the contrary I am not a demon. Well not a full one anyway. I am a half breed.

The story goes that before I was born my mother screwed around with one of Lucifer's most trusted confidants and in turn she had given birth to me. When I turned four she had gone ahead and made a deal with the devil. Literally. By the time I was five I was able to communicate with the dead and nearly departed just as Serenity could. Of course because half of my blood is demon, I have powers that other humans can't even imagine.

I had gone through life being different but also at the same time being groomed for a much larger destiny. So for every minute I spent on the outskirts of the social groups I was making up for it in rewards for the only man I've ever known as my father. Up until recently it had been a more than willing trade off. Being human was overrated anyway.

By the time my fifteenth birthday rolled around, I was able to say that I had met the devil. Lucifer had made his first actual appearance in my life that I was able to remember. It was then that he told me of my destiny. That I would be a main player in the falling of Heaven. That when the time was right, he would call for me and it would begin. Of course back then I had no idea what he meant but I couldn't deny that I was thrilled with the idea. I could finally break away from my mother, go out on my own and create my own path.

So I put up with the voices, the visions and my ability to read minds, all of which had kept me on the sidelines of what could have been a normal life. I spent every day looking at the calendar, seeing each day for what it was, just a number in a countdown that would somehow eventually end.

My mother hated me. She made sure I knew every single day what an abomination she believed me to be. There was no love lost between us. I didn't care if she up and died and honestly I think she felt the same way. While we might have never come right out and said it, it is something well known. The fighting between us the older I became just got worse, neither one of us wanting to back down. I may have gotten my looks from my father which caused no shortness of distress for her, but I'd also gotten her stubbornness.

Given my enhanced features and skills, I really have the world at my fingertips. There is nothing I could want for, other than love but given who I was, love had never played a part in my life. I could pretty well talk myself out of any situation I wanted, be given anything I craved without batting so much as an eyelash. Most people would have overdosed on that but that is where I differed from the populace. My mother may have accused me of being the spitting image of my father but this was one of the parts of him I didn't want to share.

There had been many girls over the years and then women as I got older that had thrown themselves in my direction looking for any scrap of attention but I never gave it. They never interested me. I just hadn't met one that wasn't into getting something from me and those types did nothing for me. I am much better off on my own.

I could not be like my father and binge on the humans. I may have been blessed or whatever with my looks and my easygoing temperament away from home but that didn't mean I had to use it. I did not have a sweet tooth and the world was not my candy store. I wasn't going to binge eat until I made myself sick. I suppose that is another win for my mother. I am less like my father then she believed me to be.

Two years ago, when I turned twenty I got another visit from Lucifer. He had made a few visits over the years mainly to witness my progress but it was this visit where I was informed that I am going to be his right hand man. That there is no one that showed the promise that I had and I would serve him better than those before me. He also informed me that on my twenty first birthday I would begin taking steps in his master plan. Up until that point he had only given me small details of what was to come but it was then he told me everything.

He had finally found the woman that would become his bride. It's not traditional in the way Lilith had been before. No this one is different. She is human and she is young, my age in fact. He had learned of her accidentally and after spending time watching her, or in his way, having her watched he knew she was the one. Which is where I came in. I was to go to her and put the plan that until now had been working brilliantly into action. I jumped at the chance. This was my time to show him what I could really do and essentially make him proud.

My being half human was a risk, one that he made sure I was aware of. I could not let the normal human disposition and way of being override the ultimate goal. If that happened, he warned that he would wipe me both from the world and from my ultimate high ranking spot in hell.

I would cease to exist.

Which leads me to now. I've just kissed Lucifer's bride. To an outsider, it could easily be explained as me doing whatever was needed to gain her trust. Feeding her information the way I am and then kissing her the way I did, would keep her mind from figuring me out before the time was right. I knew differently. I hadn't kissed Serenity because I needed to continue some game, I had done it because I wanted to.

She is irresistible to me, which explained why Lucifer wanted her so badly for himself. Her power was unparalleled. Her abilities were strong and only growing stronger with each passing day. The way she carried herself even though she is as horribly inept socially as I am captivated me enough to pull me right in. Add all of that to the way she looked, even while lounging on the world's ugliest blanket in the sunlight and there was no denying it.

I was hooked.

I shouldn't have kissed her not when the very thing Lucifer had warned me about is happening right before my eyes but I couldn't help myself. I hadn't been lying when I told her that as a child I prayed for someone to come along like me so I wouldn't be alone anymore. I had done it on more than one occasion and now here she was.

Nothing I said to her had been a lie.

I had been told to use whatever means necessary to get her to grow close to me and I fully planned on doing just that. At least until I walked into that classroom with her best friend and actually met her. Come face to face with her. Once that happened all bets were off. There was no way I could bring myself to lie to her.

As it is, I am so affected just being in her presence that I wanted to tell her everything about me, including just what I have been sent here to do. I couldn't do that though. Even when she inevitably became Lucifer's bride I could never admit just who and what I was and the part I played in changing her life forever. She would never forgive me and I wasn't entirely sure I could live with that.

Right now though I had much more serious things to concern myself with. Things that caused me to pull away from her and the kiss to begin with. Life and death things.

I am going to be in some serious shit when Lucifer finds out.

CHAPTER FIFTEEN

Graham

The first time I saw Serenity again I assumed she would be so different that I wouldn't be able to recognize her. Standing here, leaning against the tree as she walked up the steps with her friend, it was apparent that while she may have changed a little, it's in the most subtle of ways.

Her brown hair is now longer, hanging down her back with hints of waviness to it where before she kept it cropped tightly just above her shoulders. She'd grown a little taller but still remained a few inches below my six foot frame. She had curves in all the right places yet still remained relatively thin. I didn't want to focus on the ways her physical body had changed but shit, I was a guy, I went there.

She remained much the same in the ways that mattered to me. The ways that would always distinguish her from the others in a crowd. She still kept her head down when she walked, as if she was unsure of herself but she seemed to smile more which to me meant everything. She hadn't done it nearly enough during our time together but when she did, it had been heart stopping.

I recognized the friend she was walking with as Emma, the girl she'd told me about when we were getting to know each other. The other keeper of her secrets. While I had only gotten to see Emma through pictures it looked like she hadn't changed much over the years either. Still the more outgoing of the two of them.

Serenity had often talked about Emma and how she was constantly surprised the two of them were friends given how different they were. Emma had been the outgoing one; the one craving attention and who had a flare for the dramatic. Serenity had been the complete opposite of all of that, preferring to spend the time alone and not liking to call attention to herself. The way she was back then and quite obviously still is now is one of the reasons I liked her as much as I did.

I've always been the laid back guy. The one who would much rather spend one on one time with someone I cared about then being caught in a big crowd of people I didn't know. That was half the reason I didn't go to parties much, focusing instead on spending my time with her and my art. It had always been my passion and even now, it remained with me. Much the same way that Serenity herself did.

Right from that first meeting she'd gotten under my skin. Getting to know her had become almost like a game to me, one I needed to win. I had to get as close to her as she'd let me and given our history, that was pretty damn close. I hadn't exactly handled everything that happened between us the right way but I was planning on rectifying all of that now. I was being given a second chance to get close to the girl that had changed my life, there was no way I was letting the opportunity pass.

Content that I'd give her more than enough time for a head start getting to the class, I pulled myself off the tree and began to follow the very same path I just watched her and Emma take. I'd gotten here early enough this morning to be able to see her before she ran into me. It had become a mission for me. I needed to know what I was getting myself into. After spending most of the night restless and unable to sleep, I made the plan in the early hours and was intent on seeing it through.

It's time to make my appearance. While there is a little residual anxiety over just how she would react to me showing up here and in some of her classes, I was happy that the majority had been taken away the second I'd seen her again. That somehow solidified what I had agreed to and made it more right than it had felt the night before.

"Do not push her. Take things slowly."

I wondered if Gabriel was going to make an appearance. He hadn't said anything the night before but hearing him now was a reminder that I wasn't entirely alone in this. That he is right there with me should this backfire. At least I wasn't going in blind.

"I wasn't planning on pushing her. You've been with me before, you should know I don't do that."

"You are right. My apologies."

"Don't worry man, I got this."

102

Having the ability to talk to an angel is something you really never get used to. I found that knowing he was there had its perks but when he spoke inside of my head, it always threw me off. That was only compounded by the fact that I could answer him back.

If Gabriel had given me the right schedule, then I needed to find English Literature. Given what he told me about her dream of being a doctor, I found it amusing that the first class we shared had nothing at all to do with it. Maybe there is more to this girl now then even Gabriel is aware of.

"Hey man, you lost?"

I was lost but I wasn't about to admit it. God starting a new school, even college was exactly the same as doing it when you were a teenager. It is awkward as hell. It explained why there wasn't a person alive that enjoyed being the new kid. There were just too many variables to consider.

"Not lost, just new."

"Been there man. What class you looking for?"

'English Literature with Professor Michelson. You wouldn't be able to point me in the right direction would ya?"

The guy laughed which made me feel a little better about not knowing what the hell was going on. He pointed down the hall and motioned with his hands what I needed to do.

"Go straight, turn right where that one light is dimmed out and you'll be where you need to be."

"Thanks man." I said, shooting the guy a small wave as I began to jog in the direction he'd just explained. I reached the door but as I was about to pull it open and make my way inside, it opened from the other side. Before I had a chance to react and move out of the way, the body slammed into mine. The force wasn't strong enough to knock me over but I couldn't say the same for the person who hit me. With a squeal her body landed on the floor in front of me.

"Jesus, I'm sorry. Here let me help you up." I held out my hand for her to take and when she placed her hand into mine, I noticed how significantly smaller than my own it was, right before the shock hit my body and ran straight up through my arm. Looking down at her as I helped her up I realized just who it is that I bumped into. Serenity. The very person I joined this pointless class to see.

Talk about timing.

Helping her to her feet I watched as she began wiping at her clothes, obviously trying to brush off any remaining dust and embarrassment she may be wearing on her face. She hadn't yet looked up and caught my eyes so I admired her for the few seconds that I was being allowed.

She really is the same old Serenity. Awkward and clumsy to a fault, never paying the right amount of attention to the world around her. Always caught up inside her head. God how I missed her.

"I'm sorry. I should have been watching when I opened the damn door. I didn't hurt you did I?" She looked up at me as she asked the question, the light going off in her head as she realized just who she'd bumped into. She knew me and now the blush that had been on her cheeks spread even more until her entire face began turning red.

"You most definitely didn't hurt me."

Watching the red deepen even more I couldn't help but smile. I knew I wasn't helping her much, continuing her embarrassment but she was so damn cute doing it, I wasn't going out of my way to make it stop.

"Umm, Wow, Umm..."

"Yes?"

"Graham?"

"I wondered how long it would take you to figure it out princess."

"W—What are y—you doing here?"

I hadn't heard that stammer in years and though I didn't want to admit it, it still drove me wild. It wasn't so much that the stammer itself is attractive to me, it is more that even after all this time, she was so affected that she's reverting back to the way she used to be that did it. She was that much more attractive when completely taken out of her element.

"Just transferred in. I was told they have a pretty good art program so I figured I'd give it a try."

She nodded, obviously not trusting her voice to speak. She's nervous and truthfully, I kind of like it.

"You're taking English Lit?"

104

"Yeah, needed to fill out my schedule, seemed like an easy enough choice."

"Well I won't keep you..."

She began to move her body around me but before she could get far I reached out, resting my hand on her arm. I couldn't let it end that quickly. She had a habit just as I did of bolting when things became awkward and uncomfortable but I couldn't let her do it this time. She had no reason to feel this way around me. She didn't need to run.

"Ser, wait."

Looking at my hand on her arm and then rising her eyes to meet mine she seemed to regain her composure. At least if the stony look in her eye was any indication.

"Yeah?"

"Where are you going?"

"I stupidly left the very book we're studying in my room. I've got maybe two minutes before the professor gets here to run to my room and get it. So if you'll excuse me..."

She pulled her arm out of my grasp and quickly made her way down the hallway, the farther away from me she went, her brisk walk breaking into a run. As if she couldn't get away from me fast enough. It bothered me to no end.

I had known coming back into her life this way was going to take time. I couldn't just walk back in given our history and just expect her to welcome me with open arms but I had been hoping for a better result then what I was getting.

As I watched her retreat, I swore I heard a hushed tone inside my head, something I most definitely didn't want to deal with right now.

"Well that went well..."

"I'd like to see you do any better."

"I could have."

"Oh yeah wise one, how would you have done any better?"

"I would have gone after her."

Just the same way it happened with my mother the day Serenity had come into my life, it happened again. A light bulb being turned on in my brain. I knew what I had to do. Gabriel was right, I had to go after her.

Backing away from the classroom door I followed her for the second time that day. If I am going to do what both Gabriel wanted and also what I promised myself, I had to start now. I couldn't miss any chances. There is no way I am letting Serenity out of my sight again.

No way in hell.

Serenity

I couldn't move fast enough. Of all the times for my legs to be tired and for me to be drained, now is not it. I needed to move and I needed to do it quickly.

Graham Hudson.

What the hell was he doing here? Sure, I'd just been thinking about him this morning but that didn't mean he had to show up. I knew there was a reason I didn't like bringing him up and now I'm faced with it. I hadn't dealt with the way we left things and now here he was to dredge it all up again.

Throwing open the door to Tamara Hall and racing inside, I waited for the door to shut completely before breathing a sigh of relief. With as out of breath as I felt running my way across the campus like a crazy person, having a chance to suck in some air without fear of Graham around the corner was very welcome.

It's only when I looked up that I saw him. He was making his way to the door and within a few seconds if I didn't move then we'd be face to face again just the way we had been in front of class.

No, I definitely could not take another round of that right now. Seeing him once had been enough.

I started to take the stairs, two at a time slowing only as I heard the door open behind me. A shiver of fear ran through me. Yes I knew this guy, knew him better than anyone but that didn't mean that I wasn't scared as hell at the fact that he was following me.

"Serenity stop! Please! Don't run from me."

My feet planted themselves on the stairs almost as if obeying his command. God why did this guy have to have the effect he did on me? It had been years for crying out loud. Surely something like that wears off after enough time passes.

106

"Go away Graham."

"No. Not until you stop and talk to me."

What could he possibly have to say? He let me leave without so much as a goodbye and now here he is wanting to talk? Just who the hell did he think he was?

"We have nothing to talk about. So just turn around and go."

"I can't do that."

Spinning around on the stairs so I could actually get a look at the man I was yelling at, I was shocked by the expression I saw on his face. The pain in his eyes. The very same look I'd seen just the day before on Ryan, right after he kissed me. I am definitely not in the mood for another go round with this.

"Why not?"

"Because there are things I need to say to you. Things that I need you to hear and I can't leave until you do."

"You've said more than enough already by not saying anything at all. Leave please." I pleaded, hoping that he'd just take the hint and go. I had way too much on my plate as it is and having him here wanting to talk was just going to add to it.

The voices were starting to seem like a blessing now with the way my outside world was imploding.

I started making my way back up the stairs again, this time taking them at a slower pace. The small burst of fear I originally felt was gone, replaced instead by a seething anger just on the surface that was begging to explode. I had no idea what his game is with this but I really didn't want any part of it.

Thinking he'd taken my advice and left I began making my way up the second flight when suddenly I felt a light brush against my arm. Spinning around, I ran straight into his chest. For the second time I felt his arms spread around my body to my back absorbing the pull sensation as he brought me as close as he could to him.

"Let me go."

"Holy shit." he whispered under his breath, causing me to look up in alarm.

"What?"

"It feels even better than I imagined it would."

Now I'm confused, well more confused. Just what the heck was he talking about? Intrigued to find out what he meant but not entirely willing to ask, I began struggling against his body for release. I just wanted to get to my room and shut the door. I could block him out and everything would be fine. I just needed to get away.

"I'm not going to hurt you Serenity, you know that. Please stop fighting me."

After a few more attempts at breaking free I finally felt my body surrender into his. He's right. I knew him and knew he wouldn't physically hurt me. He just had no idea that him being here the way he is, holding me, is doing exactly what he didn't want to do. He was hurting me, just not in the way he thought.

How is it that in the span of a weeks' time I not only had a voice that drove me crazy, a guy that kissed me yet didn't seem to want to kiss me and now the first boy I ever loved all back in my life? Just who had I pissed off on the other side to earn this?

"What did y—you mean when you said it was b—better than you imagined?" I choked out, my stutter back in full force.

"Holding you. Having my arms around you. I've been waiting years to find out and well now I know."

Oh this is too much. I had to be dreaming. There is no way in hell Graham was really here and acting exactly the same way he'd always been, making my belly do flops over the sweet sound of his voice. No I definitely had to be dreaming.

"Oh. Okay."

Not letting me go, in fact making a point of continuing to hold me, rubbing his hands up and down the small of my back softly, he spoke again.

"I know that I owe you an explanation and I want to tell you everything. I don't expect to make everything right with a few words but I really hope you'll let me at least try. I just found you again, I'm not ready to walk away yet."

"I'll listen but please Graham, let me go."

He did as I asked immediately and I let go of the breath I'd been holding as my body finally began to relax. Motioning to the rest of the stairs we still had to travel, I began walking, enjoying the silence even though I wasn't naive enough to think it would last forever. No, I knew that once we reached my room, it was going to be anything but silent. I just wasn't sure how I felt about it.

Just what did Graham being here mean and am I going to regret even asking the question?

CHAPTER SIXTEEN

Graham

Finally I'm getting somewhere.

There had been a minute on the stairs where I didn't think I'd get through to her. Where I really believed I wouldn't get her to lower her walls and let me in again. I am beyond thankful that I'd finally been able to get through because I wasn't sure what I would have done if she turned me away completely. I hadn't really gotten that far in my plan.

"Since she won't be back for at least an hour, you might as well sit on Emma's bed." she said, motioning to the bed just off the wall closest to the door. If that bed is Emma's then that meant the one across the room was hers. Apparently her sense of style hadn't changed much either since I'd known her given the lack of color. Her blanket was an off putting shade of green, something that belonged more on an army base then in a room like this. Standard white pillow cases sat on top of the blanket, by far the brightest part.

Where there were posters on Emma's side, practically all running on top of each other with no space between them, it was the complete opposite for Serenity. The lone movie poster the only remnants that anyone existed here at all.

When she lived across from me and I'd been inside her room, it hadn't looked much different than this which meant she was still in constant flight mode. Never getting attached to one location. Always ready to move at a moment's notice, which saddened me. I hoped for more with her when she left. I thought she'd go away and experience life the way she was meant to. Not the way she'd been her entire life. I wanted more brightness, happiness and love for her. Not this.

Never this.

"Thanks."

"You said there were some things you wanted to say to me. So go ahead."

I was at a loss. I hadn't exactly planned how much to tell her. It wasn't like I'd gone in knowing she would react like this and I'd have to fight for even five minutes of her time. I expected her to be put off by me but witnessing actual fear from her, something we never had between us, I had no idea where to begin.

"Okay then, well I guess I want to tell you that I missed you."

Nodding at my words she finally made her way over to her own bed and sat down. She is putting distance between us already. What am I supposed to do with that?

"Speak from the heart Graham. That is what she wants. Tell her everything you feel. Do not hold anything back or she will sense it and she will remove you."

"Didn't you tell me just a few minutes ago to go easy with her? Telling her everything is not going to be easy."

"You are correct I did say that but you can see her just as I can. I think she needs to hear this now. It has been far too long. It may be the only way for you to remain with her."

He had a point. It had been far too long between the two of us. The things I should have told her back then needed to be said. Not because if they weren't I would be kicked out of her room but because if I didn't say them then I'd regret it for the rest of my life. Of that I was sure. I am already regretting it and it hadn't exactly been all that long.

"Is that all you wanted to say?" she asked lightly, fiddling with her fingers, looking anywhere but at me.

"Do you remember when you told me about hearing the voices and being able to talk to them?" I asked, figuring that if I had to start anywhere, there was no better place than that. It had been the moment she completely opened up to me and probably the moment I first realized I loved her. When she nodded, I continued.

"You scared the shit out of me that day. I really thought everything you told me about being put away for those two and a half years was true. You really were crazy." She locked eyes with me then and I put my hand up to fend off the attack I am sure was coming my way. "Let me finish princess before you threaten to cut my balls off."

"Fine."

"All it took was one look in your eyes and I mean one real look to see that you weren't lying to me. That what you told me was true. Or at least you believed it to be true. If anyone else had told me that, I would have laughed myself right out of their life but with you, it was the complete opposite. That's when it all started, at least for me."

"When w—what all started?" she stammered in obvious confusion.

"When I began to realize that I liked you."

I stopped myself and waited for her reaction. If there was any indication that she wasn't fully prepared to hear everything I had to say, I expected it now. When no reaction came, I continued.

"Do you remember the night of the party? The one you got drunk at?"

"What about it?"

"I was an idiot that night but in my own defense I really believed I was doing the right thing. Turns out I've been bothered by it ever since and I'm not really sure that what I did was the right thing after all. I think I really fucked things up. We were never really the same after that."

I wanted her to say something. Anything that would give me some kind of idea what she was feeling. Watching her fiddling with her fingers and looking away from me the way she was, is eating me alive.

"What are you talking about?"

"That night, when you kissed me, I thought you'd done it because you'd been drinking. All I could see was that I needed to get you home before you did anything else you'd regret in the morning. I didn't want to be your regret Serenity. I don't think my heart could handle it. Hell, it's been years and my heart still can't handle the fact that we don't even so much as talk on the phone anymore."

I am getting to the heart of the matter, just the way Gabriel told me. I am giving her every bit of me. All of the parts she hadn't seen back then. She affected me and I stupidly pushed her away instead of bringing her close. I didn't need an angel inside of me to know that. I had known it all along. I just hadn't wanted to admit it to myself before now.

"I am an idiot for never telling you that when you kissed me it was like you read my mind. That you were doing the one thing I'd been dying to do for months. I lost my best friend because I couldn't handle the fact that she actually may have done what she did because she liked me too."

"Okay.." she said, her voice beginning strong but fading off.

Is this the point where she told me that I am too little too late and didn't want to hear it anymore?

"Come on princess. You can't just hear all that and not respond. You're driving me crazy here."

Against my better judgment I stood from Emma's bed and made my way over to her. Lowering myself to the floor on my knees, I looked up into her eyes. I didn't want to spook her but not being able to gauge her reaction to my words was bothering me. Pulling her left hand away from her right and the consistent fidgeting that she maintained the entire time I spoke, I placed it into mine, wrapping my fingers around it.

"Say something Ser, please."

"What am I supposed to say to that Graham? It's been two years..." she replied weakly.

"You say what you feel. You yell or scream at me. You can punch me. Anything you want to really. Just don't keep giving me the silent treatment. I need to know what you're thinking."

After a few seconds of silence she spoke again, this time the stammer gone and her voice crystal clear.

"I was drunk that night, you're right. I'd never done anything like that before but I liked the way it made me feel. It gave me courage that I didn't have normally. I may have been out of it but I knew exactly what I was doing."

"So wait. You're saying you really did want to kiss me?"

Sighing she looked up at me and I could see it again in her eyes. The truth. It was dancing in them, clear as day. She didn't have to say another word more.

"I thought I was the one that stammered. Since when do you do it?" her lips lifted in the smallest of smiles as she spoke and I couldn't help lighting up at the sight. It had been so long since I'd seen her smile that I was going to enjoy every second of it before it disappeared again.

"What can I say, you inspire me."

"Yeah okay smart ass. To answer your question though, yes Graham, I wanted to kiss you that night and for weeks beforehand. You were..." she said, breaking off.

"I was what?"

"You were different. You've always been different."

"Oh you hear voices and talk to them daily but I'm the different one?"

She used her free hand to smack my arm and I sighed. This right here, the silly banter between the two of us, is what I missed the most. I couldn't do this with anyone else and even if I could it would never feel the way it did with Serenity.

"You didn't think it was so crazy when you started looking it up on the internet."

"I would have said or done anything back then Ser, if it meant spending more time with you. Doesn't matter how out of this world it sounded."

"Out of this world huh?"

"Yeah back then it was for sure but lately, I'm starting to think it might not be that crazy after all."

"What's that supposed to mean?"

I was fully prepared in that moment to tell her about Gabriel and about how I had come to have an angel inside of me but before I could form the words, I heard his voice and I immediately shut my mouth.

"One revelation at a time Graham. It is not the time nor the place for this particular bit of information. Please refrain from telling her. In time that will be up to me."

"I don't want to keep anything from her. Don't you think I can help her better if she knows everything?"

"No. You will do nothing but cause more damage with this revelation so as I said, refrain from doing so. I will tell her when it's the appropriate time."

"Graham?"

"Yeah, sorry. What did you say?"

"I asked what you meant by what you said."

"Oh, umm, ya. "I stammered, trying to come up with something that would make sense. "I just meant that having the ability you have isn't really all that bad in comparison to what you could have. I mean come on, you could be a vampire. Who the hell wants to be one of those things these days?"

The minute she laughed I knew that I redirected perfectly. While she may have wondered why I'd gone quiet when I'd been focused on Gabriel, it wasn't as important to her now as it could have been. I had done as he asked. I only hoped he didn't wait too long in telling her. I didn't enjoy keeping things from her. Especially something like this.

As far as keeping things secret went, I'm pretty sure being a host for an angel ranked pretty high up there in the bad category. With things seemingly back on track with the two of us, the last thing I wanted to do was ruin it.

"There is absolutely nothing wrong with glittering in the light Graham, Fairies do it all the time and no one gives them shit."

"Yeah but that's because a fairy looks hot. A male vampire, umm... not so much."

As we both burst out laughing, she pulled on my hand and motioned to the bed beside her. Once I'd taken my place beside her, untangling her fingers from mine, I wrapped my arms around her and pulled her into my body, a place I had been dying to have her since the moment I'd seen her again.

This is really happening. I am here with her now and she is in my arms. Just the way I'd always wanted her to be. There wasn't a damn thing that could happen now that could ruin this for me. It was perfect.

"I missed you Graham Cracker." she said and I couldn't help but smile at the old nickname. It really was beginning to feel like we'd picked up right where we left off. That the two years we spent apart hadn't happened at all.

"Graham, don't get too comfortable."

"What do you mean?"

"There's trouble. I sense it. It's coming."

Before I could ask him what he meant, I heard the knock on the door. "What kind of trouble?"

"The evil kind. Be prepared."

CHAPTER SEVENTEEN

Serenity

There had been this moment when Graham went quiet after dropping his pretty serious bomb on me that I just sat there studying him. There was something in his face, a look I'd seen many times before. I knew it so well because it was one that I wore a lot. The difference between us though is that when it happened with me, I am talking with a member of the dearly departed club and usually no one is in the immediate vicinity.

I knew the expression only because in an effort to learn more about what I was suffering from I would spend hours watching myself. I had come to be as familiar with the expressions as I am my own name. So when I saw the look on Grahams face, I really believed there was more to it.

It's crazy though because with as long as I've known him he never once displayed abilities. We spent a lot of time together over the years I lived beside him and with as often as I sat just staring at him, I would have seen it. So as much as I believed what I was seeing now, I also knew it couldn't be true.

Normally my mind wouldn't let it go but before I had a chance to even give it all a second thought he pulled me into his arms and everything I believed I saw evaporated as easily as it had manifested. All I could focus on was the way his arms felt wrapped around mine and the way my brain seemed to go wonky every time he ran his fingers down my arm.

All of my senses were heightened with the contact between us and I welcomed it with open arms. Despite the years spent apart, being with Graham in any way was second nature to me. The connection between us so powerful by just a mere touch, I found myself craving more.

Things I hadn't paid much attention to before were becoming more apparent. The scent of the candles Emma always insisted on burning, the hint of jasmine strong throughout the small space. My body seemed electrified where up until that moment it had been dormant. I could have sworn that every time his hand moved, I saw the sparks ignite in the spot where he had been resting. My hearing is heightened as I heard the footsteps in the hall before I heard the knock that followed them. Being here with Graham this way seemed to magnify everything.

"You gonna get that?" he asked me, his arms remaining tightly wrapped around my small frame, his hands not stopping in their pursuit of the rub down on my skin. Getting the door was the last thing on my mind but judging from the sound of the knock, it didn't seem the person on the other side felt the same. It sounded surprisingly urgent.

Sighing loudly, I pulled myself out of his arms, immediately hit with a chill the minute I maneuvered from his warmth. I sluggishly made my way to the door, more than a little ready to give the person on the other side a piece of my mind.

Swinging the door open, I came face to face with the last person I expected. Given that Emma is in class, the very class I'm now skipping out on, it shouldn't have come as such a shock to see him standing there but it was none the less.

"Ryan. Uh hey."

"Hey. Do you got a sec?"

Great. How am I supposed to handle this?

Graham still in his position on my bed, patiently waiting for me to come back meant that I didn't have the second that Ryan wanted with me but the pull in my body seeing him standing there was extremely hard to ignore, making it impossible for me to answer.

It wasn't like I was afraid for Ryan to see Graham in my room but for whatever reason it still didn't feel quite right. As much as a part of me wanted to tell Ryan that I had time for him I knew it wasn't fair to the man that had come all this way to make amends with me. Sure he said he was here for school but I hoped it had also been a little for me too. I owed Graham the time he requested, which meant that I couldn't give Ryan what he wanted.

"Actually now isn't exactly the best time, I've kind of got—

I felt him before he spoke but just knowing he was standing behind me, his tall frame towering over mine made my cheeks heat up in a blush. God, this is definitely not the way I wanted things to happen. Looks like my idea of keeping Ryan and Graham apart is a gigantic fail.

"Hey, I'm Graham."

I had to give it to Ryan, if he was bothered by the fact that there is another guy in the room with me, he didn't show it. His face betrayed nothing and to be honest I wasn't entirely sure how I felt about it. After what happened only a day before, shouldn't there have been something more than a blank expression?

"Uh, hey man. I'm Ryan, a friend of Serenity's."

Watching in stunned silence, both men shook hands. If I wasn't witnessing it for myself I would have sworn I was stuck in some bad movie plot. Just what kind of alternate universe is this?

Graham looked between us. I could feel his eyes on me and I watched as they moved over where Ryan stood. It's obvious his mind was trying to sort out just what kind of friend Ryan really is.

"Well feel free to come in, Ser Bear and I were just catching up anyway."

If the blush from earlier had vanished it was back in full force now. If the situation weren't already awkward enough Graham's use of his nickname for me certainly helped it along.

"Nah, it's fine. I'll let the two of you catch up. I can always come back later."

Ryan started to turn away from the door and watching him, there was a small part of me that ached to reach out to stop him. I knew it was wrong, given everything that Graham just confessed to me but I couldn't help it. I'm drawn to Ryan and just as much as he wanted to talk to me, I wanted to talk to him. There's unfinished business between us.

"Actually man, you can stay now. I need to deal with some things at the Deans office anyway. So that will give the two of you a chance to hang out."

Graham turned to me then and with a quick kiss on the forehead and a whisper in my ear that he would see me later, he slid his way out of the room and before I knew it I heard his footsteps receding on the stairs and I was alone with Ryan.

"I didn't mean to run the poor guy off." he stated, his eyes also following Graham's retreating form as he made his way further away from us.

"You didn't." I replied. "What did you need?"

Moving back from the doorway I motioned for him to come inside and immediately shut the door. Whatever was about to be said between the two of us most definitely didn't need to be heard by the rest of the floor.

I hadn't exactly gotten the chance to tell Graham about Ryan and the last thing I wanted was for him to hear about it in the wrong way.

We may not be anything to each other anymore, at least in the romantic sense but it wasn't lost on me that Graham admitting what he did meant that he wasn't opposed to the idea. I wasn't entirely sure where I stood on it either. This couldn't have come at a worse time.

"I wanted to talk about what happened yesterday."

"What about it?"

"Serenity, there's something you need to know."

CHAPTER EIGHTEEN

Graham

Leaving Serenity alone with that guy had taken every ounce of strength I had. Given the way Gabriel himself acted right before the knock it was obvious that the evil he had spoken of had to be coming from the guy on the other side of the door.

Ryan. That's what Serenity called him. It may have just been because I had an angel floating around inside of me but just the sight of the guy gave me an uneasy feeling I couldn't entirely explain. I didn't trust him.

It had nothing to do with jealousy, though I couldn't deny that there had been a bit of that when I'd seen him standing there. I could tell from her reaction to him that something had happened between them though I just couldn't be sure what. Knowing there is another guy period was enough to make my head want to explode. I didn't want anyone else around her.

Sure she hadn't exactly told me I was forgiven for the past but given the way her body had melted into mine, I'm pretty sure that is where it was heading. It may have been hit and miss before but now was different. Now it's our time. I'm back.

"Father has been trying to determine where the darkness originates and given the way you are reacting to the sight of Ryan McGregor, I think we can safely assume it comes from within him."

"I can't be sure what I felt man. I'm probably just jealous but given that I can't tell her what you're thinking I'm not sure what I'm supposed to do about it."

"Now is not the time. I need to speak with my father and brother. They will be able to give me more information than we can obtain on our own. It would seem though if this does originate with Ryan then we will need to speed up our timetable."

"Are you able to tell if she's in any danger right now?"

"She is not. He is there in a capacity that has nothing to do with evil. While he may be shrouded in darkness at this particular

120

time he is not planning on using it. I haven't been able to garner that information before now which means that there are abilities he may possess that I need to look into."

I felt better knowing that for the time being, the guy I left with Serenity meant her no harm. If anything happened to her because I walked away and left her, I would never be able to live with myself.

"Graham I know how unpleasant the act of joining was for you the first time so I need to give you the choice of what to do now."

"About what?"

"As I said, I need to speak with my father and brother. I can either separate from you to do so, or you can join me there, where I will take control of you for the duration of my visit. I will not make the choice without your input."

The choice was a relatively easy one for me given the way it felt when I became his host. How I had gone through that as a teen and not remembered is beyond me but it is definitely not something I am itching to repeat. If he had to go to Heaven, then I guess he was bringing me along for the ride.

"You know my choice. Do whatever you have to do."

Gabriel

"Well little brother, you're looking mighty human today." Michael stated as I made my entrance through the gates.

It is obvious that I had been right and they bared witness to what had taken place below. Given that Michael was standing guard awaiting my entrance could only mean that my earlier instincts, as well as those of Graham himself had been on the mark. There really is cause for concern.

"Oh Michael, if only you realized how much I missed this."

"Sarcasm does not become you little brother. Maybe you should store that until you're back on Earth with the humans where it can be more appreciated. You are planning on habitation there from now on are you not?"

Leave it to Michael to get right to it. If what Father said was true and Serenity really is my beloved then that would mean that in order to be with her I would have to also remain human myself.

Meaning I would indeed have to live life on earth. Which also meant Graham and I would remain one entity.

"What happens once the undertaking has come to pass I am unsure but we will cross that bridge so to speak when we come to it."

"As you wish brother. Father is waiting for you."

"I assumed that much. As happy as I am to see you again, I do believe that things are quite time sensitive so how about we store further conversation until later?"

"I would like nothing more. We've learned quite a bit since you were last here."

"I was afraid of that."

"It's not good Gabriel. While we still do not know all there is to know, putting us at a serious disadvantage, what we have managed to ascertain is horrible in its own right."

Walking the rest of the way to our father in silence, both of us deep in thought over the immediate danger that was to come, I wondered whether or not this is something I could handle on my own. Even with as powerful as I am in my true form there could be a level of darkness that I could be unable to control.

"It was my hope that Michael explained to you that we have learned much since your last appearance my son."

"Yes Father he did."

"It is far worse than we first expected."

"What have you learned?"

"The darkness that we felt, we have since learned it is a demon. A very powerful one which is why he was able to go so long undetected. As it would appear, he finally lowered his guard enough for us to be able to catch on to him."

"Ryan is a demon?"

"It appears that way. He is unlike any demon I have ever bared witness to. There is still much to learn about just how strong his abilities are."

I should not have been surprised that my deepest fears where Ryan were concerned had been validated but I was. Given the course of events and the timing of his appearance, it all fell on me. Had I not listened to Father, leaving Serenity alone and vulnerable then he may not have been able to get as close as he now is to her.

"This was not your fault Gabriel. This demon would have made contact in this manner regardless of what happened. You must not blame yourself. The time for that has passed."

"What do we do?" I asked, no longer wanting to hear about the problem but instead focus on a solution.

"I know I said that you needed to keep your distance and take things slow where Serenity is concerned but this news calls for immediate action. You must go against the original plan and make yourself known to her again in your true form. You must inform her of everything."

"Everything? Or just about me?"

"You must tell her everything my son. She must know her true purpose. Her destiny as well as your own. She must know who you are once and for all and you must ensure that in the end, she chooses our side."

I was confused. What did he mean by making sure she chose our side? What is he holding onto that I am not aware of?

"What other choice is there for her to make? Hasn't she always been destined to aide Heaven in creating a better existence for us all?"

"She has but it would seem there is an obstacle to that. You must ensure that she remains on her current path. You must proceed in whatever manner you can. Forget that she is your beloved and remain focused on the task despite what your human body wants."

He is being vague with me. There is still something he would not tell me and there is no way I could consciously go back without hearing it. How could I expect to protect Serenity when I wasn't aware of all of the facts?

It also didn't help that father had spoken of my human body. Was Graham going to be a problem in the future? While I believed myself to be turning at least partially human, especially in my reactions, that had nothing at all to do with Graham and his position as my host.

"There is something you're not telling me Father, I can tell. I'm afraid I cannot do what you ask of me if you aren't completely honest about what is really going on."

"You will find out in due time. As it appears, Ryan is going to be shedding more light on who and what he is at any moment. He wants to be the one to break the news to her. To reveal the master plan of the darkness. You must not allow that Gabriel. She must not choose the side of darkness or we will all suffer."

"He's going to tell Serenity everything?"

"It would seem that Serenity though gifted with the strongest of heavenly abilities very much relies on her humanity. She has spoken to Ryan on one occasion already about you. He has made his own determinations and they happen to be correct. She is aware of you and what you are though she has yet to completely come to terms with it."

She is aware of me and what I really am? How had things happened this way so quickly? Why had the option been taken from me?

I wanted to be the one to tell Serenity everything, both about her destiny and who I really am and now it looked as though it was all being stripped from me. By a demon no less.

"You must think and act like the warrior that you are Gabriel. You must not allow the way you are feeling to override your main objective. We are doing this for them even more so then we are for ourselves. You must remember that as you return to your position."

Mulling over everything I just heard, I realized he was right. I'm an angel, one of Heaven's highest and I had to begin acting like one. As much as I've been changing for Serenity, it is time that I realized my true place. I had to do things the way Father wanted because in the end I had to see the undertaking through to the end.

No matter who it hurt.

CHAPTER NINETEEN

Ryan

As I stand here in this dorm room, the entire time pretending to be something that I'm not, I find myself wishing for the most basic of material things.

With the amount of books people around the world have written about relationships, both romantic and platonic, there is one book missing. One where you admit to a girl you're beginning to feel something for that you're not exactly human. That you're in fact a half demon sent to prepare her for the dark portion of her destiny.

Yeah they definitely need to make a book about that. It would literally be a best seller. I couldn't be the only half demon guy out there with girl problems.

Oh wait, yeah I am. Damn this sucked.

Serenity is still reacting to the news that I had something I needed to tell her. Her deep hazel eyes were now widened and brighter than usual, her forehead creased in confusion. It's obvious she is attempting to sort out just what it is I need to tell her but there is no way she could know. What I told her would blow what is left of her already fragile mind and it sickened me.

I tried to prepare her before by telling her who I believed Gabriel to be. I hadn't been sure myself until she had said his name but once she did, it all became crystal clear. My mission had come full circle. This was Lucifer's plan from the start. He'd known that she is a gift from Heaven the entire time and corrupting the very entity that they had put all of their faith in was the perfect final act. Taking her as his bride is just an added benefit.

I knew why he wanted to be joined with her of course, he told me as much when he laid out the original plan but things had become much more complicated since then.

He wanted to use her abilities. Both the ones discovered and the ones we had yet to see manifested. It made me wonder just how many more abilities she held, buried under the surface just waiting for the right time to appear.

I most definitely did not want to be the one telling her this. Shit, if Lucifer wanted her so badly then why couldn't he be the one that dropped this bomb and ripped her life to shreds?

Truth is, he believed me to be of a much stronger disposition then I am. While I wanted to completely embrace the darkest parts of myself, becoming the true demonic entity he wanted me to be, I couldn't do it. Looking at her standing before me, beautiful, pure and all trusting, I allowed myself to become conflicted.

The human side of me wanted to tell her everything, take her away from here and protect her from the darkness that was coming to claim her while the demonic side couldn't wait to watch her become Lucifer's bride and see the world and Heaven crumble under the weight of her powers.

Shit. I was screwed.

"Ryan look, if this is about what happened yesterday, you don't have to explain. I mean you kissed me. No big deal. It's okay to admit you regret it."

"I...Do...Not...Regret...It." I said, dragging each word out in an effort to make sure my feelings were heard clearly.

If that's what she believed, she was sadly mistaken. I wouldn't have kissed her at all if I didn't want to. Kissing her is definitely not a regret.

Everything else that would come from it though, I wasn't looking forward to any of that.

"You don't?"

"No. Let me spell it out for you again. I do not regret kissing you."

"Well if it's not regret you're feeling what exactly is it that's making you look sick to your stomach right now?"

Here it is. The moment I've been dreading. I had to tell her the real reason for my being there. For my unease. She had to be made aware of everything and then I had to let the chips fall where they may. If they happened to land in the opposite direction of what Lucifer wanted then I had to use whatever power that is at my disposal to turn her back.

"Because I need to tell you things. Things that you aren't exactly going to want to hear. I have to tell you the truth even though it's going to rip both you and me apart doing it."

"Tell me the truth about w—what?" she stammered, her hands shaking slightly.

It physically pained me to watch her reverting into herself the way she was. She is so much stronger than this. Maybe once she realized just how much she could embrace it and let go of the human parts that made her react this way so frequently.

"About me. About you. About everything." I stated. Shit I hated this.

"Ryan, what the hell are you trying to say?"

"Son of a bitch. I don't want to do this. Not to you."

"If you don't start making sense soon I think I'm going to have to ask you to leave. It's been a hard enough day as it is and it's barely even started."

"What I have to say, it's going to be really hard to hear and you probably won't even believe me anyway but please, just keep an open mind okay?"

If I really wanted her to keep an open mind then I wasn't going about it the right way at all. Even warning before I told her anything sounded insane. If she wasn't scared by me before she sure would be now. I wasn't making any sense.

"Your abilities…" I said, choosing to start with the things she did believe in to give her the right amount of time to adjust, "Clair audience and your ability to speak to the dead as a medium, they aren't just random things that you got stuck with. There is actually a purpose for them and for you."

"Ya, I know, the purpose is to screw up my life. Same way as it does yours. Ryan, what does this have to do with anything?"

"It has everything to do with this Serenity so please just listen."

"Fine." she said politely, her eyes never leaving mine as she waited for me speak again.

"You are part of a much bigger plan. You have a destiny and you were given those abilities because of that. You're not entirely human. Serenity, you're a weapon of Heaven."

She coughed loudly, seemingly choking on my words and I knew that now that I started, I couldn't go back, no matter how she was reacting. She had to hear this even if she didn't want to.

"Excuse me, I'm what?"

"You're a weapon of Heaven. Energy and light. You were created to save the world and Heaven along with it."

"Okay, let's say I believe you, what part do you play in this then? You must be something out of this world if you know this much about me."

If she is already beginning to question my part in it maybe it wouldn't be as hard to tell her as I imagined. While she may think I'm just blowing smoke up her ass, she is actually questioning things which meant she isn't completely oblivious to her own power.

"I'm not exactly human either."

"What are you then?"

"A demon. Well half demon actually. I'm a product of a human woman choosing to sleep with a demon. I am an anomaly. By all rights I shouldn't exist but for whatever reason, Lucifer saw something in me and here I am."

"Did you just say Lucifer? As in the devil?"

"Yes. He's the reason I'm here."

"Okay I will admit, you had me at first. I am willing to believe that maybe, there is something more going on for me to have these abilities I hate so much but you really expect me to sit here and believe you're some half demon sent by Lucifer?"

"I don't expect you to believe anything but yeah, that's the truth. I was sent here because you are the chosen one. You have been chosen by Lucifer himself."

"Chosen for what exactly? What could the devil possibly want with me?"

"To be his bride."

She laughed and my stomach lurched. She really didn't believe a word of what I was telling her. It didn't help that I hated the sound of her laughter either, at least in the moment. This is most definitely not a joke and her laughing, was a hit to my ego.

"I was sent here to befriend you. To get close enough to you so that you trusted me. I think I accomplished that goal rather easily given the fact that your abilities made themselves apparent rather early on in my assignment. It bonded us, the two of us sharing the same issues as it were. The kiss when it happened only solidified it."

There it is.

The hurt. It is now manifesting itself as she turned her eyes away from mine and looked down to the floor. I know what she is thinking and as much as I wanted to stop her and explain otherwise, I had to keep going with the plan. As much as I wanted to tell her that the kiss had been more than just a ploy to bring her closer, I couldn't do it. Not yet.

"Which leads us to where we are now. With you being as powerful as you are, Lucifer wants you for himself. The problem is, so does Heaven. You are theirs so that isn't surprising. You need to realize and accept what you really are Serenity so that you can join with me, and then with your soon to be husband and realize your true destiny."

"What destiny would that be exactly Ryan? The one where I marry him? What purpose does marrying Lucifer serve?"

"He wants your power. Once you join together with him in marriage, he will practically be unstoppable. We already have an advantage in that my power is strong enough that I am able to block out Heaven and all of its abilities. They are aware of me to a point, but only because I allowed them to be. It is written that they be made aware of the threat against them."

"What is he planning on doing with this power once he gets it?"

"I'm sure if you really think about it you know the answer but I can explain."

She nodded, her body never wavering. She kept her eyes locked on the floor. I didn't need to see them to know that they were probably filled with hurt and confusion. If the roles had been reversed, I would probably be the same way. I was blowing her entire existence apart brick by brick.

"When Lucifer was cast out of Heaven and he created what is now known as Hell he carried with him a very dark desire for revenge against what he believed to be the very thing that had gotten him cast out. He had gone up against his father in regards to Earth and the humans that inhabited it. He believed his father had created an abomination speaking out vehemently against it. Shortly after that he was cast out. So Lucifer wants your power, combining it with his so that he can do what he believes should have been done a very long time ago."

"He wants to end the world?"

"The world and Heaven too. There are powers that you hold within you that even I know nothing about. He wants to use those to basically create hell on earth. He doesn't want to hide in the shadows any longer, a creature of the damned. He believes it to be his time and he wants to use you to claim his rightful place, making his father and brothers pay worst of all. If he gets his way and you do join with him whether of your own volition or through some form of his manipulation then he will severely disable them by taking away their greatest gift."

"Their greatest gift being me?"

"Yes. Your light is believed to be the one thing that sets everything right again. As long as you remain pure and untainted by the darkness then things will work out the way they want. The human race will thrive. It will be rid of violence and pain and the agony that has overpowered humans for generations."

"You've been sent here to secure my place as his bride. You want him to take my power and obliterate the human race." she stated, coming to terms with everything I'd told her and my position in the way it was all supposed to play out.

Given what the goal had been right from the beginning I knew I should confirm what she now knew. I just wasn't sure that the answer is quite that cut and dry anymore. Being around her, even taking things so far as to kiss her, knowing what her destiny is had changed me. Made me begin to question the very validity of what I had been sent to do.

Serenity is a part of that human race that Lucifer very much wants to destroy. Gift from Heaven or not, the fact still remained she is at her very core a human being. Could I really be alright with ending it all? Ending her? After finally finding the one thing that I had been praying for from a very young age, could I really be expected to part with it even though according to Lucifer it is indeed her true destiny?

In three short days she had gotten to me and made me question just what the right thing really is. I'd been fully prepared up until that point to let the world end. Meeting Serenity had affected me deeply. It was beginning to change my perceptions on everything, the least of which was my job.

"I don't know anymore."

"What do you mean you don't know? God this is all so freaking confusing!"

I shared her sentiment. It was most definitely confusing and I wish that I had more answers but I could only give her the information I had, nothing more. I am treading close to the line as it is, I wasn't ready to go over it quite yet.

"When I found out what I am, it's like the world stopped. Everything finally began to make sense. I was an outcast in life, having little to no friends. The way you have Emma, I didn't have that and I still don't have that. I couldn't form a bond with anyone or anything. It just wasn't the way my life was meant to be. When Lucifer came to me the first time I was so ready to bail out. I wanted to die. To move on from the shit life I had been dealt. He explained his mission and it was like in that moment I finally had purpose again."

"I'm still confused."

"I know, I'm trying to make sense for you I swear. Just bear with me."

"Okay, sorry. Please continue."

"I threw myself into the plan until it quickly became my entire reason for existence. I spent hours working on my powers, making them stronger so that when the time came, I would be of more use to him. Like I said, I had purpose. I fully intended to go along with the plan and make this a reality. Then I was placed here, I met you and something shifted. The more I learned about you, the closer I got to you, it just became stronger. In three days my entire world has been turned upside down. I don't know what to believe in anymore."

She looked back up at me, her eyes searching my own. I am familiar with what she is attempting to do because I had done it myself on more than one occasion. She is searching for any sign that would prove to her I'm dishonest and true to my demonic nature.

I am telling her the truth and given the way her face softened, I'm secure that she knew it now too.

"So what happens now?"

"I am at some point going to have to report back to Lucifer. One of my abilities as I told you, can block out angels and other powers from Heaven but it also appears to work on him as well. He has yet to find a way around it so for right now he has no idea that I've told you any of this and even less knowledge of my wavering feelings. I need to go and see him though, to check in."

"What do you think will happen then?"

"I can't say for sure but when he finds out that you have been made aware of your destiny I believe he is going to come to you and he will force you to choose. Though by now you have to have figured out that you really have no choice because he will do whatever is necessary until the choice has been made for you."

"And you'll let him?"

"I don't know Serenity. Even if I didn't let him, I'm really no match for him. We may have differing abilities but I am not sure on my own I am strong enough to take on the King of Hell and win."

It not often I'm shocked but when she spoke again, she did just that.

"What if you didn't have to do it alone?"

CHAPTER TWENTY

Serenity

When Ryan told me that he wanted to talk to me and that what he would have to say would impact me in ways I might not even begin to understand I didn't know what to make of it. First I thought he was here because he wanted to talk about the kiss. Now that I heard everything he had to say, I could safely say the kiss we shared was the least of his concerns and now also of mine.

I want to believe he is lying to me. That this farfetched story he told me is just that. A story. A lovely little nightmare that he thought up on the fly because in actuality he didn't much like me and this is his way of dealing with it. Simply ignoring me would have been enough but hell maybe he was inventive that way. The thing is, I looked in his eyes as he told me how conflicted he is and I know he isn't lying. The truth is there in his eyes. He wore it clear as the daylight.

He'd actually been wearing it when he kissed me. I had known yesterday that the expression he wore after the kiss meant something and now that I knew what it was, I found myself actually believing in it. Wanting to know more. What is in store for me and inevitably for Ryan as well.

Silence filled the room since I mentioned not having to go through all of this alone. I guess I should have expected that considering he just admitted to being a demon sent here to control me into becoming Lucifer's wife. He is conflicted though and if he really was willing to go against the only way of life he had ever known, the least I could do is help to make sure he didn't have to do it alone.

All of those times my grandmother had called my ability a gift came flooding back to me. I began to wonder if she had known about me. What I am and what I would mean to the world and if in her own way, she'd been warning me of it. The way Ryan spoke of me now, the real me, it made me think that maybe she had.

"Are you saying what I think you're saying Serenity?"

133

"If you think that what I'm saying is that I would fight with you, using all of this so called power to help you change the path you put yourself on and do the right thing, or at least what we believe to be the right thing then yes."

"I can't ask you to do that."

"Well it's a good thing you're not asking huh?"

"Why? Given what I am and what my purpose so far has been, how can you offer to fight beside me given that at any moment I could revert back on course?"

I hadn't really thought about it. That at any point he could turn his back on me. Obviously it was a possibility but one that I found myself not as concerned about as I should be. For some reason I just knew it wouldn't happen.

"Honestly, I'm not sure. I mean despite the fact that everything you've told me sounds bat shit crazy, I believe you. I know you aren't lying to me. I also know the risk you're taking in telling me what you did. I don't suppose the devil really enjoys having his plans given away, especially to someone like me. So if you're willing to risk everything by telling me, the least I can do is do the same and help you."

"You have no idea the tremendous danger this puts you in, despite your level of power. This isn't a book Serenity, this is real life."

"You don't think I know that? Okay granted, I'm still processing all of this but if you're telling me that you're having doubts about seeing this through, or at least your part in it than even with as confused as I still am, I want to help you. We don't have to go it alone either."

"What does that mean?"

"You said it yourself. Heaven wants me right? Well if that's true then that means for the past month or so I've had a very powerful angel visiting me. One that by his own admission has been with me every step of the way. You may have him blocked out right now, but if we really needed it, I'm sure he would help us."

"Gabriel would never help me."

"Maybe not but he would help me. If I'm supposed to do what you said then he needs me just as much as you do. He's been a pretty big pain in the ass lately and I'm not entirely sure I believe him when he tells me things but there is really only one way to find out for sure."

"How do you suppose we do that?"

"Easy." I stated matter of fact. "Lower your guards and I'll call him. If he is what you say he is, then he'll show up and if he doesn't then I know once and for all that he's the asshole spirit I believe him to be. What do we really have to lose?"

I had no experience whatsoever with the power that Ryan controlled, or even the extent of my own so while I thought the idea was pretty sound I couldn't be entirely sure. If Ryan lowered his guards and let Gabriel through would he also signal Lucifer at the same time? Would doing this put us at even more risk or could we really pull it off?

"If you do this, will Lucifer see it?" I questioned, my concern at remaining hidden from the King of Hell more important in the moment than anything else I was about to do.

"No. At least I don't think so but Serenity, you need to realize what doing this will mean. Gabriel would like nothing more than to see me dead. There is nothing stopping him from killing me the moment you call."

"I get that but what other choice do we have? Besides, I think I know him well enough to know that he won't do that, not as long as I'm here. Like I said, if Gabriel really does need me to save the world then I hold a lot of leverage and I'm not above using it."

It all seemed so cut and dry in my mind. I would call Gabriel, we would discuss this, find a way around both sides and their apparent destinies for me. Gabriel would stand with us and we would fight. I just couldn't afford to look at it any other way. I had to get myself out of this as much as I had to free Ryan. It is the single driving force in me now. I had to save him from his destiny, then and only then could I really focus on my own.

There is only one problem though. One aspect I hadn't really considered as all of this had been dropped into my lap.

How the hell am I going to explain all of this to Graham?

CHAPTER TWENTY ONE

Gabriel

I knew everything.

Before leaving Heaven, I had been informed of everything Father and Michael had been able to compile in the short period of time since my last visit. Armed with more information than I could stand I knew now what I am up against, which is driving me even more to protect Serenity.

I needed to see her but this is going to be a visit I could not do with Graham attached. For the time being he was a relative unknown. He had to remain that way. It is the only way that I can ensure his safety. I knew that in handling it this way I was going to leave the man more than a little upset but time would eventually heal that. If something happened to Serenity though, it is something that would never heal, not for either of us.

"Graham, it is time."

"Time for what exactly? Better yet, how did the visit with your family go?"

"It was very informative which brings me to what I must now do. We need to separate."

"What? Isn't the entire point of all of this for you to be human?"

I needed to be careful with the amount of information I gave him. If I didn't and he found out the severity of the situation, he would want to help and for the time being that is something that I could now allow to happen. If this all went according to plan I would need Graham alive and in one piece for my life with Serenity. His involvement now any further than he had been would only hinder that.

"It is but with what I am being called to do, I need my full power and I cannot achieve that being joined with you. You must understand that and heed my warning. Do not attempt to involve yourself. It will only bring more trouble to the very person we are charged with protecting."

136

It wasn't exactly the truth but in warning him off with mention of Serenity I knew it would prove affective. He cared about her a great deal, more than even I had anticipated when we joined and any danger that may come her way, he would want to eliminate, even if it meant pulling himself out of the situation.

Desperate times called for desperate measures as it were.

"Fine, I'll back off and let you do your thing but what does that mean for me? Is your time with me complete?"

"No. Yours will be a lifelong commitment. I will need to join with you again when the time is right but unfortunately, the plan to get closer to Serenity through you needs to be put on hold. I need to reach out to her in my true form."

"Do whatever you have to do. Just make sure nothing happens to her. I don't exactly know what that Ryan guys deal is but I still don't feel right leaving her with him."

"I intend to do just that. Ryan will be handled appropriately. Of that you have my utmost assurances."

Though it was sure to be painful for him, I began the extraction process. Father had been right, there really wasn't a moment to spare. Everything is moving at a much faster pace and even though I hadn't been prepared, I am determined to keep up with it. It must not get the better of me. Doing so could result in death.

"What exactly did you learn when you were up there?" He asked as I finally appeared in true form before him. Having come to terms with it days before, the sight no longer seemed to faze him. It is almost as if his mind embraced it as normal.

"That our suspicions of Ryan McGregor were correct. He is the one of the strongest dark entities we have come across and he has been sent here to cause Serenity a great deal of harm."

"He's human though right? So why not stay inside me and let me handle him. It's not like he's an angel and can do much to me. I can take him."

I greatly appreciated the young mans will, admiring his strength but he had no idea just what he would be up against if he faced Ryan. This is one of the things that I couldn't tell him. I had to keep him detached as much as possible.

"He is not entirely human. I will explain all in due time but now, I need to go to her. I fear that if I do not leave now, I won't get another chance."

With just a nod of his head in understanding, giving me the exit I needed, I vanished from the room, praying as I did that he would heed my original warning and not go looking for trouble. Graham Hudson is a piece of my future and he had to remain that way. I couldn't let anything that happened now fall back on him.

Ryan

I lowered my guard. The walls I have successfully been able to construct to block out Heaven were now being torn down, giving Serenity the access she needed to allow Gabriel entrance should he choose to make an appearance.

From what she had explained to me after I agreed to go along with her plan, she didn't hold out the most hope that he would show. It would seem that in his task he had failed. He hadn't been able to stick close to her at all times, which had been where I had gotten my first in and now it was obvious as much as she wanted to believe him, she still had her doubts.

*****

"He's told me so many times that no matter how it looks, he's always right here with me. Emma tried to get me to believe in him and she believes most guys to be assholes. So even she's got more faith then I do when it comes to him. I hope this time it's not misplaced."

"This time?" I asked gently, not wanting to push her but wondering just how many times she'd called to him in the past.

"I tried to do this once before. A couple of days ago. I was having a hard time sleeping and given that before he had been able to block out the voices for me and help me do that, I figured I'd give him one more try. Turns out, it was a waste of time because he didn't show."

I wasn't entirely sure what to say. Gabriel failing in his task of taking care of her made me happy because it meant it left her wide open but at the same time, it's evident that in not showing up when she called, it hurt her and I really didn't like anything that caused her pain.

"I'm not sure what to say except, things are not always the way that they first appear. There might actually be a pretty big reason why he didn't show the last time. I just hope that for your sake, this time he does."

"Why do you hope for my sake?"

"Because it's obvious that despite the ways he's let you down that you care for him a lot. I don't want those feelings to be wasted. You deserve better than to be deceived and lied to. I'm only sorry that I didn't realize that before doing the same very thing myself."

"You told me the truth Ryan, that's all that matters. Gabriel, despite having been with me every single night for the last month still hasn't done that. You're nothing like him so please don't think you are."

*****

She may not believe me to be like Gabriel but I knew better. I had been part of a plan destined to drain her of her power. I had let her down right from the minute I met her and no matter how much I confessed to her, nothing I did could ever change it.

When I told her that doing this wouldn't tip off Lucifer, I hadn't been entirely truthful. The fact is I had no idea whether or not my power was limited to each individual class or if it encompassed them all. Only time would tell but I am hoping that in letting Gabriel in the way Serenity wanted that I didn't give Lucifer open access to her too.

I want to please him, the urge is there under the surface but the pull to her is much stronger. My purpose is severely distorted. I wanted to do the right thing by her even though it may differ from the task I had been assigned. This feeling inside of me is one I've never experienced before. I've roamed the Earth for the last twenty one years with something missing. I had never been able to pinpoint exactly what it is but the more time spent around her and the affect she is having on me, I am beginning to see it.

For the first time in my life, both human and demon both, I am beginning to feel love.

Something that Lucifer would most definitely not like. A punishable by death offense. I would be banished to hell for eternity if he found out. As I watched her focusing her mind, calling on Gabriel to appear before her, it was my only prayer that he didn't.

The feeling is beautiful in its simplicity. I am now beginning to receive a real look at how the other half lived. For every moment I spent trying to divide myself from the humans, I was finding that I enjoyed the all-encompassing feeling that came with experiencing something that they were able to, each and every day. A feeling that eluded me for years.

"Well I've done everything I can. I focused on the way he made me feel whenever he was with me, even going so far as remembering the sound of his voice as he sang to me all of those times. If he really did mean what he said then he heard me call for him and he'll be here."

There was a burning in my throat hearing her speak of the way she felt when the angel sang to her. It made my blood run hot. I didn't like it that he had been the one to reach out to her that way. That is something I wanted for us, not the angel.

Jealousy.

Yes that is indeed what this was. A basic human response to something I didn't like.

I hated that Gabriel sang to her. That he came to her in the wee hours of the night and been there for her for weeks before my arrival. That he had made such an impression on her that she could easily bring her feelings to the surface in an effort to call when she needed him. It enraged me. If she hadn't been calling him to help us, I would seriously think about using his arrival as a method to take him down once and for all. A sentiment I'm sure he would share.

The light appeared then, large and blinding, spanning the entire length of the room. If I didn't already know to expect it, then it really would have been a sight to behold. It is unlike anything I had ever seen. I am beginning to see why they were described as beautiful in writings. This might be the most gorgeous sight the human eye could ever witness. It was all encompassing.

"Holy shit!" Serenity gasped, her hand instantly slapping over her mouth as the words fell from her lips.

"I told you." I threw back at her. The level of shock she was experiencing had been expected. With as much as I tried to prepare her for what Gabriel really is it was obvious she hadn't been ready to believe it. Now with him standing before us in his true and natural form, there could be no more denial.

"You didn't say shit about the light."

"Well I had to leave some things to the imagination Ser, it keeps things interesting."

"No kidding."

"Serenity..." Gabriel spoke, breaking us out of the random back and forth conversation we found ourselves in. "I heard your call. I have much that I need to speak with you about but first I must ask. Are you okay?"

It's obvious he isn't aware of my presence. If he was, then I am sure he would have ignored his concern for her and dealt with me personally. After all I am the threat to his master plan.

"I'm fine Gabe. We're fine but we need your help."

As she motioned with her hand toward me in explanation, I began to prepare myself for battle. While I may only be half demon, standing in the presence of an angel in this way, I had to prepare myself for the worst case scenario. We were sworn enemies.

"Ryan." he stated blandly before turning back to where Serenity stood. "Has he hurt you in any way?"

"No. He hasn't done a thing, well other than explain things to me."

"What has he told you?"

"He told me about what I really am. Who I am and what my reason for being is. Well both reasons really. Good and bad."

He immediately turned his gaze on me and I felt a shiver run straight through my body. When one imagined baring witness to an entity from the other side, they never imagined being met with a cold, unfeeling stare.

"Demon spawn, what have you told her?"

Sadly I had been called worse so his name calling had no lasting effect on me. If he'd been hoping to somehow engage my dark side he was failing. He would have to try something a lot worse than name calling.

"I told her everything she needed to know. Who and what I am and also a little about you, as much as I know anyway. Her destiny, whichever she chooses has also been established. She has been made aware of her impact on the world, both negative and positive."

He turned his attention back to Serenity, as if checking to make sure I was telling him the truth. I realize that in being demonic, I inspired people to immediately believe the worst but this is ridiculous. What would I gain in lying to him now? If he wanted, given his power he could easily take me out. He had to realize that.

"He's telling you the truth Gabriel."

"He has caused you no harm?"

"No, other than telling me what I should have been told a long time ago. That's kind of why I called you. I need to talk to you about this. We need your help."

"I do not make a habit of helping demons but I am willing to listen to what you have to say. I also have things of dire urgency that need to be discussed with you but we must do it in privacy."

I didn't want to leave him alone with her. That if I did I was opening the door for her to turn her back on helping me but I also knew that in pushing her and sticking around when it was more than obvious I wasn't wanted, I would lessen the chances of Gabriel agreeing to what Serenity had in mind.

Ignoring the angels dirty looks directed solely in my direction, I decided to make things easier for them.

"You can have that time alone now. I'm pretty sure things on my end are quiet so you can take all the time you need. It's time I got back to being the ever studious college student anyway."

"Are you sure?" Serenity asked, her eyes showing the concern that her voice dared not give away. She was worried. She had every right to be but it isn't just worry for herself anymore. She is worried about me now too. Another basic human emotion that I had yet to experience yet found increasingly pure.

"Yes Serenity. Everything will be fine and if it's not, then I'll deal with it. Stay, talk to Gabriel and text or call me when you want me to come back."

I knew it would cause tension but given the amount of respect I am giving him by leaving at all, I no longer cared. I made my way over to her and pulled her into my arms, as close as I possibly could. Placing my lips to her ear, knowing he'd probably be able to hear me anyway but wanting to remain as private as possible, I spoke my final words to her.

"If you need me, just focus on us and I'll be here. Despite what happened in the past, I will show up."

CHAPTER TWENTY TWO

Serenity

I'm not entirely sure how I feel about Ryan leaving.

It isn't because I fear being alone with Gabriel because in actuality I felt more than safe with him given our history. I feared for Ryan himself. I knew there is something he isn't telling me. That in doing this for me, allowing Gabriel to appear near him after spending so much time blocking him that he is risking Lucifer finding out just how attached he's become to me. He just couldn't bring himself to tell me for whatever reason.

I would let him hold onto it for now even though I knew better. I'm not sure how I felt about him leaving the room and the comfort that came from being safely between an angel and Heaven's most precious gift. Once he is out among the rest of the world he would be fair game and I wouldn't be able to protect him at all.

This is where Gabriel came in. I had to get answers from him. Ones that Ryan couldn't answer because he had no awareness of how the other half lived.

"I am not sure how I feel about you surrounding yourself with the very darkness that is threatening to end you Serenity."

"Funny thing about that, I don't really care what you think. Ryan told me more in the last hour then you've done in the past month. If it comes down to it, I trust him a hell of a lot more than I do you."

"Do you not see that he did that in order to gain your trust to further his objective?"

"No Gabriel I don't. I see a guy that wanted me to know the truth because he's gotten to know me and cares about me. He doesn't want me to lose my choice in all of this. If he really had wanted to further his own agenda, don't you think he would have taken me somewhere, blocking me from you instead of letting you in?"

I had him and I think he knew it. While he might be the powerful angel, he didn't have access to a lick of common sense. This is where being a human trumped being an angel because I was giving him a fact he couldn't deny. Win for the human side.

"You may be right."

"No, I am right, there's a difference. Now I told you I needed to talk to you about something so I'm just going to say it and then you're going to tell me everything that I want to know. No more secrets. Can you deal with that?"

It is amazing to me how easily I shifted from being the awkward girl to the strong one. Now that I knew more about who I really am, it's like the world has been opened up to me. I didn't have to hide away any more. I have never felt so strong in my life. The time for being walked on was over. It's my turn to do the walking.

"I can see that I don't have another alternative so yes, I will agree to your terms. Given the way things have been between us it is the least I can do."

"When I told you that we need your help I meant it. Ryan and I both need it and I know that you won't do it for him because an angel would never dream of joining forces with a demon but there is no other alternative anymore. You were right, Ryan was sent here to get close to me. His sole purpose is to get close enough so that he could plant things in my mind to prepare me for what he believed to be my real destiny."

"He wouldn't have been able to get close enough to do that if I hadn't let you down the way I have."

"Maybe not, but it happened. He did get close to me. In a short period of time he taught me that it is okay to be who I am and that I'm not alone in the world. That there were others like me, with the same abilities that managed to live productive lives despite the hand they're dealt. The part of myself that I let die years ago, in being able to get close to others Ryan helped nurture. I found myself caring for him Gabriel."

"Serenity, I must know. What exactly do you mean by that? How have you come to care for him?"

This is where things were going to get tricky. I couldn't say with any degree of certainty what exactly it is I feel for Ryan but I knew that whatever it is, it couldn't be ignored. He is more than just another friend to me. I had Emma for that and now Graham again. Ryan had come to mean so much more.

"It doesn't matter what I feel for him, it only matters that I do and it wasn't put there by Ryan or imagined. Everything he has ever told me has been the truth. He may have held back with the information he had about me and his true motivations but he isn't the same guy he was three days ago. What motivated him before, his end game, it's changed. This is where you come in."

"I still do not understand how I am to help him. Or you as it were."

"Ryan does not want to stick to the plan anymore. Whatever he feels for me, it's changed him and he wants me protected. He wants the choice that I am being given to be mine and mine alone. Lucifer will not let me make the decision. If I don't choose in his favor he will force my hand in whatever way he can. Or at least that's what Ryan believes. So I've told him I will fight with him. Given what I've been told about myself, I believe it can help but we can't do it alone. We need you."

I watched as the gravity of what I am asking began to set in. His face crinkled, almost as if the mere thought of helping Ryan sickened him. Ryan warned me to expect it but seeing it, especially on an angel, an entity I would believe to be naturally good was disheartening.

"You are asking me to help a demon?"

"No. I know what that means for you even though I don't entirely understand. I'm asking you to help me fight with him. If the three of us go against Lucifer we might actually be able to stop what's going to happen. I don't have all the answers yet but from everything that Ryan laid out, it doesn't look good. Not for Heaven, Earth or us."

"What is their plan Serenity?"

"Lucifer plans to make me his bride. An eternity joined with the King of Hell. I have no idea what will become of Ryan once his role in everything is complete but I can't imagine it ends in any way other than tragic. He wants me for my power Gabriel. Once married he would strip me of every ounce of power that Heaven put inside of me and he will use it to bring about hell on Earth. He will destroy Heaven and anything good that remains. We will all cease to exist."

"He told you all of this?"

"Yes. He also told me that he isn't sure he can let it happen. He can't let me go. So while you may think that he's inherently evil, I believe he may be able to be redeemed."

"Father needs to be made aware of this. If what the demon spawn says is fact then you have learned more in a short time then we have been able to ascertain in Heaven in centuries."

"Then tell them. Explain it all to whoever you have to but make sure you let them know that Ryan went against everything he was taught to believe just to tell me this. He is risking his entire existence to keep me safe, something that you claimed to be doing all along."

"You really do care a great deal for this demon don't you? I didn't think it was possible."

"Didn't think what was possible?"

"I did not believe it possible for a descendant of Heaven to protect the very thing we are sworn to fight against. It is true because I see that it has happened. You are falling in love with the demon hybrid."

All it would take is for me to open my mouth and refute his statement. Tell him he's crazy and that I am not falling for Ryan McGregor. Such an easy thing to do on the surface but when I should have opened my mouth I found that I couldn't. I couldn't deny that it was true. So I went with the next best thing.

"This isn't about love Gabriel. This is about survival and doing the right thing. Helping us would be the right thing and I don't want to do this without you. If what you said to me is true and you are always with me, then please, be with me now. Fight with me."

Trying to shake off Gabriel's statement about my feelings for Ryan, I waited impatiently for him to give me an answer. If caring for Ryan and wanting to protect him was a deal breaker for the angel, then I would just have to go it alone. I knew in my heart that I couldn't let the real plan go through. I could not become Lucifer's bride and more than that I couldn't lose Ryan. While he might be evil, there is goodness in him and I wanted to fight for that, even if Gabriel didn't.

"Before I give you an answer, I think there are some things that you should know. Once I have done that, then the decision of whether I help you or not, will be in your hands because it may change your destiny entirely. Can you handle that Serenity?"

"Yes Gabriel. So it's your turn now. Tell me your truth."

CHAPTER TWENTY THREE

Gabriel

I always believed that she deserved the truth, in fact from the very first time I had come to her I wanted to explain everything. Looking back I knew that I should have but my higher calling won out. Fact is, no matter the truth, it always won out. It is time to bare all. To let her know just as much if not more than the demon had. It is the only way I could make her see the right way and not the path she is being guided down.

Before leaving Heaven I had been made aware of everything that up until that moment had been hidden from me. Father had truly believed that in keeping it all from me he had been protecting me and the investment in his grandest creation. Knowing it all as I did now, I saw nothing but the selfish implications that soured every part of it. Had I gone in knowing the vast amount of knowledge I did now, I might have been better served at keeping the darkness away. As it is, the darkness beat me to the punch, something that didn't sit very well with me.

Serenity as I knew of her is a light made of Heaven. She may have taken on a human form but she is essentially a ball of energy bathed in the brightest light. She is a force that would inevitably change the world. As I have come to learn she is much more than that. The demon had most likely told her what I'd known but not everything. Which now left it to me to fill in the blanks and hopefully turn her away from this awful plan she thought could save them all.

"This is not the first time you have been here Serenity. You have been here in three different lifetimes. While most humans only get the chance to experience life once in a lifetime, you have had three and those are only the ones I know about. My father hasn't been the most forthcoming in that regard so there may be more that I am unaware of."

"What exactly does that mean?"

149

I know this wasn't going to be easy for her, I only hoped that the more I explained in as much detail as I could imagine, she would begin to pick up on it and things would become clear.

"Your very essence is made of Heaven. Father used you to garner information about Earth on two previous occasions in an effort to recognize the ways in which he had gone wrong in an effort to repair them. The first time you were here, you were a writer. Heaven has another name for you which is the one I recognize you as. You were a prophet. A person sent from Heaven to pass on the word of God and ultimately of Heaven as a whole."

Having learned everything that I had about her lifetimes, I knew their ends would not be easy for her to hear.

"You contracted a disease early on within that lifetime and your time was cut short before enough information could be collected. The second time you appeared, it was as a singer. It was in the 1920s, an era of great depression but one in which you made the most of. Your music touched people's lives then and continues to do so even today."

"My music is still available?"

"Yes. It is not very well known given the way you passed but it is still available. You died early in that lifetime as well, cutting your own life short way before its time. Father waited a great deal of time before sending you back again. He wanted to be sure that this time, it would end correctly and that you would be able to see your destiny through to the very end."

"Which is the life I'm living now?" she questioned.

I had been expecting some form of reaction, especially to the knowledge that she had basically been a pawn for God. With what I knew of the human way of life, it appeared they didn't enjoy being used. It seemed second nature to Serenity though as she still remained stoic listening to my words.

"Yes. He nurtured you in Heaven, spending time and using angels and spirits to work with you in preparation. There could be no room for failure this time around. He wanted everything perfect and it was. You were more than ready for this life. In fact you demanded it near the end. You wanted nothing more than to please him. "

"I wanted to please your father?"

150

I nodded in agreement. It seemed she was keeping up nicely given the subject matter.

"He decided who would be in charge of guarding you until you were ready as a human to fulfill your destiny. It had been forever since I had been trusted with a mission of this magnitude so when he chose me, I was determined to do right by him and by you. Your destiny and helping you achieve it became my soul reason for being."

"So wait, let me get this straight. You've been with me this entire time? From the minute I was sent down here, with no breaks or anything?"

"Other than your time in the treatment center and the three day break Father asked of me there has never been a moment where I haven't been with you. I had been with you then as well but I detached myself to the point that it allowed others to enter your life without my knowledge or acceptance."

"You mean Ryan?"

I could only nod in agreement. Her acceptance of the demon was unsettling to me but I couldn't let it show. I didn't want to turn her away before hearing me out. It didn't mean I had to acknowledge his name though. He would always just be a demon to me, regardless of how she perceived him.

"So you were told to stay from me? You didn't lie about that?"

"Yes Serenity. You have to believe me, if I had any other choice I would have chosen it. Leaving you or at least backing away the way I did is one of the hardest things I've ever had to do. It is during that time apart though that everything began to change, not only for you but for me as well."

"Everything began to change how?"

"I have mentioned to you before the way things feel for me when I am around you. That in being with you on those nights for as long as we were I was beginning to feel things just the same way as you. It progressively became worse for me as time wore on. Unbeknownst to me at the time, I've slowly been becoming human. Experiencing emotions and feelings that angels are just not equipped to feel and I began to question them. I came to learn exactly what's been happening and everything became clear."

"What became clear?"

"How I felt about you for one, as well as our combined destinies."

"You mean the one where I somehow use my ever growing list of abilities and change the world for the better? Or do you mean the one where I marry Lucifer and basically help him in turning the world to shit?"

"It is none of those Bella ragazza. Good or bad as they are."

"Then what do you mean? Why are you being vague with me?"

"Because given what you've told me that you want me to do and what I have witnessed with my own eyes today, I'm not sure you're ready to hear it."

Her exterior which up until that point had been relaxed and non-confrontational, quickly turned in that moment until her face hung and her lips were mirroring the upset she felt with a frown. It was obvious she had strong opinions about my decision.

"Where the hell do you get off huh, telling me what I can and can't handle? I've been pretty much told that I can either save the world or end it and I'm still here willing to figure out ways to handle it. I don't see any other human being able to do that."

"Serenity…" I said, her name falling off my lips calm yet firm. "I made what you call a judgment call and I would gladly make the same decision again. While you may be able to handle everything that has been thrown your way, you have not even allowed yourself to acknowledge your true feelings in relation to the demon and until you do, I do not believe you can handle what I need to tell you about our lives."

"If it's our lives you want to talk about then don't you think we should both make the decisions? You can't hide things about my life from me Gabriel, even an angel should know that. How do you feel knowing your father kept information from you?"

She made a valid point. I had been angry when Father had explained everything to me, informing me of his reasoning for holding back as long as he did. I owed her more than that. No matter how she felt about the demon boy, she deserved to know it all. We could always deal with the fallout later.

"In order to explain to you what I'm keeping, I need to know how much you already know and understand. How familiar are you with soul mates?"

"Do you mean the idea that God created androgynous souls which were split when they came to Earth, into one male and one female. In each reincarnation they find each other and eventually when they both reach the other side fuse back into one singular being?"

I am taken aback at her level of understanding and it must have been obvious to her because she spoke again, not missing a beat.

"I've taken a lot of classes over the years Gabriel. I was bound to pay attention to some of it eventually."

I watched as her lips curved back into a smile, again switching positions from the anger that only minutes before had been flowing deeply through her body.

"That is the basic idea yes. There are also beings known as spiritual guides and then those called the Beloved."

"Which one are we?"

"Serenity, we are two things to one another. You are my Beloved. The one being in the universe and all that it encompasses meant for me and me alone. I am also your spiritual guide. No matter what life you find yourself in, I will always be that to you and more."

"Then why the mention of soul mates then? I'm not sure what that has to do with us if we're betrothed or beloved or whatever we are."

"We're beloved to one another Serenity but the soul mate concept is also a part of your life that you need to be made aware of. I have only found out about that recently so until now I haven't even known to tell you."

"Then go ahead, explain it all. I'm all ears."

I wasn't sure if it is the ever present human part of me that is attempting to force its way through or if it is just me not wanting to get into this right now but I couldn't tell her this yet. She had to process what we meant to each other before I could even attempt to move on and tell her the rest. The demon may have turned her world on its axis slightly with his confessions but I am about to completely blow it apart.

"I will get to that I promise you but I think there are more important things you need to understand right now. Can you accept that?"

"Do I have a choice really? I'm the one that said you needed to tell me everything, state your story and it's up to you what way you do that. I guess I have to be alright with it."

"Let me make something very clear to you Serenity. You always have a choice. I don't care what it is regarding but the ability to choose will never be taken away from you. If you need to know what I meant by soul mates, then I will tell you."

She seemed to ponder what I said for a minute before speaking again.

"No, go ahead. Right now that's not the most important thing."

I waited before speaking again, to give her time to change her mind. I would never be the one to take her choice away. While Lucifer may very well want to do that with her, it is just not how I operate. She would always be the one to make the final choice.

"What the demon explained to you about your destiny as it pertains to Earth and Heaven is correct. It was Father's hope that you would reach your full potential in terms of power and be ready to save the Earth from turning on itself. When you were created originally, there had never been a threat of another destiny for you so there wasn't a need for a choice. As it would seem, the choice is now up to you."

"Do you believe that I am really the answer to the world's problems Gabe? I mean really, after spending so much time watching me, do you really believe it to be true?"

I could hear the doubt in her voice, unaccepting of her own strength and abilities and I also understood where it came from. She had always been the odd girl in life. The one that felt things more powerfully than others, sensed things that others couldn't even begin to and saw and heard things that were unheard of in a world where normal seemed to be the watchword.

"I believe it with every fiber of my being. I may have not known everything there is to know about you and what would present itself as time went on but the one thing I know for sure is that you are stronger then you realize. You will take on Lucifer if you see fit and you will win. It will not be because of your power as you believe. It will be because of your heart. As long as you have that, nothing can defeat you."

"A—And if I can't do it? What happens to m—me then?" she stammered, realization finally slamming into her at full speed. The doubt had always been there, even in the most mundane of circumstances but now that she is faced with saving the world, it is running at a new high. It is so powerful it was taking her away from the strong person she had become and back to the girl she had been.

"You will go home. "I stated. "You will go home with me."

"That's it really? I'll just go back to Heaven as if none of this ever happened? I'll just cease to exist?"

"You could never cease to be Serenity Richards. In all three lifetimes you have left your mark even if you were unaware of it. This one included. You will always exist."

She became silent and I began to worry about her. I could easily see into her soul and find out what she was thinking but wanting to be completely open and honest, I wanted her to be able to tell me herself instead of violating everything I was desperately trying to rebuild.

"I don't know how much more of this I can take. Yesterday when I woke up I just thought I was Serenity, the freak of nature with the uncanny ability to speak to the dead and talk to other people in their heads. Now, I'm beyond a freak. I'm not even sure there is a word for what I am."

"You are a gift Serenity. A most treasured gift. You always have been."

After a few more seconds of silence as she seemed to ponder over what I told her, she looked up and met my eyes.

"Who is my soul mate?"

CHAPTER TWENTY FOUR

Ryan

If I wasn't already bound for Hell, I would most definitely end up there given what I'd done.

When I left the room, leaving Serenity alone with Gabriel it had been with the intent of walking away so that she could work her magic on the pigheaded angel. In reality, I stood outside the door and using my power, listened in on their conversation.

Gabriel is bound to Serenity in a way that I would never be. While what we shared did seem to be something of another time and space, we were not bound by it. It was just a natural human experience with a supernatural twist. It is unheard of for someone of Heaven, human or otherwise, to be with someone of Hell. The odds were definitely not in my favor before but now, they were looking worse.

They were Beloved. Other than being a soul mate, there is no bond bigger between two people or in this case two entities. It would appear that Gabriel is also aware who her soul mate is, which only piqued my interest more. Where I had been open and honest with every bit of information I'd become aware of, he still could not say the same.

Heaven always prided itself on being the inherently good side. They never lied, they never cheated and they never did anything one would deem wrong. With the way Gabriel is evading things now though it would seem he did not share the same belief system. He had been keeping things from her for so long that unless he revealed everything now, things would not play out well for him. Even being her beloved she could still turn away and choose to stand with me.

Things had been quiet in Hell. I hadn't heard anything since bringing myself out of hiding. At some point I knew the time would come for me to return home with an update but I'm happy that it isn't going to be now. It gave me a little bit more time to figure out what I am going to do. Am I really prepared to go up against Lucifer and the hounds of Hell, even with an angel standing by my side? Have I really changed that much in such a short period of time?

What I had done, listening in the way I did was not right and I am more than a little afraid of what Serenity would think when and if she ever found out. She believed me to be a person of redemption and having this come to light, even as trivial as it is could ruin that. She is already standing on a precipice in terms of the information she'd been privy to today. All it would take was one slight nudge and I might lose her and the faith she had in me forever.

I could not let that happen.

I heard footsteps making their way up behind me and I spun around, ready defensively for whatever was coming my way. I'd been careless letting my guard down with Serenity, now that I wasn't with her, I couldn't afford to do the same. It could mean life or death.

"What are you doing out here?"

I knew that voice. It was the guy from earlier, Greg or Graham, whatever his name is. Of course I'm going to be caught eavesdropping by the very guy that we essentially ran from the room earlier.

"I was just heading out, she got another visitor. Figured I better split. I could ask you the same question though."

"Something didn't feel right when I left. Figured I'd give you two a little bit of time but circle around and check on her."

"What's that supposed to mean man? You really think I'd hurt her?"

It's obvious by the fact that his eyes locked on mine, his posture stiff that it's exactly what he believed. I didn't even have to ask the question. I wasn't entirely sure of his history with Serenity but it's obvious he is the protective sort. Maybe if she struck out with Gabriel, we could find a way to use this guy. Nothing was better in a fight where you wanted to keep the girl safe then a protective asshole. They always had the ability to go above and beyond in the strength department.

"Yeah I do. I don't know you and more than that, I don't trust you. Serenity has had enough assholes coming in and out of her life, she doesn't need another one. Comprende?"

If he wasn't being completely serious I would have laughed at how stupid he sounded. He really had no idea who he was talking to. The last thing he wanted to do is piss me off. Hell hath no fury and all of that. I wasn't in the mood for his attitude.

"Well you have nothing to worry about from me. I care about her. I don't expect you to understand that but I do. The person in the room with her right now though, not so much."

"Wait. Who is in the room with her?" he questioned, his concern over me now replaced with a need for information.

"Some guy named Gabriel. When I first met Serenity I had no idea she had this many guys interested in her. Given her annoyance with most of the populace, I got to admit I'm a bit surprised."

"Yeah, well how do you think I feel about you then?" he shot back at me, making me seriously debate giving my true nature away and doing away with him once and for all.

"Then it seems we have something in common. We both want her safe."

"Maybe that's what Gabriel wants, you ever think of that?"

I did. I knew exactly what the angel wanted because she is his charge. Well he was more than that given everything I overheard but he had been guarding her for the past twenty years keeping things like me away from her. I had no doubt he wanted to protect her. He just hadn't banked on me being, well…me.

"I can't say I've given it that much thought. Now if you don't mind I'm going to get out of here before I get accused of stalking again."

I began to walk away but before I could make it more than two steps to the stairs, I felt myself being pulled back under Grahams strength.

"What now man? I stand here you throw evil looks my way, I go to leave and you stop me? What's next? You gonna wanna make out?"

Rolling his eyes he released my arm. "You wish."

"That's doubtful. I don't know what way you go but I definitely don't swing that way."

"You want to leave, I won't stop you but answer me one thing first."

I didn't owe this guy anything though I was going to entertain him just a few minutes longer. Things seemed to be heating up in the room and I didn't want to leave until I'd gotten everything I possibly could from their conversation.

"Okay. What do you wanna know?"

"Do you love her? And I mean really love her man, because if you don't, walk down those stairs now and don't come back. Serenity is special and unless you understand her completely, you aren't going to last very long around here or with her. Trust me on that."

Oh this guy is too freaking much. I didn't even care anymore what was being said on the other side of the door. All I cared about now is putting this asshole in his place.

"I'll last a hell of a lot longer than you and you wanna know why? " I snapped. "Unlike the other people in her life, I won't ever leave her."

I slammed my way past him then, pure adrenaline fueled with the need to slam my fist in his face running through me. If I didn't bail out now, I wouldn't be responsible for what happened to the silly human. I might have feelings for Serenity but not enough to put up with some stupid guy thinking he knew it all. I didn't wait to see if he would say anything in response. I was done. She would call me when she needed me and that is all I needed to know.

Halfway down the stairs, I heard a door open and focusing all my energy into hearing just who it was, I realized it was Serenity.

"Graham, it's you."

It was then that I knew. I had gotten my answer.

Son of a bitch!

CHAPTER TWENTY FIVE

Serenity

I can't believe I am about to say it but I actually missed the time in my life where I'd been utterly and completely alone.

It was quiet for me when I'd been the outcast. Back then I didn't have to worry about the voices in my head anymore and I could focus on being me while being surrounded by people the world deemed the most like me. There had been no judgment there, no overload of information being thrown at me, no drama of any sort. As long as you didn't count the fits some of the people had while I'd been there. That was as dramatic as my world back then had been and I missed with it with every fiber of my being.

When Ryan explained everything that he knew about me I handled it. Not because I understood it or because it was coming from someone I may or may not have feelings for but because the information had been solid. It made the most sense to me given everything that had already taken place in my life. It was easier to accept on the surface. It's even more tolerable given that he didn't seem to want to follow through on his initial orders. Ryan didn't want to help me prepare for a life with Lucifer. He wanted to get me out of it. It is those thoughts that brought me to where I am now and with who.

Gabriel telling me the truth isn't having the same reaction. I guess a lot of that had to do with the fact of what he really is and what I expected of him based on that. Waiting as long as he did to tell me everything damaged the relationship we'd been building between us. I had trusted him, felt things for him I hadn't felt since the short time with Graham. When he vanished even if his reason had been pure it had still broken me. Which made every word he said to me now seem unbelievable.

He asked me before not to give up on him, that he would fix everything he had broken but that wasn't happening now. No, all that seemed to run through my brain the more he spoke is how to make him stop. I am reaching a point where the unbelievable is bleeding over into the believable.

I am his Beloved. His one true partner but I am not his soul mate. This is where it all began to fall apart. I mean how is it possible to be one way but not the other? If we were meant to be together in whatever form we were given then how is he not the other half of my soul? The one being that my soul searched for and found in every lifetime?

I couldn't separate the two and that meant that for Gabriel, he wouldn't have all of me, at least all my trust. I couldn't hand it over until my mind could make sense of it. I had to know all the facts. Including but not limited to the name of my supposed soul mate. He definitely owed me that if we were to ever get past this standstill between us.

"If you allow yourself to look deep enough Serenity, you already know the answer to that question. It is most obvious though I have no idea why I didn't know of it sooner. It is something I should have easily picked up on given its magnitude."

We were back to talking in circles again. He seemed to be unable to give me a straight answer. What had started out as something he would tell me in its right time, had turned into him believing that instead of telling me I should just figure it out on my own. I'm beginning to see that living with angels even in your mind is a gigantic pain in the ass. One I wasn't sure I wanted to deal with, even if it meant saving Ryan from his fate.

"You say it's easy to see, yet you didn't see it. A powerful being such as yourself and you had no idea. So why not just tell me and spare me the aggravation?"

"It is true that I did not know but given your earlier reaction to things I've said, I feel as though putting any more information out there will only cause more undo pressure for you. Your mind will more readily accept it if it comes to the realization on its own."

He's right. It is obvious that I wasn't processing much of what he was telling me because of my lingering distrust of him. If I did figure things out on my own, the way my mind worked, it would definitely go over better.

"Before I try and figure this out I'm going to need a little more information in order to understand it. Do you think you can give me that much?"

"It is not about being unable to give you the information you seek Serenity. I only behave in this manner because I know that the more you come to realize on your own the easier it will be for you to accept and come to terms with in the long run. I want you to believe everything I'm telling you but I understand the reasons why you cannot."

"How are you not my soul mate? If what we experienced with each other during the time you came to me is real, and I believe that it is, why aren't you the other half of me?"

"Father planned it differently. Your soul mate was made for you before your first incarnation on Earth. He has been with you in every lifetime since. Our bond was created later, before your third lifetime began, though I was not made aware until recently."

"So even though I can't remember anything from the lives I lived before, you're telling me that the other half of my soul has been with me every single time, and you haven't been. If that's true then who guarded me in previous lifetimes?"

"Michael."

"Is it Michael? Is that why you can't tell me? I know enough about angel lore to know who Michael is to you."

"You would be correct in your knowledge of Michael. He is my brother but no he is not the other part of your soul. The way you described soul mates earlier is important in this regard. It is you essentially. It will mirror you in every single way, aside from being the male counterpart to your female one. Michael has the ability to inhabit a human host but he is not made of you. He was made long before."

The way Gabriel described it, the way my soul mate would be made me instantly think of Ryan. I hadn't exactly interacted with many people over the years and the only one that seemed to jump out at me that's male and the most like me, either in physical comparison or in abilities is him. Is that why he wouldn't tell me? Because my soul mate happened to be a demon, something Gabriel had been trained to despise?

"Ryan."

"No, though he does seem to manifest the image of one. He may very well be a part of your life but he is not the one that your soul searches for throughout each lifetime. He has only been apparent in this one and you know the reason why."

Yeah I most definitely did. Ryan had been sent into my life this time to groom me to be Lucifer's bride. It had been that cut and dry. As similar as he is to me in every way imaginable, Gabriel was right, he couldn't be and it had nothing to do with angel and demon feelings for one another. That left only one other person, at least of the male variety and I am almost positive it couldn't be him. If it is to be the way Gabriel described it to me than he is actually the least likely candidate.

"You've figured it out haven't you? You can't get your mind to agree but you have become aware of it."

"The only thing I am aware of is that I have no idea who it could be. If it isn't Ryan, the person most like me, then I am at a loss. Graham is nothing like me."

"You are wrong."

"What's that supposed to mean?"

"The demon as you said is the most like you, but you need to be able to open your heart and look deeper than that in order for the true answer to make the most sense. Ryan has the ability to make you believe anything about him that he sees fit. Whether or not he was truthful with you, he still did it under false pretenses, something that a real and true soul mate would never do. You would call to each other, be most open with each other because you share the same soul."

"You're telling me Graham Hudson is my soul mate?" I asked in utter disbelief. I kept imagining the way Gabriel explained it to me as well as what I knew of it on my own and I couldn't make it add up.

"Even though I would like nothing more than to tell you what you want to hear considering the bond we share, yes. That is exactly what I'm saying."

While I'm having a hard time believing it, my body seemed to respond and recognize it as the truth. Maybe this is how it worked between us. My mind was the most human part of me which explained why it is having such a hard time coming to terms with it. Something my heart and the very soul inside of me knew and recognized instantly. It knew who its partner was.

"Does he know? I mean is he aware of it?"

"No. He is much like you in that regard. Until this moment you would never have believed it, though I can see by the way

163

your body seems to have relaxed you are indeed aware of it on some level now. He is unaware of the bond between the two of you other than the more human aspects of it. You feel drawn to one another; caring and protective; unable to walk away. It is there on the surface but neither of you had the knowledge to explain it."

It made me feel better knowing that Graham is as unaware as I was.

"You know of my lifetimes but do you know anything of his?"

"I am not aware of all of the details but I am sure that given some time I could find out as much as possible if you want to know more. When you came to earth as a prophet, your writings were all very biblical in nature. You explored the art of good and evil and ways to ward off the inevitable battle that waged on the horizon. You were known by some during that period as a heretic. You spoke truths that most people were not ready to hear. Graham was one of the people that believed in you. Before you began your own writings, he is the one that wrote the things you would see."

"So he was like my ghost writer?"

"That's a very human way of describing it but yes. The two of you worked closely together to the point where it became romantic. He crossed over from the same illness as you, though he happened to go first."

"What do you know about the second time?"

"The second time is a little shadier. The two of you never got together, as your suicide prevented the two of you from reaching your full potential. He was your manager at the time, a man that didn't have the best of intentions though his adoration of you was pure and untainted. The man was very much in love with you and through that became a better man after you left him. You altered his course. Where he should have taken a darker path upon your death he went on to change the world through music, one artist at a time until his untimely death about twenty years later."

Sitting here able to hear that Graham had been a part of my life even though I had no recollection of it amazed me. He had become such a focal point in my life this time around that hearing how he affected me in past lives only solidified my belief in what my heart and soul already knew.

"There's one thing I don't get. Has he had more lifetimes then me?"

164

"Yes. He would return to Earth shortly after each life ended. For some he wandered the world lost. Those were the times you were not there with him. He was even a murderer in one lifetime but not for the primal reasons you would think."

"He killed someone?

"In his search for you, he became close to a woman, one he believed in his heart to be you returned to him though that wasn't actually the case. When she was attacked in an alleyway one evening, like a man on a mission he hunted those responsible and in the end, was the reason for their departure. Those two souls went on to reside with Lucifer."

Hearing his name sent shivers down my spine yet reminded me of the real reason I was having this conversation. I had to help Ryan. I had to get him out of this.

"He killed someone believing they hurt me?"

"Two people and yes but there's more."

"What more could there possibly be?"

"The very man that attacked Rosemary during Graham's lifetime without you was one of the most powerful demons in hell."

"Okay, well what does that have to do with me?"

"The demon I speak of is a descendant of the very man you want to help."

Graham had hurt someone close to Ryan?

"What kind of descendant?"

"He killed Ryan's biological father Serenity."

"Graham killed Ryan's dad?"

Gabriel only nodded which didn't help the swirling of information now spinning around in my mind. Graham had looked at Ryan in a way that I'd never seen him do before. Is it possible that even though neither of them had been in contact with one another in this lifetime, they were predisposed to be wary of one another?

"I could easily find out what you're thinking but I don't want to invade you in that manner so please Serenity, tell me what you are thinking."

"I need to find Graham."

Having heard all of the information that I could handle, not even caring that Gabriel hadn't given me a response on whether he

165

would help me fight against Lucifer to save Ryan from whatever fate awaited him, I made my way to my door. If Graham really was my soul mate then he needed to know.

I would not keep this from him.

Gabriel called out to me as I opened the door but I wasn't in the mood for him to stop me. I had to find Graham and make him understand everything I just learned.

As I made my way from my room, I came face to face with the very person I'd been hoping to find.

"Graham! It's you."

CHAPTER TWENTY SIX

Graham

Man there is something about that guy that just rubbed me the wrong way. When he finally walked away from me, I was thankful. First he had the nerve to question what I was doing at Serenity's dorm room though from the way he looked when I arrived spoke volumes about what he'd been doing there. The only thing missing from the way I found him to complete the stalker profile was his ear to the actual door. As it is, the way he just stood there had made the hairs on my arms stand on end.

As much as I didn't want to admit it, his words had gotten under my skin. It was as if he knew about my past with Serenity and was throwing it back in my face. Did she know this guy well enough to tell him about us? She had never been that open with anyone other than Emma before and knowing that now it wasn't just Emma and I she would turn to bothered me.

I didn't want some random guy knowing my business, least of all this guy. He is pure evil. It's written all over his body language and attitude.

As much as I hated dealing with the guy, all it had taken was Serenity's face and the sound of her voice as she ran into me to remind me of the reason I was really here. I had come back for her. I was here now because Gabriel had told me he would be explaining everything to her. That he was going to protect her on his own. I tried to stay away but the urge to know if he had succeeded in what he wanted won out. Given the flushed look on her cheeks, I obviously had nothing to worry about. She was fine.

I saw the glow of light from her bedroom and recognized it. Gabriel must still be here. The only concern I had now as I scanned her face, is how she was handling it all.

"Were you expecting someone else princess?"

She blushed again and shook her head. If I wasn't so focused on her wellbeing I would have enjoyed deepening that blush of hers. As it is, the sight of it drove me crazy.

"Then what's the hurry?"

"I was actually coming to find y—you." she stammered, again the sound causing my body to react. It seemed everything about her made me lose control.

"Well here I am. What's up?"

She motioned back toward her room and backed up against the door to let me pass. "Come in and I'll explain."

"That sounds ominous. Is everything alright?" I shot back to her as I did as she wanted and moved into the room. Taking a look around I noticed Gabriel and his light instantly.

"No. Everything is far from alright."

Well she definitely had my attention now. What had Gabriel said to her?

"Well I'm all ears."

She sighed and motioned to Emma's bed with her hand. "You're gonna want to sit."

"Okay but on one condition."

"What's that?"

I patted the bed with my hand and smiled weakly. "You sit with me."

Thinking over my request, hesitant to move forward in my direction, obviously bothered by whatever happened in the room before I arrived, she sighed as I patted on the mattress a second time. Conceding to my request she sat down beside me, leaving just enough space between us to where we couldn't touch.

If she was unwilling to even risk brushing up against me, then whatever she'd been told must be pretty damn bad. I'd seen her through a lot of stressful situations before but none had given this type of reaction. Physical touching at least where I was concerned had never been a problem for her.

"Why don't you start with the elephant in the room. He may he standing there like a statue but I think we both know he's probably got a whole lot to say."

The look of shock that appeared across her face was alarming. Obviously Gabriel hadn't gotten around to telling her just how close the two of us had become. If he hadn't confessed that truth to her then what had he been doing since he'd left me?

"You can see him?"

"Yeah I can. Big bright light, angel wings and what looks to be a very irritated face. Who could miss that?"

"Wow...umm...okay."

Given the fact that she didn't seem to understand how I am able to see him, I turned to him. "You didn't tell her?"

"Not as yet. There were more pertinent issues to be handled first."

"Wait," she interrupted, her gaze fluttering rapidly between the two of us. "Tell me what?"

Well this was turning awkward pretty fast. I had been under the impression that given what Gabriel had gone to Heaven to learn that nothing could be more important than cluing her into the fact that I am his very real, very human host. Apparently I was wrong.

"You wanna tell her man, or you gonna make me do it?" I asked, fully prepared to tell her everything.

"This is really not the time human."

"So I've been promoted to human now? Geez, just what have you two been talking about?"

"Will the two of you just shut up and tell me what the hell is going on here? I think I deserve to know how the hell Graham can see you Gabriel and what exactly you haven't told me."

There she is, my Serenity. The take no prisoners' girl I met that day under the tree. Though the circumstances weren't the best I had to admit I really liked seeing that side of her again. Gone is the stutter and nervousness, replaced with her inherent bullshit detector.

"I can see Gabriel. I've been able to see him since he came to me a few days ago in Green Haven and asked me to help him."

"Help him how exactly?" she shot back, her expression blank. Almost as if what I told her about Gabriel meant nothing.

"Help him with you."

"Okay your turn now. " She said turning her body to where Gabriel stood bathed in light. "How did you want him to help you with me?"

Where Gabe's face had looked pained before, now it looked completely destroyed. I could only imagine he hadn't wanted it to come out this way.

"I had ruined things with you when I stayed away. I needed Graham to help me find my way back to you."

"You were going to use him to get to me again? Please tell me that's not what I'm hearing."

"It is not as you believe it to be. You are taking it the wrong way." Gabriel stated though from where I was sitting, it looked exactly the way she was taking it. He had never been entirely truthful about why he needed my help so I am learning the same way she is.

"So you lied to the both of us? You told me that you needed my help with Serenity alright but you didn't tell me that it was because you'd botched things up on your own."

"That was not of import Graham."

Serenity, her body turned again towards me rolled her eyes and I couldn't help but laugh. Apparently we were in agreement on what we believed to be important. We didn't enjoy being used, especially by the person that did it.

"Well Gabe, for the sake of argument let me just tell you that our versions of what is important are extremely different, like other planet sized different."

"He really didn't tell you what he was planning?" Serenity asked, quietly, looking at me, her eyes searching mine for any sign of dishonesty.

"No. He told me that you were in danger and that he needed me in order to keep you protected. He knew how I felt about you because he'd been there three years ago and he knew I'd help him because of that."

"What do you mean he was there three years ago?"

This is not something I had a whole lot of knowledge about. I knew the basics but if anyone was going to explain this to her, it had to be Gabriel. He had been the one that had lived it. I didn't even remember him.

"Gabriel, I don't know why you're choosing not to tell her any of this, but I think you need to suck it up and do it. I can't answer this since I don't remember it."

"When you moved to Green Haven with your mother many years ago, I was there watching over you. As I said, I am your guardian, you are my charge. I needed a human host at that time to be able to get close enough to you for that purpose and given your relationship with Graham he is the host I chose. The two of you had become close on your own, I didn't involve myself in that aspect but what came later is where I made my entry."

So…" Serenity began before Gabriel cut her off.

"If you want to know everything then please let me finish before you attempt to figure out my motivations."

"Fine, go ahead." she snapped back at him, crossing her arms over her chest and angling her body into mine again. She was willing to listen but she wasn't interested in looking at him anymore. I couldn't blame her, I wasn't happy with the angel much myself.

"Graham held all of the traits that the perfect human host could have and at that age he had been more than willing though I will not say that alcohol didn't also play its part in it because back then it had. When you moved away for college I left him and carried his memories of that time with me. Not all but most of them. The way he felt about you remained, as did his nature before he even met you. I would not allow him to forget you."

"It is only now, with the knowledge I have that I truly understand why things were the way they are between the two of you. It was not my intent to deceive you Serenity but I had run out of options. You are my beloved and I couldn't let you just walk away from me, especially with the undertaking underway. I had to think quickly and Graham was my only available option."

"You couldn't have known how I would react to seeing him again, so your available option was a pretty big risk wasn't it?" she asked, after we both waited a few moments for him to speak again.

"There is no risk I won't take where it pertains to you and your destiny. Surely you must realize this by now."

"Why not just tell me all of this from the beginning man?" I interrupted. "I may not have been as agreeable right away to what you wanted from me but I would have still done the same thing. You knew that though or you wouldn't have come to me at all."

"There was no time to waste. Why do you think I made sure you ended up here on this campus only two days later?"

He had me there. According to him even from that first visit he had maintained that time was of the essence. He had taken the easy route, the one that wasn't exactly angelic but it had gotten the job done. I had come here and could now watch over Serenity again the way I'd been wanting to for years. He'd helped me just as much as I had him.

"You are not as angry at me as Serenity is. Why is that Graham?" Gabriel questioned.

"You needed my help with Serenity and even though I didn't want to admit it I needed yours too. That's why I'm not mad Gabe. I get it. I had to make things right with her or I would never have moved on with my life. I would have been stuck in that same damn place that I was two years ago." I turned to Serenity then and taking her hand in mine I looked her straight in the eye so she would feel and see the honesty in my words. "I'm sorry Ser. I want to hate him the way you do but I can't. He gave me the chance to have you back."

"Graham..." she whispered squeezing her hand in mine. "There's something you still don't know."

From where I'm sitting I knew everything, at least as much as I needed to.

"Well then tell me."

In a move so unexpected I didn't even have time to react, a light shot down between us and we immediately jumped back, our hands separating with the sheer force of it.

"I apologize but Serenity now is not the time. You brought me here to ask me for my help and I will give it to the best of my ability but my only concession is that what you feel you need to tell Graham, you hold back on."

Standing from the bed, her eyes blazing with venom, all leveled in his direction she made her way over to him and lowering her voice spoke again.

"He...deserves...to...know." she said drawing her words out carefully, obviously attempting to tame the anger still burning inside.

I expected to hear him respond but looking between the two of them, even though Gabriel remained tight lipped and serious, it hit me. He was speaking to Serenity the same way he'd done with me when we'd been joined together.

"I'm sorry but if someone doesn't tell me what's going on here, then I'm going to have to go and find someone who will." Remembering Ryan standing outside of the door the way he had been and some of the things he said to me made me think he knew more than I originally thought.

Perfect, if they were going to fight over whether I should know or not, I knew Ryan wouldn't miss a chance to tell me. "Maybe I can just go and ask that Ryan guy. Seeing as he heard whatever you two were talking about before I got here."

Serenity and Gabriel both turned towards me then, surprise registering on their faces. He spoke first.

"Graham you have no idea what Ryan truly is. You must not go anywhere near him."

"He wouldn't hurt him Gabriel. I told you, Ryan isn't the demon you assume he is."

Demon? What? Did I just hear her right? Gabriel had told me that he wasn't entirely human, but a demon?

"Someone better start making sense or I swear I will go find this 'demon' you speak of and get him to tell me everything."

"Graham, are you sure you want to know?" Serenity asked, making her way back over to me and sitting back on the bed, significantly closer than she had before. Whatever she had to say, it was obvious that with all we had learned, it had lowered her defenses. She trusted me enough to be close again.

"I want to know it all."

"Well okay then. I guess it all starts the first time I met you, in 1860."

Ryan

Graham Hudson is her soul mate.

He is the other half of her soul that had been split from her by the very entity that Lucifer wanted nothing more than to destroy. All in an effort to learn more about the world he had created. They were two souls, born of one entity, tasked with finding each other in every lifetime until they were inevitably brought back together in harmony in the future.

While I might have been able to compete with Gabriel as it pertained to Serenity's heart, Graham and his connection to her is the very thing I'm not made to fight against. I might stand a chance against the King of Hell, I might even be able to adequately fight

173

God and his army but to break through the seal of the soul mate, I definitely could not do it.

What is written in the annals of love cannot be broken or shattered.

How many times had that been drilled into my brain over the years, from none other than the man himself. Lucifer had been the first to inform me of the bond of soul mates and exactly what they meant to the world. In fact he had informed me that the girl I was being sent to watch and grow close to is the only being he ever witnessed that didn't appear to have one. How wrong he had been.

I meant what I said to Graham. I would never walk away from her. She is giving me the one thing I've been missing, the reasoning behind the very beat of my heart. Even if I wanted to, I could never walk away, especially now that the connection had been made. Unfortunately it seemed the universe is the bitch Lucifer made it out to be and the fates were against me. While I might not be able to walk away from her, I couldn't exactly fight for her either.

"Ryan. It's truly delightful to be able to find you on my first attempt."

Shit. This is not going to be good.

Turning around, I faced him, trying as I did to block all emotion off my face.

"Father, what are you doing here?"

"It would appear that all of my attempts at reaching out have gone unanswered. One might even say blocked. Would you care to explain to me why that is and how long you've had the ability to do so?"

Shit. He knew I was blocking him. The very thing I feared bringing down the walls and allowing Gabriel access to me had happened. Lucifer had been able to break through as well.

"I don't know what you're talking about Father. I haven't been in contact because I have been doing as you requested and remaining as close to Serenity as one can possibly be."

He seemed to accept my explanation but it was obvious he didn't entirely believe it. I was going to have to think fast with the bullshit before he caught on to the fact that I did have the ability that he had previously been unaware of.

174

"It would appear that I have gotten to a point with her where she finds herself to be in love with me. When she is without me she longs for me. I seem to occupy a great deal of her mind."

"Is that so?"

"Yes Father. After the kiss we shared, it seemed to draw her closer. She brought down her walls and allowed me entrance to the most private parts of herself. This may not be the way we planned it initially but works out very well in our favor. For if she loves me then it will only be a matter of time before she is to fall in love with you."

The more I spoke the more his expression changed. He no longer seemed to be wary of my intentions which meant that on some level he believes what I am telling him even though not a word of it is true. Thankfully the walls inside my mind were still very much intact, or my thoughts surely would have gotten me killed.

"I am most pleased to hear that we have reached that point so quickly in the assignment, which makes what I have to tell you that much easier. You see, there are parts of the plan that I kept from you, mainly for your own protection but also because I could not risk your humanity becoming a problem. It is time, not only for the plan to move forward but for me to lay out the things in which I kept hidden."

I'd gone into the mission believing that Lucifer wouldn't be treating me as he did the other demons but now I'm finding out he didn't trust me at all. I was a means to an end and he had been withholding from the start.

"What haven't you told me?"

"It had been my original intent to bring her to Hell with me when the time was right. Of this I had made you aware, but given this recent turn of events and the information I have been compiling from the beginning, plans have changed. I no longer want to use her power from Hell. I believe it will be much better served here on Earth."

What the hell is he trying to say? Is it even possible for him to maintain that type of power in a vessel?

"I am unsure of how that is possible Father."

"Well that is quite simple my son. In order for me to maintain my power as well as that of my brides, I need to find a vessel worthy of carrying that much power within it. I have found such a vessel and now it is up to you to help me so the plan can begin."

"Who is the vessel and how can I help?"

"Why Ryan, it is you. It has always been you. You will be my vessel. You will be joined with Serenity and be the very one to drain her of the power that resides so strongly yet dormant inside of her. It all revolves around you."

CHAPTER TWENTY SEVEN

Serenity

"1860? This is a joke right?"

Despite Gabriel's claim that Graham wouldn't be able to handle the intensity of what hearing about his past lives would cause I still wanted to tell him. I would take that risk because not only did he deserve to know given the position that Gabriel put him in all of those years ago but we also shared the same histories and I wanted him to know so that I wouldn't be so alone in it.

Sure it's selfish but I can't help it. I had already been alone with this my entire existence. It couldn't be entirely wrong to want someone to share it with. Much the same way Ryan wanted someone when he heard the voices.

"I assure you, as much as I would love to say it is a horrible joke it most certainly is not. I am also going to let it be known that I am against her telling you this. You are blatantly human, hearing this will break you."

For an angel Gabriel seemed to always run on the worst case scenario which made being around him hard as hell. I knew Graham better than anyone and if anyone could handle hearing this, it was him. After all he had been the only person other than Emma I had broken down and told about hearing voices and while I had assumed back then he would run as fast as his legs could carry him, he stayed with me and hadn't let it get to him.

"He's stronger than he looks Gabriel. For someone that spent a great amount of time inside of him, I thought you of all people would know that." I shot at him, garnering the result I had been craving. His lips grew tight and drawn and he remained silent.

"I know how this is going to sound but hear me out alright, because every word of it is true. Or at least I believe it to be."

Drawing the rest of his body back up and onto the bed, he completely stretched out and turned to face me. As his eyes locked with mine, he smiled. "If you're going to tell me a bedtime story, I'm gonna make sure I'm comfortable."

How many times had we done this very thing? Sitting in our bedrooms, one of us lying on the bed while the other sat up and told stories of the day, or even the past without a care in the world? It had been so long since we'd done it that I lost hope at ever having it in my life again but here we were, just like old times.

"According to Gabriel, we've shared more than one lifetime together. The first happened in 1860, the second one taking place in 1920 and now this newest one."

"How is that even possible?"

"You'd have to ask sour pants over there but the way I figure it, your soul was chosen to span over multiple lifetimes, some with me and others without. I know now what my goal was in living as many lifetimes as I have. I figure it might be the same for you."

"So you and I, we've been around each other in these lifetimes?"

"Yes. We have been together in all three of my lifetimes."

"Well at least I had good taste those other times."

Blushing I covered my face in the hair that was now falling out of the ponytail I'd placed it in hours before. I definitely didn't want him to see how affected his words made me. I've never been able to flirt adequately. There is something about it that always made me feel strange. This time is no different.

"Either that or you've got the worst taste imaginable. Either way, we've been in each other lives before. The first time, in 1860, you were my ghostwriter. You would scribe for me. We were actually together romantically in that lifetime, until we both died because of some sickness. Fast forward to 1920 and that's where it gets a little more difficult. We were close in that lifetime as well but from what Gabe tells me, you were a real asshole, so no romantic entanglement."

"We dated, for real?"

I was a little surprised with how easily he was taking it though also content in the knowledge that I had been right all along. Graham wasn't fragile in terms of information. He might think it is out of this world but he would never let himself be changed by it, even when it had everything to do with him.

"Yes. You were my manager in the second incarnation until I committed suicide. According to Gabe, that's when you changed your ways and turned good."

"Shit, that's horrible. So no matter what lifetime we live in, we lose each other?"

"It seems that way. I mean that didn't happen to us in this lifetime so I don't think it's a sign but it's definitely something that we seem to like to repeat."

"You're wrong. It did happen in this lifetime." he said, his voice so low it was almost a whisper.

"What did?"

"We did lose each other. Sure it wasn't to death the way the others seem to be, but we lost each other just the same. If it hadn't been for him," he said motioning to where Gabriel stood his face still made of stone. "We might never have found our way back to each other."

I wasn't willing to believe that. I chose instead to think more optimistically, believing that no matter if it had been five years or twenty-five we would have eventually found our way back to each other. Even putting the past lives aside, I couldn't entirely imagine a life without Graham in it.

"We will never know if it was Gabriel's doing or not. Either way we didn't lose each other to death like you said. So this time really is different."

"I've got one question." he stated, lifting his head from the pillow and leaning it on his hand, his eyes never leaving my face.

"I'll answer anything I can, otherwise you might have to ask him and he doesn't exactly look like he wants to help much."

"Why did our lives intersect so much? I mean I get that it's possible that we may have known each other in other lives but I mean that often? What is it about us that makes us keep repeating the same cycle and coming back to one another?"

He asked the question that would bring everything I told him full circle. The very thing I was still having a hard time coming to terms with in my mind despite my heart knowing and feeling differently. Despite Gabriel's reservations, I fully intended to tell him, no matter what the reaction.

"We were marked for each other Graham Cracker. Our lives have to intersect even though you did live through lifetimes without me."

"Right, but what does it mean?"

"Oh come on, for crying out loud!" Gabriel interjected, calling our attention away from each other and focusing again solely on him. "The two of you are soul mates. Do you really need it spelled out for you?"

"We're soul mates?" Graham asked, the words falling from his tongue slowly testing them out for the first time. Listening to the way he said it, even after hearing the very same thing from Gabriel not that long before was different. As it all seemed to settle in, his face changed. Where he had been relaxed yet dazed minutes before, he is now sitting himself up, his gaze alert and focused.

"Gabe's right. We're soul mates."

As I confirmed what Gabriel said, his gaze fluttered between both of us, making me question what was going on inside his head. Is it something he expected to hear or is this coming completely out of left field the way it did with me?

"Well, finally." He said. "It all makes sense."

Gabriel

It is common knowledge that there isn't much that can break a bond between soul mates given that they shared the same soul. With as powerful as being a beloved is, at least in a higher power context, it paled in comparison to that of the soul mate. There really is no comparison and now that Graham knew, it made me want to fight that much harder for Serenity.

Graham was meant to be my human host for the remainder of Serenity's time on the planet, of that I could be secure in but given what I had promised him when I gained his approval only days earlier, I realized that it could all still end in a less favorable way for me.

If I am to give him the ability to lead his own life, being a part of him but staying on the sidelines the way I planned, then I would lose her to him. They were unable to fight the natural inclination they both had for one other. They would always end up together.

In helping Serenity with Ryan I hoped I would endear myself to her. That she would realize that I wanted what was best for her and would accept her role as my beloved with ease. Unfortunately Graham is now a wild card, one that I hadn't been expecting to deal with quite so quickly. It was always a given they would make their way back to each other but I had been the one to light the match this time.

She longed for him even now. I had seen it before I left. That there had been the one that got away that played heavily on her mind on more than one occasion but I had believed in my ability to make her forget so I hadn't given it much thought. Watching them now, and seeing the way he looked at her, his eyes lighting up until they were practically glowing was turning my stomach.

Her growing feelings for Ryan were no longer visible in the way she is with Graham now. I once believed the demon to be my greatest threat but now I knew differently. I could easily deal with a demon when it was called for but going up against the other half of Serenity's soul, I wasn't sure that is something I could manage. Any damage done to the man before me now would only damage her, something I could never do, no matter how badly my heart wanted me to.

It was in watching them then, moving toward one another in slow motion that I realized what I had to do. I had to help her protect the demon even though everything in me was fighting against it. Not only that but if the demon really did have feelings for her, we were going to have a talk before facing Lucifer.

His feelings would be nothing compared to what Graham and her shared but maybe if I helped him he would repay the favor by helping me find a way to destroy what is happening in front of me now.

I would gladly give up the chance to be with Serenity on Earth joined with a human host if it meant that she remained with me for an eternity in her rightful spot as my beloved. I know it's wrong and that Father would not be happy but I have to do it. I couldn't lose her to Graham not before I even had my chance.

I would let them have their moment for now but when the time was right, I would speak to the demon and we would fix this situation once and for all.

CHAPTER TWENTY EIGHT

Ryan

I am the key to everything. I am the one that will bring hell to Earth and destroy the world as we know it.

It's a little hard to take in. I mean how had I not known that this would be my fate when the plan was put into motion? Why, given what I am had I not questioned everything thoroughly and figured it out before now? I am a demon hybrid for Christ sakes. Nothing that happened in Hell had ever been above board. Why had I blindly accepted it so easily this time?

I thought I was so smart blocking out Heaven and Hell at the same time. Letting my selfish impulses where Serenity is concerned guide me without any real admonishment.

At least I had been, until now.

Lucifer's news that I would in fact be the very person that would execute what I could only see as the end of everything shocked me. When he determined he wanted to take a bride, one that he could siphon power from to execute the plan he had in mind I'd been all for it. I was his biggest supporter, wanting nothing more than for him to achieve his goals.

I knew that once he achieved what he wanted that my time both on Earth and otherwise would be in jeopardy. Lucifer never did anything without figuring in every factor. I also knew that any deviation from that plan would render me nonexistent, which is where shading myself came into play. He couldn't deal with me if he didn't know I'd done anything wrong.

Unfortunately for me though, he knew. Whether or not he believed my feeble excuses, he knew I had overstepped my bounds. He was going to work with it and turn it around in his favor. I may not be taken out of existence the way I originally assumed but his fate for me now is far worse.

I would have to kill Serenity, at least the very parts of her that I cared for and the ones that distinctly made her who she is. I would have to drain her very life force bringing about the end of the world at the same time.

I wanted out before and really believed it was achievable but now, it looked grim. Between the realization that she has a soul mate out there in the world that stood between whatever we might share, I also had to worry about the consequences for my deceit to the only man that had paid me any mind over the years. The only real father I've ever known. Given the magnitude of what I just learned, I am filled with even more doubt that I would make it out of this alive, let alone being able to do the right thing.

"Why my son, are you so affected by what I planned for you? I would have thought you would have jumped at this chance. Given what you have just told me, you being joined with the angelic one, draining her of the light she carries should make you ecstatic."

He is right. I should be happy given that in the end I would have Serenity. Sure it isn't the way I really want her, which is as she is now but I would still have her. I would also have the most powerful position in hell. Everything could work out the way I wanted it to and I would hold more power than I ever thought possible.

Except I wasn't happy about any of it. I didn't want it this way. If I am bound to be with Serenity, defeating not only the angel but the soul mate as well, then I wanted to do it the natural way. The right way.

"Father, while I am most appreciative of the chance you are giving me, I am just not prepared for the change of plan."

When all else failed, deviate back to what you knew and lie. That is how I am going to deal with this. I could only hope that in doing so I would give myself enough time to warn Serenity. I could not let her walk into this blind or I might not be able to protect her. If I was going to be forced into this, then I am going to do whatever I can to make it as easy on her as possible. It is the least I could do.

"Understandable. The more time that passes, you will begin to feel more comfortable in your new position. Now that I have informed you, we need to put things into motion."

"How?"

"You must go to her and prepare her for what is to come. She will reach her real and true destiny. You have until tomorrow evening. We begin then."

Great. Now I'm on a clock. Sure that worked in my favor as it gave me time to reach Serenity and inform her of what is about to happen but it isn't enough time for me to figure a way out of this. I couldn't let this actually happen. I couldn't be the one that took her life and turned her dark. While I didn't agree with Heaven having her either, it was by far a better alternative to what Lucifer had planned for her.

"Yes Father, I will begin the preparations for tomorrow evening. You can count on me."

"That is exactly what I hoped to hear. Keep me abreast of any issues and Ryan?"

"Yes?"

"Do not attempt to hide from me again. I have put a great deal of energy and time into you, grooming you for this very moment. I have no qualms about taking you out if I need to. Prepare the girl for her destiny and also for your own."

He vanished before my eyes and I let out the breath I'd been holding in tightly since the moment he appeared. I was right. He didn't believe my excuses and he knew that I tried blocking him. The next time I would have to be sure it worked better because now that he had given me the time, I couldn't waste a minute of it. I had to warn Serenity.

Before it was too late.

Gabriel

I hate demons.

No matter how much power I put into tracking this one, it would seem he was stronger and able to block me at a moment's notice. I had no idea where to look to find him.

It is becoming trying, this search and I am aware that there isn't much time to waste. It is only a matter of time before Lucifer put his plan into motion and I had to find a way to counter it as well as bring Serenity around to my way of thinking before that time came upon us.

Just the mere thought of what I am about to do reminded me again of just how much I changed in such a short period of time. I am now willing to go against everything I believed in, to garner a life with Serenity. I would disobey my father, brothers and all of Heaven to achieve this goal. Something that I am already doing in agreeing to help redeem the demon but something that would be made worse by the steps I was now about to take.

"Gabriel…"

Michael.

I knew his voice anywhere. What he is doing inside of my mind now though I couldn't be sure. Is he aware of what I am about to do and has come to stop me?

"Yes brother."

"You are treading down a path that I fear I will be unable to bring you back from. You must not go through with this no matter what your heart wants you to believe. You must remember your place."

"I have not forgotten my position Michael. I am merely attempting to keep the original deal in place. Father kept the information from me for far too long, allowing both souls to come into contact with each other again, throwing a wrench into my plans. I am merely fighting against that."

"I know that you believe yourself to be doing the right thing, but you are not. Father made a mistake in not telling you of Graham and Serenity's bond before now but it will still happen as written. He will still be your vessel and you will still be with her. In the way that Heaven intended but not if you go through with what you are planning."

"I would have Serenity only in a manner of speaking. Michael, she is my beloved. I deserve more than to be with her on the sidelines. I will not let the soul mate bond change what is meant to be."

"What would happen when she passed on from this life? When she ceased being Serenity Richards. Where would she end up little brother?"

"Heaven of course, what kind of question is that? You already know the answer."

"I am aware that I know the answer but I want to be sure that you know. The moment she enters the gates she is yours. Father

185

will have no further use for her which means she will become yours."

"After her soul has been joined back together with Grahams. That is what you mean isn't it Michael?"

"Yes but once her soul is whole again, there will be no other cause for concern as it pertains to the soul mate bond. Isn't that ultimately what you want?"

It is exactly what I wanted of course but given that Serenity is being given a full human life, I wasn't willing to wait that long for us to be together. I had been promised life on Earth with her and I wanted that to begin now, not when she wi finished and back in Heaven.

"Yes of course that is what I want but it is also not what was written."

"Gabriel, if you choose this path of darkness, I will be left with no other choice then to strip you of your powers and position here on Earth and bring you back home. I cannot in good conscious let you do this. This was never your path."

Being threatened with losing my powers and spending the rest of eternity locked away at home should have scared me more but honestly, it didn't. Michael is right, this isn't my path but given the way everything seems to be happening, I wasn't sure what my true path is anymore. All I knew is that I had to have Serenity in it. There could be no other option.

"Do what you must brother."

I am nowhere near Michael but I could hear the exasperation in his tone loud and clear. He is bothered by my determination and lack of caring as it pertained to my powers. He had never been through something like this and I figured he had to be close to his limit now. It was only a matter of time before he gave up on me completely.

"Brother it is your lucky day."

"What is that supposed to mean?"

"As much as I would personally love to take your power from you and banish you back home for an eternity alone, it would seem there has been a change in plans."

"How so?"

"Well little brother it seems that Lucifer has put his plan into motion which means we are both needed in Heaven now. We need

186

to come up with a plan before this time tomorrow or he will
succeed. It looks like your punishment is going to have to wait."

Did I just hear him right? Had Lucifer really put his plan into motion and if so, was the demon aware of it? Maybe I wouldn't have to find him after all. It would only be a matter of time before he came looking for me. Maybe this could work out after all and in the process we could kill two birds with one stone.

"Then what are you waiting for brother. Let's go."

CHAPTER TWENTY NINE

Serenity

I'm not entirely sure when it happened or even how but somewhere along the way, after explaining everything to Graham, both about us and about me, we'd both fallen asleep on Emma's bed. It was only when she came slamming through it in the wee hours of the morning, making as much noise as humanly possible that I woke up and realized just what had taken place.

An entire day had seemed to pass after I walked away from English Lit and the rest of my classes that day in a desperate attempt to run away from the man I am now sharing a bed with.

I had learned about myself and about the three people closest to me. I now knew my true purpose in life and that I wasn't as big of a freak as I'd believed myself to be. With the look I'm getting from Emma now though, it all came flooding back.

"Well this explains why I didn't see you the rest of the day."

"It's not what it looks like." I managed to choke out, my voice dry and still riddled with sleep. As she rolled her eyes in my direction I focused on the fact that I wasn't the only one who found herself in a shady position. Emma obviously stayed out the entire night, which meant she had spent the night in another's bed. Calling her on it would surely take the heat off the way this looked.

"Where have you been?"

"A party. I drank too much and just passed out there, now though, I need my bed and a day off from classes, so if you and Romeo don't mind, can I get on with it?"

Sitting up in the bed, I nudged him in the arm, hoping that I wouldn't have to do something more drastic to wake him. Having Emma catch us this way was bad enough, I didn't need to do anything to make it any worse. As he stirred under my fingers, I rose from the bed and slipped my body over his, chills running down my spine as our bodies connected. This must be the soul mate connection at work, something I'd felt on more than one occasion but am paying extra attention to now.

188

"Wait, is that who I think it is?"

"Depends." I said standing up off the bed and wiping my hands over my clothes, smoothing them out. "Who do you think it is?"

"Well given everything that you told me happened between you and Mr. Wonderful the other day, I was assuming that I'd find you with him, but that is most definitely not Ryan."

"No you're right it's not Ryan."

"When were you going to tell me Graham was here?" Emma asked, as we watched him begin to stir in the bed.

"Well since he only got here yesterday, I suppose now."

"Oh shit." He said, interrupting our conversation as we watched him become more aware of his surroundings. "How long was I out?"

Emma winked at me with a smile before moving herself closer to where Graham was now beginning to sit up on her bed. "Awhile from the looks of that bed head. Might I add, I could definitely get used to finding you in my bed."

"Ems!" I said, my cheeks heating up, turning a whole new shade of red in the process. This is something new to me, having my best friend catch me with a guy. I wasn't entirely sure how to act about it. It is made even worse by the fact that we'd been caught in her bed.

"What Ser? You know you were thinking it."

"Well I'm glad I can entertain you ladies but I think I've probably overstayed my welcome." Graham said with a smirk, pulling himself off the bed and slowly beginning to move over to where I now stood. "Sorry about the bed Emma."

"Oh don't be. I think I'm going to like sleeping with the smell that's wafting off of you."

Reaching out as he made his way past her, she slapped his ass, causing my cheeks to burn again, turning away so neither of them would see it. I'm easily being reminded of just how different Emma and I really were again. I would never be able to do what she is doing with Graham right now. I didn't have it in me. Higher calling or not.

"Well glad I can be of service. I do aim to please." he stated with a small laugh before turning to face me and lowering his voice. "Grab coffee with me?"

189

"Of course. We should let Emma have the room anyway. From the night she had, it seems she needs it more than I do anyway."

Turning back to Emma, Graham smiled one last time in her direction. "Enjoy the bed Emma, I know I did." He winked then, causing Emma to break out in a fit of giggles and me to blush again. There could be no denying what he was implying, which meant that the next time Emma and I were alone, I wouldn't hear the end of it.

"Hey Ser, you think you can come back and wake me up before Psych later? I don't care about missing any of my other classes but the professor will fry me if I miss that class again." Emma asked, the giggle fading off leaving only a smile behind.

"Of course."

As Emma made herself comfortable in her bed, using a couple of minutes to clean myself up, complete with a new outfit and a quick finger brush of my teeth, we made our way out of the room towards the coffee shop.

We walked in relative silence until we reached our destination when more than once I wondered what was on his mind. He had taken everything so well last night that in the light of a new day, I wondered how he was handling it.

"Is everything alright Ser?" Graham asked, his voice light.

"Yeah I'm fine. Just thinking."

"Hold that thought. I'm going to go and grab us drinks and then you can tell me everything."

As I watched him walk away I let the fear set in again. Knowing what I did now about Graham and I and how revered it is in Heaven, I had to wonder if this life really would end up like the others before it. Would we lose each other this time too? Given what my destiny is, I am inclined to believe that it would. No matter what side I ended up on at the end of the day it would mean changes to my life, ones that he couldn't be a part of.

Then there's Ryan. I may have been able to deny things to Gabriel but the same couldn't be said for Graham. I wouldn't lie to him, not when through everything he stood by me. I owed him the truth, always, even when it might mean hurting him. He may very well be my soul mate but there is a connection between Ryan and I that went deeper than me just wanting to save him.

There it is again, the doubt. My mind wanting to believe Ryan to be that guy, the other half of my soul. He just seemed to fit better with the image I conjured of it. With that being the way my mind worked, it meant that in helping him that I would also be saving a part of me.

We were the most alike and I really believed that it wasn't because Ryan had faked it the way Gabriel claimed. No, we were two sides of the same coin. We were bonded together because of that but also through our need to do the right thing even if it was wrong to do so. Ryan may be a demon at least in part but he was also very human as well, which meant he could be redeemed. He could change sides and want a better end then the one set for him.

"Penny for your thoughts."

As I looked up and met his gaze, I smiled, before taking the second cup from his hands and motioning towards the tables to the left of us. If he really wanted to know what was on my mind then I am going to make damn sure he is comfortable while doing it. Well as comfortable as one could be with the brisk wind that blew around us, a sign of the season which still remained my favorite.

"They probably aren't even worth that much honestly."

"I doubt that. Now what's going on in that pretty head of yours princess?" he asked, taking his seat across from me.

"Last night. What all of this means for us and some other stuff too."

"What other stuff?"

"There's something we need to talk about. I just don't think you're gonna wanna hear it."

"That sounds bad. Look, as long as it doesn't have to do with soul mates and destiny, I think I can handle it. I've had my fill on those things though."

I couldn't blame him. I had more than enough of them and I was the one that they were about. As accepting as he seemed to be about hearing me out though, I knew that once he knew, that would all change. There is no way it couldn't. He is a guy after all.

"It's about Ryan."

Judging from the way his face contorted my suspicions were correct. He didn't like him which meant he is definitely not going to like where this is going.

191

"Before you came back, something happened between the two of us. Well, really something has been happening for a few days before but I think you get the idea."

"Did you sleep with him? Is that what you're trying to tell me?"

"No! It's nothing like that. This isn't about sex Graham."

He didn't believe me. After having the innate ability over the years to be able to see deception through facial expressions, I knew the look that Graham wore now very well. He is having a hard time believing that this isn't about sex.

"I connected with him. He hears voices and well, he can talk to me inside of my mind, the same way Gabriel can. I'm sure we have even more than that in common but it is that originally that we bonded over. I care about him."

"Care how?" he asked, slowly drawing the words out, almost as if he was cautioning himself against what I might say. "Are you in love with him?"

This is it. The point where I admitted not only to Graham but also to myself what I knew to be true. That yes, I did think I loved him or at the very least am beginning to, though given my lack of experience in that department it was hard to say just how much I felt. Sighing loudly, not yet wanting to hear myself say the words out loud I just nodded. It was going to have to be enough for now.

"Fuck." he swore under his breath. "You fell in love with a fucking demon?"

He wasted no time in showing his disapproval, the very reaction I had been expecting. I knew he would never understand how I felt and what had happened over the course of as many days to create this feeling inside of me. There is really nothing I could say that can make him understand either, which is depressing.

"What exactly did you expect to happen Graham?"

"Well it wasn't that."

"We haven't seen each other in two years. While I didn't really think about dating much during that time it doesn't mean that I'm wrong for doing it. I didn't know he was a demon when this all started. I know what you and Gabriel believe him to be but I see him differently."

"Of course you do, he created himself in a way that you couldn't resist obviously. You let him take advantage of you."

While I understood how he felt he was taking things too far. There is no way I was going to allow him to sit here and blame me for having feelings for someone else, soul mate or not. I may have spent my life allowing people to treat me like shit but that wasn't going to happen anymore. Call it a reflex of the revelation about my life or whatever, but I am not the same girl anymore. Not by a long shot.

"I didn't let him to do anything. The only thing I'm remotely guilty of is giving a damn and feeling something other than crazy for the first time in my life."

"You really don't see it do you Ser? Gabe was right all along."

What the hell did any of this have to do with Gabriel? Despite what he believed himself to be where I'm concerned, he had nothing to do with the way I felt about Ryan, other than stepping back and allowing it to happen, which to me wasn't exactly a bad thing.

"Does it even matter to you that while he may be a demon he's also human?" I seethed out in a whisper as I watched people make their way past us and not wanting the audience. "He feels something between us too, which is why he's determined to not follow through with his end of the plan. He doesn't want me to reach that part of my destiny. He wants to protect me from the darkness."

Graham's eyes grew big and I immediately wondered why.

"That's what Gabe meant last night when he said that he would help you if you kept your mouth shut about what we were to each other isn't it? You asked him to help Ryan." The last part coming out as more of a statement then a question, already knowing the answer.

"Yes. In order to protect me, we need all the power we can get. Ryan isn't exactly happy about it but he let me call on Gabriel for help. Given how he feels about me I was pretty sure he would agree to help me. Though as you can see, there were strings attached."

"He was right when he came to me. Even though he kept the truth from us both, he was right. He wanted to protect you from the darkness but at the time he couldn't figure out just what that was. He came to me for help because he thought I'd be able to save you before you make a stupid mistake. Obviously we were both too late for that one."

Not knowing where it came from but being guided by a force larger than myself I reached across the table and slapped him, his final words leaving the worst of tastes in my mouth. How dare he accuse me of making a stupid mistake when he had waited over two years to come back and admit how he really felt? If anyone made a stupid mistake it had been him but I would never be so callous as to accuse him of it.

"You know, I thought that in order for you and I to sort through everything, I would take a chance and tell you the truth. I can see now that it was stupid of me. Just forget I even said anything."

Where two years earlier it would have pained me to walk away from him this way, it is something that I knew I had to do. If he wasn't willing to hear me out, instead choosing to make me feel bad for the way that I felt about someone then I couldn't be around him anymore.

Ryan had been the first person since Graham himself to make me feel something other than loathing, there is no way I am going to let him sit here and belittle it and make it seem like something other then what it is.

As I walked away I made the decision. I didn't need Gabriel and I damn sure didn't need Graham and his judgment. I am going to help Ryan and I am determined to do it all on my own. No one is going to determine my own fate but me.

I could hear him calling my name as I put more distance between us. I wasn't going to break down and give him the satisfaction of turning around. If his goal had been to hurt me then he succeeded. I wasn't going to allow him the chance to get a real look at the damage he'd inflicted. Swiping at my eyes as the tears came I picked up my speed from a walk to a run.

I ran as fast and as far away as I could, not caring in that moment where I ended up. Only knowing that it had to be somewhere far away from here.

194

CHAPTER THIRTY

Ryan

I have no idea where she is.

I've been by her room, the classes we shared that neither of us had shown up for and the quad where we'd been together only days before. The very place I'd taken her and proceeded to kiss her. I don't know why I expected to find her there but it was somewhere to look none the less. Part of me hoped that in some sentimental way she would have found her way back here the way I did now.

After what felt like hours of searching for her on the vast campus as people milled about all around me, I am all but ready to give up. It was then that I saw the familiar shade of brown that I had come to know so easily. It moved out of my view so quickly that I thought I imagined it but using my power, strengthening my eyesight and scanning over the very area she just passed through I found that it was indeed her. Serenity is here.

She is running in the opposite direction, away from me, which explained why she disappeared in a flash but she was there none the less. I breathed a sigh of relief as I ran to catch up to her. Given the way she was running it was obvious she wasn't going to be in the right frame of mind for what I had to say but there wasn't any time to waste. We were only a few hours away from Lucifer returning and I had to make sure she is ready for it. No matter what the fallout.

"Serenity!" I called out, catching up to her speed easily but still remaining a few steps behind her. "Wait!"

She turned then and seeing me slowed down to a crawl, making it so I was able to finally catch her. The first thing I noticed when I drew close enough is the sweat running down her forehead, running down into her very pink and puffy eyes. Noticing the small streaks down the front of her face I realized she'd been crying. I didn't like it. I never wanted to see her that way.

"Ryan...umm...hey." she said her voice giving her away and choking up between every word.

"What's wrong?"

"Nothing. Just ran so much that my eyes watered."

If that's her story, I could easily let her stick to it but I just wasn't feeling that generous, especially when I knew instinctively there is more to it than that. "I don't believe you. Wanna try again?"

Sighing and dropping her eyes to the ground she spoke "It's nothing. I was just an idiot that's all."

"You're a whole lot of things pretty girl but an idiot is not one of them. Now tell me what's really wrong. Does this have something to do with that guy from yesterday? Graham or whatever?"

She looked back up at me, her eyes giving nothing away.

"How would you know that? Wait, never mind. Seriously Ryan it's nothing."

"Stop lying to me. I think we've moved past that point in our relationship."

It was a risk I knew, using the R word the way I did but I didn't care. It's a risk I would take. I had to know what happened between her and Graham. It would have everything to do with how we moved forward.

"I told him about you. Well, I told him how I felt about you. I thought it was only fair he know that there is something here. At least for me. It was a mistake. He didn't get it, not even a little."

"What did he say to you?"

Given that the human had created this I had no problem returning the favor the next time I found myself in contact with him. No one hurt Serenity while I'm breathing. Not even the other half of her soul.

"That I was basically an idiot for trusting you. Nothing I didn't already hear from Gabriel. It's just coming from Graham, I don't know, it hurt more."

That son of a bitch. He is going to pay for making her feel this way. Supposedly he is the one that understood her best. That she had been the most open with before me and here he was ruining all of that by treating her the way everyone else in her life had. He was definitely not going to get away with this.

196

"He's wrong Serenity. Please trust me on that. Just say the word and I'll make sure he gets the message loud and clear."

Through her tears I saw the faintest smile trace her lips which given the way I'm feeling did wonders for my ever growing heart. This is the way she deserved to be at all times, not riddled with tears and emotion because of some asshole that didn't really know her at all.

"Thanks Ry." she said, the smile growing even larger across her face, covering my body in warmth at the sight of it. "I need to go home and get changed and ready for class. Can we talk later?"

"Actually, I was hoping we could talk now. Something's happened."

"What happened?" she asked, her eyes going wide.

"Lucifer."

"What about him?"

"His timetable has been moved up. He's aware that I've been blocking myself from him and he isn't pleased about it. Ser, he's changed the plan. He's changed everything."

"How much time do we have then? Gabriel was a long shot and I know now that I can't depend on him to help us."

"It happens tonight."

"Tonight? Why so soon? Don't you have to do more work on me before he can have his way?"

"Not anymore. Not since he changed the way everything is supposed to happen."

"What do you mean Ryan? How has he changed things?"

"I'm his vessel. He is going to join with me and then I'm supposed to take you and make you my wife. Oh and did I mentioned drain the very life out of you? I'm the one that has to take everything from you Serenity. If I don't then he's going to kill me, or worse."

She went silent, her consistent breathing the only give away that she was still there with me. The look of realization and the fear that followed killed me to witness. I thought we'd have more time to make all of this work. Knowing that we no longer had that option, instead having only a few short hours to figure things out, it is no surprise that she looked the way she did. I had done this to her. I failed her.

"I'm so sorry Ser. I don't want this to happen but I have no idea how to stop it anymore."

I could hear my own voice choking under the pressure. For the first time in years I felt utterly useless and even though I'm filled with power, I am powerless to stop what awaited her. Unless there was a miracle, she would be lost to me forever. I would lose her, the girl filled with light that I loved more than anything Heaven or Hell could create.

"Don't stop it." she said with a whisper focusing my attention back on her.

Did she just say what I think she did?

"What are you saying?"

"Don't stop it. Call Lucifer here. Tell him that he wins. I've made my decision."

I can't believe what I'm hearing. When I'd come to find her and explain I never expected this to be her response. I had no idea what she thought she was doing but she had to realize that nothing good would come of it. She had to know I didn't want this and that even if I did, I couldn't go through with it. I would not hurt her.

"Think about what you're saying Serenity. What it really means. I'm going to have to marry you in one of the darkest ceremonies known to all humankind and once we do that I have to drain you of your power. Of the light inside you. The goodness. You'll be lost to me. We will never be able to go back."

"So then we don't go back. I know what I'm saying Ryan and I know how much you wish I wasn't saying it but if all we have is a few hours before he comes and takes me anyway, we might as well just accept it and move forward now. I want to do this. Please let me do this." She said, her last statement pleading.

"I don't think I can. Serenity, before I allowed the darkness to become such a large part of my life years ago, I spent my entire life praying to meet the one person in the world that would save me from feeling so alone. I've finally done that. I've found you. Please don't make me give you up."

"Don't you see Ryan? If we go through with this, then you won't be giving me up. Yes I will lose myself, at least the human parts of me but no one can take me away entirely. I want to do this. Let me do this. Let me be with you in the only way possible."

I couldn't argue with her logic even though the very heart she helped me find wanted me to. The darker parts of me wanted to let her go through with this. To accept our fates and go through with the original plan even though it had changed. It would enable me to be with her and in a way that wouldn't be as wrong as it is now.

"Serenity..."

I knew what I wanted to say, what needed to be said but I had no idea if she was ready to hear it. I needed her to hear it even if it would be too much. I couldn't let another moment pass given what she is willing to do for me. It had to be now. I may never get another chance.

"I love you."

"As crazy as it may sound, I love you too."

As the words left her lips I pulled her to me, wrapping my arms around her as tightly as I could manage, never wanting to let her go again. Not even for what we were about to face. I wanted to stay just as we were now, right in this moment, locked forever. If I had to leave existence, this would be the way I wanted to go. There isn't anything that could tear me away from her now.

She owned me.

"Call your father, and tell him that we're ready." she mumbled against my chest. "I've made my choice. I will be his bride."

CHAPTER THIRTY ONE

Gabriel

I lost her.

I knew what Father and Michael had been attempting to do in showing me this and I didn't fault them for it. They wanted to show me the error of my ways. That in stepping away from the main objective the way I did, instead choosing to embrace the jealousy and fear that had overpowered me during my time on Earth, I am at fault for what is now about to take place.

Watching her with Graham the way she had been wasn't easy. I fully expected to see the two of them finally give into the history that surrounded them, a culmination of all of their lifetimes and become one. What I had been privy to though had been the exact opposite of that, proving my brother's earlier words to be correct.

I am an Angel first and foremost and somewhere along the way I lost sight of that and became immersed in the very darkness that had been attempting to take her. I have become a casualty in the war that Lucifer very much wanted to wage against Father and the rest of Heaven. I played right into his hands.

When I saw her meet up with Ryan I knew what would come of their time together. That they would give in to one another faced with a destiny neither of them could fight. So when Ryan said the three words that normally would have broken my already damaged heart, I had been prepared. I should have been more upset but given what followed, all I could seem to do was feel sorry for myself for the horrible position I put her in.

It all began and ended with me. Father made that crystal clear upon my arrival back home. Lucifer had known that I was the guardian for his bride and he had used that to his advantage, overriding my more basic instincts and making me believe in something that wasn't true. I am not becoming human the way I assumed. Instead I am very much the same entity I've always been but one with a clouded sense of self. He preyed on the fact that I am the weaker of the archangels and easily twisted me up inside by using my ever present doubts. I had been the perfect target. In trying to protect Serenity the way I'd been sworn to, I put myself on a platter and he used it.

Instead of making things right, I only pushed her further from me to the point that now, as I watched, she is prepared to choose a fate that did not suit her. She is meant to save the world not be the very thing that brought it to its knees.

I had to do something. I had to make sure that this didn't happen. Lucifer could not win. It is only now that I realize that whatever I felt for her; what we were to each other could not come to fruition at all if she died in the process. Something that I had no doubt Lucifer had planned. Once he had her power he would no longer need her, which meant she would make her home in Heaven far sooner than Father wanted her to. I am already having a hard time living with myself for having let it get this far, if she died, I wouldn't be able to live at all.

Coming home to Heaven would make her able to be with me but she wouldn't the same ball of light that I have come to love during this time on Earth. No she would something entirely different and I didn't want it that way. It had to happen naturally or not at all.

Why didn't I just agree to help her and the demon? If I had done that instead of focusing all of my energy on the soul mate, this may not be where we were now. I would have her trust again and we'd fight alongside one another instead of on opposite sides.

"Tell me what I have to do to fix this Father. I will do anything."

"Gabriel, the time for you to fix this has long passed. As a warrior of Heaven you are expected to resist the most basic of temptations and remain guarded not only with your charge but within yourself so that what has taken place is not a possibility. In choosing to answer to the darkest of instincts you have not only put your beloved on the path of destruction but you have also put all of Heaven and Earth at risk."

"No! I refuse to believe that! There has to be something. You can't let it end this way. I won't let you."

"Michael took pity on you before bringing you home. Where he was charged with draining you of your powers and position he chose to bring you home and let me hear you out. I have no doubt of his love and admiration for you, a sentiment that you are unable to return given the monster you have turned into."

I wasn't a monster. I am Gabriel, Archangel of Heaven, fighter of all things right. My soul purpose for being to protect and nurture all things on Earth as they should be in Heaven. I may have made some bad choices but deep down I am still that person. I could fix this if I am just given a chance. Surely he had to see that.

"I know what I have caused Father but I beg of you to please let me continue on. Let me try and fix this to the best of my remaining ability. Do not let it end this way knowing that I may still be able to stop it."

He stood now, his eyes locked on mine, his face betraying nothing about how he really felt. I knew he was disappointed in me and that I had a lot I needed to make up for but is it so wrong that I wanted him to show his feelings rather than just stand there robotic the way he is?

Michael, in his rightful position beside my father, turned to face me, his urge to question written all over his face.

"How do you propose to fix this?"

"She is choosing this course because of what happened mere minutes before. Graham Hudson without realizing it broke something within her. As much as I believe she does care for the demon, she cares more for him and having him turn on her the way he has, inspired her need to want to give in when every part of her made of Heaven wants her to fight. I propose that we use that."

"Use the soul mate? Gabriel your time on Earth has obviously messed with your brain. What good can that human be to us now?"

"On his own, he will be of no use but if you give me one more chance, and allow me to join with him, I may be able to turn this around. She has been in love with Graham from the very first moment she saw him in this lifetime. Her soul speaking to his clearly. Let me use that and win her back. Let me change her destiny to the one that is right."

It is obvious that what I suggested interested them. For the first time since my return home, Father's face seemed to betray him. I could see the light in his eyes, the one he often got when faced with a solution that worked. While he may not trust me given how easily I had been led astray, he could not deny that my plan held a great deal of merit. It could work and work well if executed correctly.

"You may be on to something my son but how can you be sure that it will work?"

"One can never be entirely sure of anything. As I think this entire undertaking has taught us. I just know her. I've spent the last twenty years guarding her, paying particular attention during her teenager years. She loves Graham Hudson with a passion that even the darkest of demons could never match. I do believe her love for him can override what she is about to do. It will change the course of everything, but that can only happen if you allow me to prove it to you."

"The soul mate bond is one of the strongest in existence. I believe when you say you can use that to your advantage but Gabriel you're still weakened from everything that Lucifer put you through. There is no guarantee that you will be strong enough even within the human host to stop what is already being put in motion."

"Then do the one thing you speak off so freely here. The one thing you wish all of your followers on Earth would do. Have faith. I can do this but not without your faith and trust in me. Believe in me."

Serenity

There's a sense of calm that comes over your body when you make a decision. Especially one that determines the life or death of a particular being. The world goes from being on your shoulders, wearing you down to the point where you don't think you can take anymore to being carried away where all that you're left with is peace. At least that's how I felt after I chose my path.

Where I expected to feel torn, ripped apart from the very best parts of me, I am anything but. I am completely centered and happy, both with myself and with the decision I made. While I am embracing a destiny born out of darkness, I could still very much feel the light burning its way through me. I didn't fear what came next, instead choosing to embrace it, knowing that in doing so I am embracing a life with a being that wanted nothing more than to treasure me for the rest of my days.

When Ryan said that he would end up dead or a fate much worse than death there had been this moment where my breath caught in my throat that I knew what I had to do. I'd seen it with such clarity that I knew that this was my true path. The very thing I had been sent here to do.

While Heaven might believe that I've been sent to save the entire human race, I knew better. I was sent here to save him. To redeem him in the eyes of those much more powerful and bring him into the light, where he belonged.

That's what no one from the good side seemed to get. He deserved to be in the light. I hadn't known it right away but from the moment I'd seen him on the quad, the white light surrounding him, a force in its own right pulling me in, I'd known it. He is made of the light just as I am. In that moment I knew it as easily as I knew my own name.

He is my destiny.

Ryan

"She truly is a gem to behold Ryan. There is no finer specimen to stand side by side with me then her."

The sound of his voice, like a viper, made my stomach turn over in disgust. When I called on him as Serenity asked, he'd been more than willing to oblige her, unable to mask his excitement. For Lucifer it was all coming up roses. His plan to capture the very essence of the woman I loved is now complete and she had come to the decision all on her own, no manipulation from him required.

The last remaining part of me that was joined to him is also jubilant with the reward we had been given but the rest of me fought against it. This is not something to be happy about. Serenity is not made for this life, for the fate she would soon meet and time is running out on me being able to do anything to free her.

"Don't you mean stand side by side with me Father? That is still your ultimate plan is it not?"

The grin on his face only magnified his evil. He is genuinely happy about what he had planned for us and unless I earned a miracle there would be no wiping the grin off his face permanently, the way I wanted to.

"Of course it is. I can think of no better punishment for you than to take the very life force of the woman you love while I watch. It causes me supreme amounts of happiness knowing the pain you must be feeling in this moment."

So this is a punishment. He hadn't believed me when I said that I would deliver her, nor did he believe me when I said my feelings for her were a means to an end. He knew everything and now he is basking in the glow of victory, not only by securing Serenity's place by his side and therefore her power but also in triumphing over me.

He was using her as a means of torture for me. This was not meant to be a rising of the ranks for me. It was meant to destroy me to the point where all that was left is the shell Lucifer himself would inhabit. I really would be the perfect vessel, he had maneuvered it quite nicely.

"You knew how I felt about her the entire time." I stated wanting to hear him say what I already knew.

"Ryan, where do you think the powers you have come from? They are the parts of me that I deem to share with certain demonic individuals I believe worthy of them. In trying to hide from me, all you did was lead me straight to you and the ridiculous notion that a being of your type could ever love. You gave yourself away."

Of course I did. He had known all along. The only one I truly blocked out had been the one being that could have actually helped me. Son of a bitch, knowing this now, it stung.

"The way things happened, you must realize that it wasn't my intent. I didn't go into this task believing that I would fall for the very target I had been sent to destroy."

"I am aware, which is why you are the vessel I plan to take and you are not completely obliterated where you stand. I understand what happened between the two of you, it all goes back to the very reason I am doing all of this. Human nature is an abomination and it must be stopped. You and the way this situation was handled are perfect examples of that. Before this day my son, you were the perfect specimen, a demon worthy of succeeding me in Hell when the time came for me to take a lesser role. Human emotion and the nature that I have come to despise so deeply changed you."

"My punishment."

"Indeed. Think of all the ways the human side of you will suffer when you drain the life force and light successfully from your lovers' body. Think of yourself as a test subject. If you survive and that is a strong if, then I will know just how much damage I will need to inflict over time on the Earth to eventually make it destroy itself. You will be helping me through your own personal torture."

Why had I never seen this before? How deeply disturbed Lucifer is and just how wrong his plans were? I am beginning to see as we stood here just why he had been cast from Heaven. With an end result as dark as the one he is planning for human kind it was no shock he had been ousted the way he had.

How could a dark entity such as himself exist in a place purely built on love and acceptance? If he had stayed given his level of darkness he would have destroyed the very light that made him.

"It is not enough that you've won Father, must you proceed to rub salt in the wound? Why not just drain her in front of me, the damage would surely be the same and your end result would be reached."

"Oh Ryan, how naive you are to the ways of the world as it were. You love her. I know you have no experience with love given your upbringing and those that you surrounded yourself with, myself included but there is no greater torture to a person in love then to be the very thing that kills them. While the end result may be the same, the agony between them is significantly greater. Your pain at having killed the only woman you will ever love will destroy you from the inside out."

I don't know what possessed me to say it, or even how I am going to go about making it a reality but I knew I couldn't sit here and listen to any more of this without doing something. Anything is better than just laying down and accepting.

"I won't let you do this."

"Spoken like a man deeply in love. Accept what is happening around you Ryan because in only a few short hours, I will have achieved the previously unachievable. Life as you know it will cease to exist and all you will have left is the knowledge that you failed in saving the only thing that truly ever mattered to you."

CHAPTER THIRTY TWO

Graham

I am the king of bonehead moves. I was the king two years ago and apparently I'm still the keeper of the crown now.

I'm a guy. When the girl you've been in love with for what feels like your entire life tells you that she loves another man, the caveman instinct clicks in. It's like all rational thought leaves your body and you become a Neanderthal. I swear if they would allow it, I'd fit right in at the zoo with the other apes.

I became territorial, I admit it. I saw red but for more than one reason. She is in love with a guy that I knew was bad for her. He is a demon for crying out loud. How that is any good for someone is beyond me but what did I know? I'm just a silly human who never seemed to get the one thing in any lifetime that I wanted more than anything. Jealousy does not become me. A lesson I had never actually had to learn before now so I didn't exactly handle it the best.

In fact I'd chased her off. Like I said, king of bonehead moves.

Instead of listening to her, hearing her out, I went caveman and proceeded to tell her how stupid I found her feelings to be. The same girl that years before had gotten herself moderately drunk so she could kiss me without fear, I told that her feelings were shit. There wasn't an award special enough for the idiocy that I let fly out of my mouth.

I did all of this because I love her. I've been with random girls over the years since she walked out of my life but none of them clicked the way she did. Whether that had something to do with our soul mate bond or because she is different than ninety percent of the girls out there, it didn't matter. There wasn't another soul alive that seemed to get me the way that she did then and the way she seemed to now.

Even though she yelled at me I couldn't help but feel proud of her. For years she had hidden herself away, been the strong yet silent type, letting people walk over her like she was dirt under their feet and I wanted her to change that, to be the girl I knew her to be, sarcasm and all but it never materialized. At least until today it hadn't. No today she had told me off and she walked away and as depressed as her leaving made me, I was still proud.

Taking Gabriel's intentions and his words and throwing them back in her face may not have been the smartest move but if there was a choice between an angel and a demon, whether he was half human or not, I would always choose the angel.

So I used him against her. I had taken her heart which part of me believed after the night we spent in each other arms had been open and ready for me and stomped on it all because she wanted to be honest with me about her feelings.

I really am the lowest of the low.

Even with as pissed off and upset with myself as I am, I still can't allow myself to completely understand where she's coming from where Ryan is concerned. In the end I just knew he would screw her over and I didn't want to be there when it happened. Serenity is strong, there is no doubt about it but if someone who claimed to love her, hurt her I'm positive she might never recover. For as strong as she is now, she's still that fragile girl underneath.

"Graham..."

Turning around in my seat I began scanning the crowd of people around me, looking for the voice. I'd heard my name, crystal clear but not recognizing anyone as I scanned each of the faces, I had no idea who was calling out to me. At least until they spoke again.

"Graham, it's Gabriel. I need to speak with you. It's important."

"Isn't that what you're doing right now?" I asked, amazed at my ability to speak in my mind even though Gabriel was no longer sharing my body. This must be a side effect of spending time being a human host.

"Yes, I suppose it is. I need your help."

"Didn't you make enough of a mess the last time we tried this? Why come back for more?"

"Because just as before, you are the only one that can do this and it's for the reason you think. I need the bond between you and Serenity."

208

"Sorry to burst your bubble man but I think I'm the last person that can get through to Serenity now. I sort of fucked it all up."

"I am aware of that. I witnessed the entire thing. I need the bond in this regard but I do not need you. Just your body."

I know he is serious but I couldn't help but laugh at the way he worded things. Someone needed to teach the angels proper ways to speak. Him wanting my body wasn't something that appealed to me very much.

"Why do people always just want me for my body?" I asked, unable to stop myself. I'll be damned if I wouldn't get a little entertainment out of it considering the way my day started.

"This is not the time for humor Graham. This is a matter of life or death. More importantly, Serenity's. She has gone and done the unthinkable."

Of course he had my full attention the minute he mentioned her name. No matter how I felt about her, or her choices as far as Ryan was concerned, I would always look out for her and want her safe. Just what had she gone and gotten herself into?

"What happened?"

"She's gone to Ryan and despite his attempts at changing her mind she made her decision."

Her decision. I knew what this meant and none of it was good. If Gabriel is here now than it's painfully obvious that her choice had not been to side with him and Heaven. If she chose Ryan and in turn Lucifer, it meant that it had everything to do with what had happened earlier between us.

I caused this.

"How do I help?"

"Be my vessel one final time. Let me right my wrong here. Let me get to her, use the bond between the two of you and save her life before she is lost to both of us forever."

"How do you plan on doing that?"

"The bond between the two of you is stronger than anything both made of darkness and light. It is the only thing that can save her right now. I know I haven't been honest with you in the past but this time, I need you and I need to save her before it's too late. Please help me right my wrongs."

"Of course I'll help you, but before we get this show on the road, I need you to answer me one thing."

"Time is really of the essence here Graham. We only have a few hours left."

"Then I figure you better answer my question so we can get moving."

"Fine." he stated, his tone obviously exhausted and in no mood to argue with me. "What would you like to know?"

"Why do you think this is your fault?"

"I do not think it is my fault, I know it is and if Lucifer is allowed to go through with this, I will spend the rest of my existence paying for it. I handed her over to him. All because I let him get into my mind and manipulate me. All of this is happening because of me."

"Not only because of you. I played a giant sized part in it too. So what do you need me to do?"

"Go back to your dorm room. Once there, we will join together and I will proceed. I only hope that I'm not too late."

I wasn't entirely sure how I knew it but he vanished then, out of my head off to god knows where. Standing up from the table and making my way in the direction of my dorm room I thought about everything he said.

He is taking the blame for everything despite the fact that he had been a witness to what was probably the single event that threw her over the edge.

Gabriel isn't the only one that needed to make things right.

I couldn't let it all happen this way. After spending the night with her, hearing her tell me what she was facing in the future I knew with every fiber of my being that I couldn't let her go through with this. This is not what she was meant to do. She is meant for so much more and if I died trying, I was going to make her see it.

I just had too.

CHAPTER THIRTY THREE

Serenity

This is happening way too fast.

What felt like only minutes since I told Ryan to call on Lucifer had actually been hours. The sun is still visible on the horizon but lower in comparison to where it had been earlier that day with Graham. We were no longer on the campus, instead having been transported to Green Haven, my old home town.

I hadn't been back to Green Haven in three years and even then it had only been to gather up what remained of my stuff and successfully bring it to where my mother now called home, a larger city almost three hours away. Why Lucifer had chosen this place is beyond me but given what was about to take place, it wasn't as if beggars could be choosers. If he wanted me to die here then I would.

I haven't seen Ryan since he'd taken off before I'd been moved. Something didn't feel right about it. Is he alright? Did Lucifer chang his plan yet again and Ryan had already been taken from me? I thought of asking the demon that moved me but given that his focus the last time I'd seen him had been solely on making sure I was unable to escape, I doubt he'd be willing to give me the answers I desperately needed.

Green Haven Memorial Park. That is where I am now, rope wrapped around my body and knotted at my wrists. I spent many a night in this park, content with just bringing out a blanket, laying on it and looking up at the stars. Sometimes Graham had been with me, other times Emma when she came down to visit but mostly it had just been me. I preferred it that way. It was the one real time I could be alone and think about my future.

The girl who heard voices still had a life to live and a future that she had to plan even though there had been times where any type of future seemed pointless. I wasn't proud of those dark moments in my past given what I knew my future held but I had them none the less. Life couldn't be painful if you weren't around to feel it.

Even with the sun going down, casting shadows over the park it still looked pretty much the same as when I spent time here. The only difference seemed to be the children play area, complete with slides and swings. That wasn't something the town wanted to invest in back when I lived here. Even though I couldn't exactly enjoy it from my vantage point, I was happy they'd finally done it. Where the park had felt so lonely before, it was now filled with life.

"I can't believe they've done this to you."

Looking up at the sound of the voice I saw Ryan, standing just a few feet back from me, the expression on his face grave. I sighed in relief at the sight of him. I could handle being tied up to the tree while preparations were made, as long as I knew he was alright.

"When I imagined being kinky for the first time, this was definitely not what I had in mind." I said lightly, smiling just a little, sensing the distress he felt and wanting to make light of it.

"Not funny. You do not know how badly I want to release you right now."

"Then what's stopping you?"

"He's controlling me. If I make any attempt to do anything that isn't according to plan, he has the ability to destroy me right where I stand."

Moving closer to me until he was standing directly above me, he knelt down until his knees were digging deeply into the dirt below. He reached out and ran his fingers across my cheeks, pain evident in his eyes. I didn't have to be a mind reader to know he is tortured seeing me this way. I only wished I could take it away but in choosing this, I had given up my ability to. We were stuck.

"He won't keep you tied up forever, though knowing him he's going to find the marks that these leave," he stopped fingering the ropes around my wrists. "beautiful."

"He likes torture marks. Of course he does. I sure know how to pick them don't I?" I said with an awkward laugh.

Having him here, as close as he is to me was hard enough. I couldn't allow myself to focus on it or I wasn't sure I'd be able to make it through without falling apart. I knew what the end result is going to be and would do everything in my power to put off thinking about it as long as possible.

"How can you make jokes at a time like this? You shouldn't even be here. This is not your destiny. This is my punishment."

"I'm tied to a tree with no foreseeable way out, what would you rather I do? Break down and cry? I can't do that Ryan. I made the choice and I've got to live with it. For however long I have left."

"You shouldn't have to. I should have gotten you out of this. I wasted so much time. I should have just told you everything the moment I felt the shift."

"Maybe so, but you still told me and that's all that matters. What do you mean this is your punishment?"

The sadness in his eyes is like daggers being shoved into my heart. I hated seeing him this way. In telling me everything he had and allowing me the chance to reach out to the one person who might be able to help us, he had sacrificed everything. Life as he knew it is over now, if his words were any indication. He betrayed Lucifer. I doubted anyone lived once that happened.

"He isn't making me do all of this so that I can take over for him when the time comes or to stand by his side. He is doing this because in falling in love with you, his choice for a bride I betrayed him in the worst way possible and he wants revenge."

"By letting us be married, even if it is demonic in nature? Seems like a weird type of revenge."

"The wedding is not the revenge Serenity. He is giving me the one thing that I would want as a human with you before the real act of his revenge kicks in."

"Which is you killing me?"

He nodded slowly, his eyes instantly lowering away from mine. As he moved I caught what looked like the coloring in his eyes changing, becoming more dark.

"What's happening to your eyes?"

"He's forcing my demon side through. He's been trying for the last hour or so but now I am unable to deflect it. He wants to turn me so that when the time comes, I can do what needs to be done. Then he'll allow me to be human again in order to watch the result."

"He plans on torturing you." I said calmly, not allowing a trace of emotion to come through in my voice. Given the current state we were in, me sharing how much it upset me wouldn't help. I had to stay strong.

"Yes and there is not a damn thing I can do about it."

The air around us began to change then, going from a slight breeze which to me had been rather enjoyable to an overwhelming blast of heat. It didn't take either one of us long to figure out just what the change meant.

"Such a beautiful sight is this. Seeing two lovers torn apart by circumstance, come together to say their final goodbyes."

"Were the binds really necessary Father? She already agreed to see this through. You've branded her so that she cannot change her mind. Surely you realize you have won."

"They weren't needed, you are right but they amuse me. I see how much pain seeing her trapped this way causes you and it brings me immeasurable joy."

"Wow, you really are an asshole." I said, letting the words fall from my lips without much care about the punishment they may inspire.

Lucifer laughed and pointing his long bony finger at me, he looked to Ryan. "She really is the perfect choice. It's a pity that she won't be around much longer. She would definitely inspire hours of entertainment for me."

"You're here, you got to see how much this bothers me. What else could you possibly want?" Ryan asked in complete disregard for what he just heard.

"I came to inform you that it is time. You must come with me while Serenity is taken and prepared. It is time for a wedding."

Gabriel

When Graham made his way back to his room mere minutes after we'd spoken we had done as I said and joined right away. I made sure that he was aware of what would be happening now and after hearing his acceptance, I had completely taken over his being. It was now mine to do as I saw fit, something that given my earlier attitude was a gift I am not deserving of, yet I had.

Having gotten word from Michael as to where Lucifer was keeping Serenity and the demon, I prepared my vessel for transport and immediately put myself back where I had been only a few days before.

Lucifer had chosen Green Haven as the main focal point of his plan for a reason. It had been the place that not only had I inhabited when I'd taken Graham as my host many years before but it was also a place both close to Serenity and unknown to the man she is intending to marry. He had not known her during the period of life that she had lived here, which meant that if he did attempt to go against the master plan his execution would fail given his lack of knowledge.

If I wasn't so intent with making him pay for everything he had done, I could almost admire his choice. As it is though, I knew the area and given the information that had been passed on from Father to Michael, I now knew where this would be taking place.

There were only two churches in the small town of Green Haven. One hadn't been used in years, the other a mecca for the religious. The sad reality for humans though is that when worshiping in my father's name, a place is not needed. Father actually preferred the times at which he was one on one with the people that believed. It is in those times he could give them his full attention. Churches were made simply because humans let their egos become far too large for their bodies to contain.

The abandoned church seemed out of character for Lucifer to use as a home base given the religious overtones but given the way he had been ejected from Heaven, it did seem that my brother was coming full circle. What had ended for him that day when Father cast him out would begin in a place seemingly blessed by Heaven. The irony is not lost on me.

As I stood in front of the church, taking in the boarded up windows complete with the color of spray paint, I felt the wind change around me. This is indeed the place. I could feel his power as strongly as I could feel my own burning inside me.

Closing my eyes and focusing on the way Serenity had looked the very last time I'd seen her, I scanned the area for any trace of her. I felt her fear first, evident through the heat emanating off her body, her form coming to view completely as I locked on it.

She is alone in the room, sitting on a wooden pew in front of a mirror, her hands slowly running a brush through her hair. She is dressed all in black, the material of her clothing hugging each and every curve of her body. On top of her head, held in a knot was the veil and it is then that I realized just what was about to take place.

In saying yes to Lucifer's plan it is almost time for the wedding that would join the two of them together as one. It would be from there that Lucifer would cut her, draining her of her life force and consuming it into his own body. From there he would be at his most powerful.

I couldn't let that happen. I had to stop this now, and given that she is alone, now was my best shot. Focusing again on her, in her present form, I felt my body begin to dissipate until it formed again, this time directly behind her.

"Serenity."

Spinning around on her seat her eyes went large as she took me in standing before her. She would have no idea that I wasn't Graham, which is exactly the way I wanted it. While he may believe that he had been the cause of her choosing to join with Lucifer and live out that aspect of her destiny, he was not. It had been me.

"Graham, what are you doing here?"

"I can't let you do this."

"Oh really? So earlier when you told me I was stupid for caring about Ryan, not even bothering to hear me out, you weren't pushing me to do this very thing?"

Maybe appearing as Graham given the heated anger she now displayed hadn't been the best idea after all. While I believed that my actions had caused this in its entirety, maybe Graham had at least partially known what he was talking about.

"I was jealous. How the hell am I supposed to feel Ser? You pretty much told me you were in love with another man, a demon no less. Am I supposed to just hold you and say congratulations?"

Thank you. I whispered as I let Graham take control of his body again. I knew there was no way I would be able to do this on my own. If he really did believe himself to be the cause of this then no one could fix it but him.

"No, thank you. I needed to do this."

216

"You left me Graham. You let me believe for almost three years that kissing you had been wrong. That you didn't care about me the same way. Not once in that time did you reach out to tell me differently. Of course I fell in love with someone else. What was I expected to do? Wait for you when I didn't even have a clue?"

"No. But you weren't supposed to fall in love with a demon for Christ's sakes. Not when you can do so much better."

"Oh yeah, because you know, I've got a ton of guys lining up around the block to date me. A girl with the voices of the dead in her head, yeah I'm a real catch."

Graham moved closer to her then, in a move so fast, that being inside of him I had to take a moment to adjust to the rapid change. He pulled her up from her seat even though she fought against it and pushed her into his body before wrapping his arms around her, closing her in.

"It has nothing to do with the amount of guys interested in you Ser. You are a catch and as far as I can tell there are three people more than willing to prove that to you."

"Three people? What the hell are you talking about?" she questioned, her voice a muffle against his chest. Even as she questioned it I knew what Graham would tell her. That not only is there Ryan and him but me as well.

"In his own way, Gabriel loves you. He's wanted nothing more in the last twenty years then to protect you from this very thing. Then there's me. I think I've already told you how I feel but if you want to hear more than fine I'll tell you."

" I was awake in Emma's bed last night after you passed out in my arms. I got to feel the way it felt having you pressed up against me and the way your heartbeat seemed to slow to a crawl while you slept, probably the most peacefully you have in years. If I didn't love you before that moment I damn sure did then."

Her body relaxed against his and I felt the temperature in the room begin to shift. No longer was it filled with heat and anger. She was allowing her body to relax with his words and I knew I'd made the right choice in giving him the control. We might be able to fix this after all.

"Why are you telling me this now? You see the way I'm dressed, you see the result of the choices I've made. Why come

217

here and tell me this?" she asked, lifting her head just slightly away from his chest, a lone tear slowly making its way down her cheek.

"Because if I let you go through with this, I will never forgive myself and neither will Gabriel. Serenity, you don't need to do this. You can come with us now, we can leave here and never look back."

"I know you think that it's that easy Graham but it's not. I made my choice and I'm going to see it through and nothing you say will change it. I'm sorry."

She began to pull away from his body and I could see the finality written all over her face through his eyes. As hard as I fought to save her, I couldn't do so if she first didn't want to be saved. I had thought that in coming here, I would find her wanting to be freed from the choice she'd made but what I am baring witness to instead is the complete opposite.

She accepted her destiny.

The door to the room opened and a shadow covered the room. Pulling Graham back, I took over control, ready for battle if called for. While I had needed him to try and get through to her, now that I knew it was impossible, there was no way I am going to let him suffer. Whatever happened now would fall on me, I would take the damage.

"What the hell are you doing here?" Ryan asked as he made his way into the room, his eyes scanning between the two of us, and landing on my arms that were still very much wrapped around her.

"He was just leaving."

"I am most definitely not leaving." I stated, fully prepared to stand my ground and fight the demon for her. While I understood that I couldn't make her change her mind it didn't mean that I couldn't use my powers to get her out of here against her will. Something I was fully prepared to do.

"What do you want Graham? Did you finally realize how stupid you are and want to make up for it?"

Given the heated glare the demon was leveling in my direction I knew that she had told him of what happened earlier in the day. While I liked the soul mate bond no more than the demon himself,

I understood what he was attempting to do here. Protect Serenity from what he perceived to be the real threat.

"This is not her destiny. Serenity says that you know that. If that is to be believed then you must help me get her out of here now."

His expression changed and he let his eyes scan over Graham's body again. Realizing too late what he was attempting to do, my attempt at blocking him from learning the truth failed. He now knew who I really was. While I waited for him to react, to give me up and turn on me, time seemed to stop. He lowered his defenses then and his eyes became clear, though this time not filled with anger but with sadness.

"While I would like nothing more than to do just that, I'm afraid it's completely impossible. Even if she wanted to leave, or I wanted you to take her far from here, she can do neither. Lucifer made sure of that, which means he was expecting you."

I understood what he was getting at. He knew exactly who I was and what I was trying to do and agreed with me, wanting nothing more than to free Serenity from the plan that would ultimately destroy her. He also knew my brother and knew that he had made sure of every conceivable problem before putting his plan into motion. He had been expecting me, or someone just like me and had warded against it.

"He bonded her with a brand didn't he?" I asked, wanting confirmation for what I truly believed is the issue we now faced.

"Yes, which as you know means she isn't going anywhere."

CHAPTER THIRTY FOUR

Serenity

If I hadn't seen it with my own eyes I might not have believed it even happened. Ryan and Graham seemed to be in agreement about what they wanted for me. They had both not minutes apart admitted their true feelings for me, both of them wanting to be the one my heart chose which should have put them at odds. It seemed to have had the opposite effect.

They may have both loved me but in doing so they wanted the best possible outcome for me and neither one of them believed this to be it. I didn't really believe it either but I had my own reasons for seeing this through. It is that reasoning that despite my growing fear kept me moving forward in what is increasingly becoming the most insane thing I've ever been a part of.

I knew insanity. I had seen more than enough of it when I'd been put into the center. I lived with varying degrees of it for two and a half years and it hadn't even made me bat an eyelash. This though, the ultimate fate that I had waiting for me beyond these doors, this was a level of insane even the center couldn't help.

Graham is gone now, Ryan going out of his way to make sure that he was able to get out safely and now the stage is set to begin with the first phase of Lucifer's plan.

The wedding.

According to Ryan in the few minutes we had alone so he could explain, this wedding is incredibly sacred to all that have taken part in it before us. It is something Lucifer himself held dear and would fight to make sure went off without a hitch.

I am about to take part in my first demonic wedding. I always imagined that if I ever found the right person for me and we progressed toward marriage, I'd be doing so donning the white gown, not the tight slip of a black dress that now gripped my body. The veil would be see through and made of white satin and I'd wear the world's biggest smile as I walked down the aisle toward the man that would keep my heart safe for the rest of our lives.

Instead, my veil is made of the same flimsy material as the dress and if I didn't focus completely where I was walking I'm doomed to fall flat on my face. Never having walked a day in heels before today, now I was expected to cross from one end of a church to the other in them, which served only to make my feet scream at me in agony.

There is a light at the end of the tunnel though because while the rest of it didn't match up to the visions I had as a child, there is one thing that did.

Marrying a man that would hold my heart until my very last breath. Ryan would be the keeper of my heart. My last breath may only be until the end of the day but I knew without question that Ryan is the one I wanted it to be with. It didn't matter if he is half demon, what matters is the light inside of him, that is even more present now than ever before. That is what made him the right choice. The only choice.

"It is time." the demon with the disfigured face said, motioning toward the doorway that would inevitably take me to where Ryan would be waiting.

As I moved my feet forward, careful with each step as I made it, the fear I felt earlier began to manifest itself. Chills began rolling through my body and the faintest of goose bumps broke out over my arms. While I couldn't see my legs I am sure the same effect is happening to them. This is really happening. I am really about to marry Ryan and then give my life up in an effort to save his.

I'm scared as hell. Well if anything really could be scared in hell. Maybe if I lived long enough I'd be able to ask Ryan. He'd know about that better than anyone.

The descent down the hall took less time than I expected. Soon the demon that escorted me opened a large wooden door and I was making my way through it. As I took in my surroundings I realized this was as close to hell on earth as I was ever going to see.

The only light in the room came from black candles, dozens of them placed strategically throughout the room manifesting just enough light to be able to see only directly in front of you but not bright enough that it called any extra attention. There were symbols on the walls, some I am able to recognize, like the

221

pentagram and then the others I'd never seen before. The walls were a deep red, the symbols blending in nicely all painted perfectly in black. Whoever had done the symbols had obviously taken great care as not one smudge seemed out of place.

There is a woman standing directly in the center of the room, Ryan to her right and Lucifer behind her on the left. Given my lack of knowledge in the wedding department I could only assume she is the equivalent of a priest and would be the person to marry us. If she's even a person at all.

Ryan, as he had before looked troubled yet beautiful standing there in the black tuxedo, his hands clasped firmly together in front of him his eyes locked on me. His eyes had been black since the moment in the park, now they seemed to be the color of clouds, clear white and glowing under the illumination from the candles. His hair which normally is more closely pressed to his head seemed to fall away from him now in a way I've never seen before but couldn't help but admire.

He truly is the most beautiful person in the room and once my eyes locked on his, I found myself unable to look anywhere else. I saw all I needed to see. I wanted to look at him this way forever. Seeing him as he really was for the first time in the short time I'd known him. He is here, he is as beautiful as always and he's safe.

I could do this. I would do this. For him.

In quick succession I found myself at the front of the room and was positioned by the woman to stand to the left of her, facing toward Ryan who followed suit, moving his body to face me.

"She truly is a sight for sore eyes Lucifer. You have done well with this one" the woman stated before turning back to face me. "I am Marishka, the high priestess and I will be joining you and Ryan today."

Breaking eye contact with her and choosing instead to put my focus back on Ryan, whose face gave away nothing, I just nodded my head in acknowledgment. I wasn't going to give them anything more then what was necessary. They didn't deserve it. I would be as emotionless in this moment as Lucifer himself.

"Shall we begin?"

"Yes Marishka, with these two time is definitely of the essence. The longing between them is undeniable."

I had no idea how he could know what I felt as I watched Ryan earlier but it seemed he did. Either way I wasn't going to react, that was what he would be expecting. I refused to be a victim to him. Just based on the reason this is happening at all, what he hoped to gain, I knew I am better and stronger than that.

The high priestess picked up the bell from the pulpit and tapped it with her fingernail causing it to shake and ring out. She began moving her hands around in the air and it was then I realized that she was drawing a pentagram, which meant it must be the go to symbol for the ceremony. Which explained the appearance of the ones surrounding us. I swallowed the huge lump growing in my throat and prepared myself for whatever came next.

"In Nomine Dei Nostri Satanas, Luciferi Excelsi. In the Name of Satan, Ruler of the Earth, True God, Almighty and Ineffable, Who hast created man to reflect in Thine own image and likeness, we invite the Forces of Hell to bestow their infernal power upon us. Come forth to greet us and confer dark blessings upon this couple who desire to become as one in the eyes of Lucifer."

Jesus, this is a lot worse than I thought. She was spouting off some form of incantation.

What had I been thinking saying yes to this?

All it took was one look across from me, locking eyes with the man about to become my husband and I am reminded exactly why I agreed. To be with him as long as we were able. I would say yes again in a heartbeat if given the choice over again.

Picking up the chalice that stood where the bell had been, she lifted it to her lips and drank, waiting only a split second before continuing on with what came next.

"I invoke thee, the four crown princes of hell. Satan from the East; Beelzebub from the North; Astaroth from the West, and Azazel from the South. We come together in the name of our Father and Lord Satan to join Ryan and Serenity together in marriage."

Again picking up the blade she used when tracing the pentagram in the air she began drawing a circle around Ryan and I, which sent shivers down my spine as she made her way around me. I wasn't sure I could maintain my composure much longer. This is really beginning to freak me out.

"Almighty Satan, look with favor upon your disciples Ryan and Serenity. Both have come here of their own free will. They come before you to ask your blessings as they set forth on this very day as husband and wife. We ask that you bless this union with lust and the pleasures of life, that their mutual affection and desire for one another continues strong and enduring."

"Do you Ryan desire of your own free will to take Serenity as your lawfully wedded wife, to love honor and respect; to become one as one in the eyes of Satan and before the powers of Hell?"

As the priestess turned to face him, I studied him. He seemed to be as uncomfortable with this as I am. Lifting his hands to his nose, the stress obviously getting to him, he looked up again and the pain in his eyes was evident.

"Yes, I do."

She turned to me then and repeated the same thing. This is where it began, the result of my decision. I had put myself here; there is no way I could back out now.

"I do."

Ryan reached his hand out then and motioned with it, fingering the ring he held. Slowly bringing my hand out in front of me, I watched intently as he slid the ring down the length of my finger until it reached its inevitable resting spot at the end of my hand. He handed me the other ring and I followed what he'd just done, my hand lingering a few extra seconds longer than his had as the ring rested on his finger.

No matter how strange this was, I couldn't take my eyes off the way the ring he wore looked. The way it seemed to belong there. Looking up and meeting his eyes, he smiled just slightly, as if he could hear exactly what I was thinking. I smiled back, before stepping back to my original spot, preparing myself again for what was to come.

"In the Name of Satan and before all of the Demons of Hell, I pronounce you Husband and Wife. May your union be powerful, strong and abundant with pleasure. HAIL SATAN!!"

I wasn't really in the mood to pay homage to the very man that was about to take my life from me but I played along anyway, following suit as all of the demons around me began chanting his name. How much longer am I going to have to pretend I really want all of this? When could I finally admit I had gotten in way over my head?

Before I could think more about what I had just been a part of the priestess began speaking again, this time in a language I couldn't make sense of. The more she spoke though, the more I found myself wanting to know exactly what it is she was saying.

"Ol sonuf vorsag goho Satan lonsh Calz od vors caosgo; sobra zol Ror i ta nazps od graa Ta malprg: Ds hol-q qaa nothoa zimz Od Commah ta nobloh zien od luciftian Oboleh a donasdogamatastos. O ohorela taba Ol nore od pasbs ol zonrensg Vaoan od tooat nonucafe gmicalzoma. Pilah Farzm znrza od surzas Adna od Gono de Satan, ds hom od Toh. Soba croodzi ipam ul vls Ipamis. Ds loholo vep nothoa poamal Od bogpa aai ta piap piamol Od vaoan. Zacare ca od zamran! Odo cicle qaa! Zorge! Zir noco! Hoath Satan bvfd lonsh londoh babage."

"I'm sorry." I interrupted. "What is that?"

Ryan stepped forward smiling the same as he had when I put the ring on his finger only minutes before.

"First Key in Enochian Serenity. It's tradition at weddings."

"Not any weddings I've been to."

"I bet." was his reply and if my ears weren't deceiving me, I heard a slight chuckle that he failed at holding back, which in turn helped me relax and return his smile.

"What does it mean?"

"I will take this one Ryan. Serenity my love, it is quite simple. Let me translate." the priestess said, a smile also evident on her lips. While I knew what Ryan and I had smiled about I was at a loss at what this woman found amusing.

"I reign over you, saith Satan/Lucifer In power exalted above the firmaments And over the earth; in whose hands The sun is as a sword And the moon as a thorough-thrusting fire: Who measure your garments In the midst of my vestures And trussed you together as the palms of my hands And brightened your vestments with infernal light. I made a law to govern my sons and daughters. I delivered truth and furnished to you The power of understanding. Moreover, ye lifted up your voices And swore obedience and faith to Satan/Lucifer Who liveth and triumpheth, whose beginning is not Nor end cannot be. Who shineth as a flame In the midst of your palace and reigns amongst you As the balance of righteousness and truth. Move therefore and show yourselves! Open the mysteries of your creation! Be friendly unto me! For I am the servant of the same! The true worshipper of Satan/Lucifer In glory and power exalted, Of the kingdom of the south."

"Oh…" Was all I could manage as she finished. While I still didn't understand any of it, at least I now knew what the language was.

"Go forth as one, keep each other strong in Satan as you now walk together on the Left Hand Path. May Satan grant you many blessings along the way. Ave Satanas!!

I watched as Ryan repeated her final words and I followed suit. Again I had no idea what they meant other than another way of worshipping the asshole that we were doing all of this for and this time I found myself not even wanting to know. I'd just play along with their stupid tradition.

At least in the end I'd have Ryan.

She picked up the bell again and repeating much the same motion as she'd done at first, she clicked her nails against it, causing it to ring out. With the final sound of the ring permeating through my head I was overcome with a feeling of finality. We were one step closer to the end. Gulping down the lump in my throat I took a chance and looked at Ryan.

While he may have never done this before he had to know what came next. I needed him to tell me, otherwise I wasn't sure I could go through with it. My fear was finally getting the better of me.

For the first time in my life, the end was in sight and there was nothing I could do about it.

CHAPTER THIRTY FIVE

Gabriel

Father is not pleased. When I begged to go to Earth one more time, determined to change her mind I hadn't expected to find what I had. I let him down again though this time, it is through nothing I did but what Serenity had done.

"It has been thousands of years since anyone, demon or angel has ever branded a human, forcing them to remain locked into their decision. Lucifer really has thought of everything."

Since I left Graham and come home this is the way the conversation had gone, though it almost seemed as if Michael is more upset about it then Father himself.

I understood Michael's disappointment given that I had underestimated our fallen brother even more than he had. He'd done a lot of things over the years that turned us away from him even more than we had been but this was by far the worst.

Lucifer, in an effort to achieve his goal had set the world and Heaven itself back to a time most of us wanted nothing more than to forget. He had enslaved Serenity, forcing her into a situation that even when she changed her mind and there was no doubt that she would do just that, she is unable to break free of it. She'd essentially become his slave and knowing Lucifer, I knew he would more than enjoy it.

"With her locked into the darkness it is only a matter of time before he releases hell on earth Gabriel. I know Father told us not to get involved anymore but I don't think I can do that."

"Nor can I brother but what can we do? She was adamant in her decision and even when she changes her mind Lucifer owns her. There really is nothing that the two of us alone can do."

Michael's face became pensive as he racked his brain much the way I had been doing since I heard the news. Searching for some way that we might be able to undo what Lucifer put in motion.

"I know what Father said and I know how we will be regarded for disobeying but I think it's been far too long since we spent time with our eldest brother."

"What did you have in mind?"

"There is no one that knows Lucifer better than we do. For centuries before he was cast out we learned everything there is to know about him inside and out. If we have any way of saving Serenity and changing her fate then we need to take it. All of us."

Michael is the strongest of the remaining archangels and if anyone stood a chance against Lucifer it's him but what he is proposing isn't going in alone. He wanted to take all of the brothers with him. He wanted to wage a full scale war against Hell.

"Do you really think Uriel and Raphael will agree to this? You know how they are about displeasing Father. They would rather feel the burn of the holy fire then go against him."

"Of course I know how they are but what other choice do we have? Not only do we have a demon that is doing everything he can to be redeemed in the eyes of our Father but we have one of Heaven's own down there, choosing this life because of Lucifer's manipulation of you. We can't just sit here and hope Father finds the answer."

As much as I wanted to disagree with him, I couldn't. Where I had originally hated the demon for the hold he had on Serenity and the way she trusted in him so easily, I couldn't deny that he had done everything in his power to try and change the fate she'd chosen. He had been the one to inform me of the branding bond and even helped me get out of the church undetected so that I could stand where I am now. He deserves to be redeemed. The only way that could happen though is for us to do what Michael was suggesting.

"Then go to Uriel and I will go to Raphael. Maybe between the two of us we can change their mindset. I only pray that it isn't too late."

Ryan

I'm a married man.

I'm pretty sure there isn't a man alive that finds they want to be married at twenty years old. There might be a few but I have yet to meet one. No, the twenties were a time to sow wild oats; get as drunk as possible and live life as if there were no tomorrow. Not preparing to witness a woman walking down the aisle toward them, her face a mask of the most frightening of fear.

Yet here I stood, surrounded by the highest order of demons, all a part of Lucifer's army, as well as a variety of other random ones, drinking various drinks of their choosing and living it up party style, a married man.

Serenity since the party started has been glued to my side, moving her body with mine with every step I made, even the involuntary ones. She's afraid for me to leave her because she knew the moment I did what it meant. As frightened as I know she is, her concern for my well-being won out. By keeping me with her she is keeping me safe. I couldn't help but enjoy it even though it was wrong.

"Can I ask you something?" she asked quietly, as we both stood looking out over the crowd. "About the ceremony."

"You can ask me anything Serenity. Especially now given what we just went through."

"The blade she used when she was tracing the pentagram and the circle around us, it seemed important, like almost sacred to her. What is it?"

Out of all of the questions I knew had to be swirling around in her brain, I was thankful to have such an easy one to answer. I wasn't sure how I would tackle what was to come between us later. There is no way to make even the most understanding of human beings understand it, so I couldn't imagine Serenity being any more accepting.

"It's called an athame and to her and Lucifer it is a very sacred blade."

"Does that mean that it's going to be the thing you use to kill me?"

"How can you say those words so easily? Have you really conditioned yourself to your fate already? Just thinking about it makes me sick and all I want to do is take your place."

She went silent and my heart broke for her. I hadn't meant to sound as hurtful as I did but I was not willing to accept this as our fate tonight. I couldn't even begin to imagine doing as Lucifer wanted and draining the life out of the beautiful and inherently sweet woman before me.

My wife. I did not want to kill my wife.

When after a few minutes of silence she still hadn't spoken, her eyes lowered, masking her pain, I chose to speak again.

"I know why you went through with this Serenity and no matter if I live through the night or for years after this, I will never forget the sacrifices you are making for me. I know it seems contrite but the day I realized you were exactly like me was the happiest day of my life. My destiny was to walk this world in darkness and never once experience what it feels like to be in love and you in such a short period of time changed all of that."

"I haven't accepted this.." she whispered her eyes scanning the room as she did, obviously still on high alert for any sign of Lucifer. "I want nothing more than to leave here but I know that I can't. I have to see it through, even if it doesn't end the way I hope it does."

"What do you mean? How do you hope that this plays out?"

"That you are redeemed and get to spend the rest of eternity either in Heaven or on Earth, with multiple happy lifetimes."

Her soul is the purest one I have ever seen, not because of the words she spoke but the way it shined. Not many knew it but souls had different colours for varying emotions and experiences and now, hers was shining a bright gold. The purest kind imaginable.

She really did believe in a brighter future for me even though I didn't and I wanted that to be a reality but I also knew that the havoc I created over my years on Earth, all of the damage I caused and left in my wake had not earned me favor. If Lucifer did not succeed in killing me tonight he would at the very least damn me to hell and honestly, I deserved to be there.

"That's a nice dream, I only wish it could become reality."

She turned into me and looking straight up, meeting my eyes she smiled the biggest and brightest smile I have ever seen, showing the faith she had in what she is about to tell me.

"It can become a reality Ryan. Don't you see it? The reason we connected so deeply so quickly wasn't because we were similar in our experiences although that did play its own very big part. It wasn't because you were so beautiful I couldn't help but focus on you whenever I'm near you. It is none of that. It is because of the light."

Now I'm confused. "What light?"

"The light that even now surrounds you. You can't see it?"

I shook my head. I had no idea what she was talking about but there is no doubt with the way she is reacting, that she saw it and believed in it strongly.

"It's there. Its faded yellow in colour but with each passing day we spend together it becomes brighter. I know you think that because you're half demon and have done horrible things that you can't be redeemed but through your love for me I believe that you can. It's the purest part of you."

Before I could respond, I saw the shadow appear over us and my breath caught in my throat. I didn't even have to turn around to know who would be standing there. The shadow alone was enough of an acknowledgement.

"Ryan." he spoke, the icy cold tone of his voice making my stomach churn. "Serenity. I hope you are enjoying the party in your honor."

"Y—Yes." Serenity stammered catching it and herself. "It's wonderful."

"I'm pleased you think so. Ryan, may I have a word?"

Nodding, I turned to where Serenity stood, her eyes again a mask of fear yet also filled with what I could only believe to be loathing of the man that stood before us.

"Ryan please don't go."

"Baby, I don't have a choice but I'll be fine. He just wants to talk which means we still have some time."

I kissed her lips gently before moving upwards and kissing her forehead. I knew what she thought was happening and I wanted to do everything in my power to make her feel secure that I would return before it was time.

"Do you trust me Serenity?"

"Yes.." she said, her voice breathless as she leaned her body into mine, her hands resting on my arms tightly, still unable to let me go.

"Then let me go and trust me when I tell you that I will figure a way out of this before it's too late. I will come back to you."

She released her hold on me and I walked away slowly, my heart breaking with each step that led me away from her, my mind still swimming with everything she told me about the light and the possibilities it might contain. Could it mean that there really is hope in this hopeless situation? Could Serenity and I really make it out of this alive?

Making my way over to where Lucifer stood and eyeing the wide smile on his face I felt my stomach drop again. If he was this happy then it meant that there wasn't much time left before the next phase of his plan was put into motion.

"What do you want to speak about Father?"

"Can you feel it Ryan, the pull of your heart to hers? Has it happened yet?"

What kind of stupid question is that and what did it have to do with anything? "Why bother asking questions you already know the answer to. It does not become you."

"As always you're correct but there is one thing I wanted to discuss with you."

"And that would be?"

"I wanted to pull you away from your most blushing bride to inform you that the time has come. Say your goodbyes now and meet me in the chapel. Oh and Ryan, do not dream of keeping me waiting or finding a way to escape because I assure you, I will not look kindly on either."

He walked away and I turned back to where Serenity stood, her eyes still locked on my form. Her concern for me is written all over her face, which now again is lowering itself to the floor. I knew I had to make my way back and do as Lucifer wanted because he'd been right when he said he wouldn't take lightly to tardiness.

I just didn't want to.

How am I supposed to go back to her and say goodbye when every part of me not being controlled by Lucifer wanted me to grab her, hold her and never let go?

CHAPTER THIRTY SIX

Serenity

There's this small flicker in time when you're looking down the barrel of a gun and instead of your life flashing before your eyes, it's all of the moments you missed out on. The things you didn't experience but secretly wish you had. The boy you liked but didn't ask out, the girl you wanted to be friends with but were too shy to speak to, a vacation to a faraway location that you never had the nerve to get on the plane for. They all flash by in sequence and once finished it leaves you feeling emptier then when it began because the reality is, you'll never get the chance to go back.

That's how I felt as Ryan led me into the chapel. The place where we had stood not two hours before and pledged to love one another until death parted us, which with my timetable would be in the next couple of hours unless a miracle took place. As dark as the ceremony had been I wanted to remember this place for the feeling that I'd gotten when I looked into Ryan's eyes as I said I do. Not for what he is about to do to me.

Ever since he told me that it was time, he held my hand and didn't let go. The nervousness and fear we were both experiencing is evident with the sweat pooled between our tightly entwined fingers. He led me along slowly, hopefully wanting more time just as I did. He told me that we needed to prepare ourselves to say goodbye but I just couldn't do it. Given that he had yet to mouth the words meant he didn't want to either. I held onto that, the realization that we were both experiencing the same thing as he led me even closer to my impending fate. It is the only thing keeping me going.

Lucifer stood where the priestess had earlier the smile on his face still covering his otherwise tightly put together features. I expected that in meeting him I would find him to be as dark as he is often portrayed in writings and movies, cold, both inside and out and a person that very rarely smiled. He actually smiled a lot more than most humans did, though that might be because he was getting his way.

Who didn't smile when they knew they were winning?

"Please say something Serenity. I know you said that you wouldn't say goodbye to me but with what's about to happen, I can't stand not hearing your voice."

"Now would be a good time for a miracle." I said, the only words I could manage as we finally reached our destination.

Laid out before us now, instead of the pulpit is a bed, or at least the bare makings of one. A mattress, complete with black sheet laid where the pulpit once stood, candles surrounding it. What looked to be two super-sized goblets laid to the left. I knew what it meant but I was unwilling to let my mind accept it.

When Ryan told me about taking my life force, I always imagined that it would be like air releasing from a balloon that was never tied shut. I just thought he would somehow reach inside of me and pull the force out as if it is some object buried inside but I knew better.

He is going to exsanguinate my body until there is little to no blood left within me to contain the force of what resided inside of me. In doing so he would release me of my heavenly destiny, taking the very best parts of me with it. Leaving only a shell behind.

The athame laid across the bare sheet, its dark wooden handle standing out from the rest of the decor, almost calling to me to acknowledge its presence. There would be only one use for it now and the realization made the bile rise quickly in my throat. Looking up at Ryan, searching his face though not exactly sure what I was searching for, I squeezed my hand in his which he quickly answered back with a squeeze of his own.

"Traditionally when such an event takes place, there is a more ceremonial feel to it but in this particular instance, I have chosen to do away with tradition and just get down to business. So Ryan, if you would, place your bride on the bed in the most desirable position for her."

If that had been his way of telling Ryan to lay me down so that I was most comfortable, well there is no position in creation that would make me feel comfort in this moment. He is going to be shit out of luck.

234

"Do you trust me?" His voice asked, coming through my mind clearly, reaching straight to my very soul.

"Yes of course."

"Then please do as he instructs."

Leading me up the small amount of stairs to where the mattress lay, he stopped, levelling me with a determined stare before lifting me up into his arms and bringing me slowly and carefully down on the bed.

"I always thought that when this happened for the first time, there wouldn't be an audience."

He smirked as he smoothed me out to the point where I could almost forget what was happening around us. I felt comfortable in his arms, safe even and I didn't want it to end. Even with the King of Hell only steps away watching.

"Trust me, if this was actually going to lead to where your mind imagines, there definitely would not be an audience. For a very long time."

As I gasped at his words, he smiled again pleased at the reaction I awarded him. Even with death on the horizon, nothing could tame the magnetism between us. The desire was there, right from the very start and even now could not be denied.

"How touching it is when the two of you even as you face your end can still smile at each other." Lucifer remarked, bringing the both of us out of our moment of brief privacy and back to the reality that was now laid out before us.

"I thought I would find a way out of this before it got this far but I can't Serenity. So you must trust me implicitly from this moment on. Never letting it waiver. Can you do that?"

"Yes but what exactly are you going to have to do first?"

Before he could answer me, Lucifer spoke again doing nothing for my fraying nerves. If Ryan could just tell me what to expect then when it happened, maybe I might be able to fight my way through it.

"Pick up the blade Ryan and do as you are instructed."

As if guided by a hand other than his own, Ryan did as he was told, sliding his way back from where he laid me and picking up the blade in his hands, running his fingers slowly up and down the dull end as if preparing himself mentally for what came next.

"I'm going to make two incisions on your body, one on each wrist, which is what the derrynaflan chalices are for. I am to collect your blood in them."

It all made sense as he walked me through what he was about to do. The chalices were there beside the bed to capture my blood. I could only imagine that Lucifer would then drink of it, taking all of my power within him before moving on to the final step.

My body shuddered as the impact of his words set in.

Ryan's eyes grew dark then and I knew that the demon side of him is about to take over. Soon all traces of the man I agreed to save in doing this would be gone and I would be left with the shell of the creature that lived inside of him.

Knowing that these might very well be the final minutes of my life and wanting to say everything before I am lost to him and the world forever, I spoke, praying that by the time I finished that he would still be there and have heard every word. I wasn't quite ready for how his demonic side would react to me.

I doubted that any wife ever was.

"Ryan, I know you don't want to do this and that you wanted something better for me but just know that if I had to do it all over again I would make the same choice because in the end it brought me even closer to you. I love you. Please do not let him win and break over this. I know where I'll go from here and I'm okay with it."

"If this works the way I intend sweet angel, you will not be going anywhere. I will not drain you completely. I would never have done that. I will leave you with just enough blood so that you can begin to heal. I can't offer much time to do so but I'm hoping to buy enough so that you can make it out of here safely and alive. Please trust and believe in that. I will not let you die, not while there is still breath in my lungs."

His words calmed me, focused me on a possible change in the plan, giving me hope that I might indeed be able to make it out.

I trusted him and I would do as he said, no matter what the end result would be. I would go to my death knowing I had chosen the right thing because in the end, I redeemed him.

What he is about to do for me only strengthened that. I only hoped that Heaven became aware of it in time to save him. If they did then this would not all be for nought. My death would really have meant something.

I felt the sharp pain as the weapon pierced my skin, travelling along my wrist as he moved slowly across. Sucking in a breath of air I called on every bit of strength I had left in me to make it through this. Before I knew it he had moved away from my body, positioning the chalice under my wrist as he went, moving on to the next one.

As the athame pierced my skin a second time the pain was unbearable. The deeper he slid the knife in and across, the more I screamed and wriggled my body in absolutely agony. The crystal colouring of his eyes broke through again as I screamed and the painful look that came over his face matched that of my own. He was hurting just as much as I am feeling it.

"We are almost there Serenity. I will place the second chalice and move back from you now. It will appear as if I am gone but I'm not. I will heal the wound as soon as it looks as though you've been drained. Please do not fight the urge to pass out. It will be the very thing that keeps you from dying."

True to his word he backed away from me and out of the corner of my eye I could see him, just on the precipice, doing exactly as he promised and standing near enough to stop the flow when it got to be too much. The pain had subsided and my body was now numb, the pressure on my eyelids becoming stronger with each passing second.

"I love you Ryan..." I said one last time before allowing myself to finally begin to succumb to the darkness that threatened to take me under. The last thing I saw as my eyes shut was Ryan moving with the blade not closer to me as I expected but further away, to something I couldn't make out.

As I blinked one final time, I saw Lucifer looking down on me, a smile of triumph on his face. Before I could react though, the world around me finally went dark.

Ryan

I wasn't sure how much Serenity was still aware of but as I wiped the blade with the end of the blanket, using my power, I closed her wound just enough to stop the consistent flow, just as I promised her I would before stepping back and bringing the chalices one by one to the small altar Lucifer had resurrected while we acted out the second portion of his plan.

I knew what was to come next. I had to drink of the chalices, letting the blood slowly make its way into my body mixing with my own, giving me infinite amounts of power but not before he made me watch her final moments which judging by the look on his face as he made his way over to her, he is going to enjoy immensely.

"She is just like a fairy tale Ryan. Beautifully at rest in the same way the princess was. It's a shame that rest will soon turn to death for her. I would have rather liked seeing how she would adapt to being a demon."

"Are you telling me that you not only want her power but to damn her to a life such as ours as well?"

Looking up at me he laughed. "Surely you do not believe the last twenty one years of your existence to be a complete damnation. I fondly remember you enjoying yourself on more than one occasion as you possessed someone."

He's right. There had been a time in my life not that long ago where possessing someone had been the ultimate thrill. It is not an image that I like remembering now, least of all fondly the way he described.

"You're right but she deserves better than that. Better than us."

"Well will wonders never cease, the demon really does have a soul after all."

"What is it that you told me not so long ago Father? That you would stand by enjoying my reaction to her death because you knew that I loved her? Well could it be that I don't have a soul the way you assume and that I am just a human in love?"

"The time for petty conversation had passed Ryan. Take the first chalice and drink, and make sure to not leave behind even one small drop. Every bit of her blood will have to be ingested in order for this to work."

As he barked orders, the demon inside of me complied and I did as he requested, moving quickly to where I'd let them rest, taking the first one in my hands steadily and bringing it to my lips.

Taking a small sip first, the taste of it making its way slowly down my throat, I felt the hunger within me rise and I lifted the chalice even higher in the air, taking more and more with each gulp, acquiring a taste for the sweet substance that would soon override my very own powers.

"''Its exquisite isn't it my son? The blood of an angel such as her. Such a shame you won't be around to benefit from its effects."

He is taunting me, knowing full well I am under no control of my own. I had to comply yet also couldn't deny that what he said is the truth. I drank blood before, another thing I wasn't the most proud of but nothing I had ever tasted had been as sweet as Serenity's blood as it began running through my veins. It is definitely a delicacy that I am becoming addicted to feasting on.

"Now drink of the second chalice and make it quick. Time is running out."

Following his orders again, this time moving more rapidly than before, I brought the blood to my lips, fully prepared or at least it would appear to again drain it dry. Except this time he had given me the loophole I'd been hoping for. This time he hadn't been as specific which meant I didn't have to drain it.

Drinking just long enough for it to appear as if the chalice was empty, I placed it back on the altar, sliding the athame from the table as swiftly as I could, sliding it into my pocket before Lucifer could tell that anything was amiss.

"Do you see the colour draining from her skin Ryan? With each passing second she becomes more pale. It won't be long now until her body begins to go into the beginning stages of rigor and her skin, her perfectly peach coloured skin will turn to grey. How the thought of that must make you feel."

As I made my way around him, turning my eyes away from the sight he wanted me to witness, and praying that I stopped her blood flow in time to secure that it wouldn't be her fate, I pulled the athame from my pocket. In one sharp and quick movement I slammed it into his body, causing him to stumble but only for a second before he turned his widened gaze on me.

"You stupid foolish boy." he choked out, before gripping the handle of the weapon and slowly pulling it out of his body, tossing it to the floor. "Did you not think I would have seen that coming and prepared myself against it?"

The stagger now gone, he lifted himself back up straight, the look of hatred so hot that it turned his naturally black eyes the very colour of the blood from the chalice. He moved towards me his hand outstretched and before I knew it, began yelling in Latin.

"Da da per cultellum Ryan!"

Bending down to where it had fallen and unable to stop myself, I lifted the athame from the floor and reaching back up to a standing position, passed it over to him. When his hand grasped it, yanking it from me, I saw my life or what is left of it, flash before my eyes.

He plunged the weapon into my chest, using his strength to push it all the way through me, blood immediately beginning to pour down the front of my shirt as it escaped from the now wide hole he created. Looking down and seeing it, the colour slowly staining my shirt, I realized that Serenity would never get to see the one thing her faith had afforded me.

She would never get to see me redeemed.

Falling to my knees, my hands with a mind of their own clutching at the spot where the knife still resided, it came to me that this is my ending. Knowing I had to die to ensure that she lived made the pain I was feeling lessen. She would carry on where I could not. She would live in the light and that would be my redemption.

As I pulled the knife from my chest, my body crumpled to the floor and before everything went black, I saw the most beautiful ray of light.

Serenity's light.

Gabriel

In the last two months I have gone against not only Fathers orders but that of Heaven itself more times than ever before. It had all been in the name of the light known as Serenity. While there were instances that I would never repeat should I ever have the chance to redo them, for the most part I would always do what I had done as it pertained to her. Not because of my feelings but because apart from all of that she is special.

One of a kind.

After securing my brothers cooperation, each of us agreeing to use our powers to block out our Father as much as possible, we began to plan what we would do upon our entry into Lucifer's grand design. I filled everyone in on where he was located, what the overall plan would be and just what we would be walking into. We were all aware of the risks but this is something that none of us could back away from.

It was time to come face to face with Lucifer again.

We spent centuries of time away from him, only interacting with his minions rather than the man himself. Each of us had a great deal of love for our brother, even going so far as to not give up on him even after he had been cast out. We'd always wanted a better resolution to the problems he and Father faced and we still had hope, even now that one day they would come together again. We wanted to believe the best of him, choosing to hold onto the belief that he was just misguided.

What is happening to Serenity now was not happening by the brother that we knew and remembered fondly. No, this is what became of him after he believed his entire family to have turned on him. If we could just tap into that then maybe we could save him as well as Ryan and Serenity from the fate that beheld them.

Before apparating to the run down church, Michael and I agreed to go to Graham and secure his help but when we arrived back to where he had once called home in Green Haven, we found the location abandoned. Focusing my mind on him, I scanned the college and the area in search of him, all of which had me coming up empty handed. Rather than let my concern for him take over, Michael made sure I focused back on what is most important.

Which led us to where we stood now.

All four brothers, standing side by side, angel blades at the ready, preparing ourselves for whatever possible scenario we might walk into the minute we walked through the chapel doors.

I could only hope that we weren't too late. Lucifer had taken precautions against us, as there were markings placed all around the church that were set to disallow us entrance, but it wasn't enough to stop us. Uriel, being an expert at getting into places that entities of our sort were normally forbidden from, dropped the magic easily and once he did, we executed our plan.

Michael and Raphael began to make quick work of the demons guarding the doors, using their blades fast and efficiently, obliterating our brothers' army so that no trace was left behind.

Once done, they turned to me, and motioned for me to move forward.

I am at the center of the plan. Without me and what I'm about to do, we might not make it out of here alive. I had to make sure that no matter how horrible the situation is for her when I entered, I stayed on task. There was only one chance at this which meant no time for mistakes.

I am the one that has to get Lucifer's attention. Distract him long enough for Uriel to wipe the brand from Serenity so that we could get her and the demon if he wasn't already too deep in, away from Lucifer and certain death.

Standing outside the chapel doors, I mentally prepared myself for what happened next.

"Does it strike anyone as poetic that Lucifer chose a church to do this in? I always knew there were parts of him that the darkness wouldn't change and it appears I was right." Michael stated as he situated himself in seclusion as I placed my hand on the handles of the large wooden door.

"He always did have a flair for the dramatic. This is no different then what he did in Heaven." Uriel stated, his face frozen in determination, not betraying one single feeling that he might be experiencing about this reunion we were all about to have.

"Are you all in position?" I whispered, scanning around me and noticing all three brothers, locked into their spots, their faces blank slates.

"Let the party begin." Raphael muttered quietly from his corner behind the right side door.

Pulling back the door with my hand, wide enough for me and the girth of my now glowing wings to make it all the way inside. The deeper I entered into the room the more I took in the devastation around me.

Lucifer is bending over Serenity, whose still body lay unmoving above a dark covered mattress, stains of blood visible on her pale arms. I swallowed the lump of bile in my throat as I realized that he had already drained her, making us possibly too late for her to be saved. Off to the right of her, I saw the demon, also lying in a pool of his own blood, a weapon hole visible in the clothing he wore, his once clear eyes vacant and cold, with only a little remaining spec of black within them. The remains of his demon self.

"You always were the smarter of us all Gabriel." Lucifer boasted as he moved forward, his expansive size calling my attention away from the cold bodies I witnessed around me. "How you managed to get past my warding spells is beyond me but I can't say I'm not happy that it happened. It's been far too long little brother."

"What you have done here Lucifer I cannot allow to continue. You have forsaken the very part of yourself that we as your brothers believed to still be intact. You must be punished."

"Look around you dear brother. You are already too late. The plan is a complete success. In a few short minutes I will possess the rotting carcass of my most trusted confidante and I will be completely unstoppable. It is of no consequence to me now that you believe me to be evil."

From the looks of the destruction around me I knew that there is no argument I could make. Between Serenity's cold and stiff body to that of the very demon that had most likely died trying to protect her, it did appear as if he had everything perfectly planned out. Except I knew different. He hadn't been planning on the arrival of his brothers.

"I will not allow you to take Ryan as your host and neither will the others."

For the first time in as long as I could remember, I witnessed a look of shock appear across my brothers face as his eyes grew wide and his lips grew tight.

"Others? Who has agreed to meet their demise along with you today?"

From behind me I heard my brothers move from their hiding spots and felt the ground shake as they all moved forward at once as a unit. The human saying of there being strength in numbers was no more real than it is in this moment now. The most powerful of Heaven all in one room, ready to take down the fallen one.

"If it isn't a family reunion! How sweet. I'm actually amazed you could get that one there out of Heaven at all. That is quite the accomplishment Gabriel." He replied with a smirk as he pointed to Raphael.

"Where we may not see eye to eye on most things, in this regard we have and we are here together as one to stop you from going through with what you have planned to do."

"How do you propose to do that Gabriel? As I said, the stage has been set. Even though I am wounded, I still hold more than enough power to take you all down."

I heard the smash before I saw it, as the bottle flew up and over my own head and landed squarely at Lucifer's feet, breaking with a crash into hundreds of small shards, the liquid from inside pouring out all around him.

Before he had time to react, using every bit of the power I still had at my disposal, I shaped the fire ball in my hands, building it more with every movement my hands made until it was large enough to encompass his body the minute it impacted with the holy oil.

With one more burst of strength I pushed it at him, and backed away as it collided with its target. Within seconds Lucifer went up in flames, the fire ball mixing together with the oil and creating a wide open circle of fire around his now burning body.

"You are only postponing the inevitable young angel." he shouted through the fire, barely legible through the sound of the flames building and crackling as they grew higher around him.

"Maybe so but all I need is a brief interruption." I stated as I motioned with my hands for Uriel to begin his part of the plan.

I watched in awe as Uriel made his way to where Serenity lay and as her body began to glow under his power I knew that soon the branding would be gone and we would be able to remove her from this place. Even if I had arrived too late, at least when it is all said and done, I would have gotten her body back to where it belonged.

In Heaven.

"Saving the girl brother, how typical of you. Too bad I don't care about her; she was just a means to an end. An end that as you can see has most definitely been reached."

Before I could respond I heard Uriel's voice loud and clear in my mind.

"She is still alive, her power growing a little more each second. We must move her now before he learns of his mistake."

"Do it. Take her home brother."

Focusing my attention back on Lucifer I watched as Uriel lifted her into his arms and within seconds vanished out of the chapel. Releasing the breath I had been holding I smiled at back at him.

"Michael you must remove Ryan from here as well, before the oil burns out. There isn't much time left."

As both Michael and Raphael made their way over to where Ryan lay fallen and motionless, I watched as Lucifer began to step out and around the ball of fire that until now he had been trapped in.

"You will do nothing of the sort brother."

As he made his way toward me, I summoned my blade to my hand, preparing for the fight. How he walked out of the holy fire I didn't know but I couldn't let that little surprise stop me. As much as I didn't want to be the one to kill my brother I knew now that it might be only way to make it out of this thing alive. He was stronger than I'd originally given him credit for.

"Do you not see Gabriel? I can walk from the very fires of Heaven practically unscathed. I can surely deal with a silly little angel blade. You know Father only liked those as props anyway."

He reached out and grabbed me then, lifting me from the ground by my neck, squeezing harder the higher he lifted me up. Michael who had left Raphael to deal with the moving of the demon turned and shot a blast of lightning from his palms, hitting Lucifer in the back and releasing his hold. As I hit the ground, the blade clanging against the cement floor below me, I dived toward it, as my brother grabbed tightly on my leg in an attempt to stop me.

Kicking him off of me, I turned and sat up, and much the way Michael had just done, I grew the ball of energy in my hand and whipped it toward him, knocking him completely backwards until his body lay still.

"Now! Get Ryan out of here now!" I yelled, again turning my attention back to the angel blade, securing it in my grasp before bringing myself up by the wings to a standing position above Lucifer. As I stared down at him, realizing that at any moment he could get back up, I saw the weak look in his eyes and the blade markings protruding from his chest. While there was no sight of blood I knew that the marks had damaged him.

As Michael and Raphael vanished from sight, the body of the demon disappearing with them, I breathed one last sigh of relief before turning my attention back to the brother laying broken in front of me.

"Your plan was flawless my fallen brother. You really did think of everything. You just did the one thing we all expected you to do."

"What...is...that?" Lucifer said, struggling with each breath to get the words out. What looked to be his final ones.

"You thought you had it all figured out of course. You let your head get bigger than the rest of you. By the power of Heaven this is where your darkness ends. You will never see the light again."

I plunged my blade into him and watched as the black blood began slowly pouring from his chest, staining the ground below. As I watched him inhale his last breath, content that I was the one here for his final minutes, I whispered a prayer for the dying, placing one last kiss on his brow before bowing my head and apparating.

Darkness has a way of creeping up on you, making its presence known before you even realize it's happened. Taking over your life and turning you into the very thing you are sworn to destroy. That would happen no longer because it is a new day. The darkness would no longer have its chance to reign supreme.

Today the light had won.

EPILOGUE

Serenity

When you're born you come into the world with no real understanding of anything. Your only real goal is to just get through each day, learning and taking in as much as you can and making the best of the bad situations. There is no discussion of destiny or fate and for most people they never even realize that they have one. They go through life blindly, never giving the ultimate goal much thought.

I was one of those people. I grew up with a unique ability but instead of wanting to learn everything I could about it and use it to its full potential, I saw it as nothing more than a curse. A flaw in God's design. I had never given much thought to a master plan for me. What I would eventually mean to the world. I mean really, what could a girl that could speak to dead people and have back and forth conversations with random strangers in her mind really be capable of in the grand scheme of things?

I am capable of a lot as I came to find out as my life continued on. I spent the majority of my life pushing people away, fearful of getting close and my secret disability getting out, so I'd run them off before they chose to do it themselves. In the blink of an eye that seemed to change. I was no longer alone in my life. Not only did I have Emma, I had Ryan, Graham and Gabriel.

For the first time in my life I had a family and more than that, a real destiny.

Not a day will go by in the remainder of my life, which as I'm told from Michael (who just might be the most egocentric of all the angels I've met) will be a long and fulfilling one, where I won't be aware of what my true calling is and that I achieved it. According to our Father, God himself, my calling has not yet been achieved but honestly I think in this one way I may know more than him because I know it has.

Saving Ryan or at least realizing the light within him when I did, that is my true calling. Even Gabriel thinks so. We don't talk

247

as much as we used to and that's not okay with me. While I may not understand the whole concept of the beloved, I do know that for the time period I'd been aware of him in my life I enjoyed it. He had more than succeeded in his goal of keeping me safe, I only wish sometimes that he would see it that way too. Life just isn't as fun without an angel coming to me at all hours and singing in my ear.

He's still healing, Ryan that is. He's been in this coma for the last six months. Apparently according to Michael he really died in his effort to save me and for that I would forever be grateful. True to his word he left me with just enough of my life force in order for me to regenerate more. Within two weeks of so called bed rest by Gabriel and his brothers I was back at full working capacity. I hadn't died and in the process, his sacrifice had redeemed him.

Ryan's sacrifice only solidified what I knew all along. He may have been born of the darkness but he was destined for the light. His father had been the demon and in sleeping with the mortal woman the way he had, he set his son on a path that wasn't of his design. Ryan had never been given the choice. When Lucifer came to him as a child, the choice had been made for him. In deciding to save me, it turned things around. Ryan is finally making his choice and it is the right one. The one meant for him.

After spending practically every waking minute with him in an attempt to get him to wake up and come back to me, Michael finally kicked me out but only after promising that he would continue watching over heaven's newest addition. It is because I loved him that I did as the angel asked. I knew if the roles had been reversed, Ryan would have done the same thing for me and in knowing that, it made it easier to comply with what everyone wanted of me.

Everything seems to have worked out well, or as well it could have given the awful situation my choice had put us all in. The only thing that wasn't right is Graham. According to Gabriel who tried in multiple ways and times to reach out to him, he couldn't be found. In much the same way that Ryan had been able to block himself from Gabriel it's almost as if Graham is doing the same. His soul is unable to be found anywhere, something even the man himself tried and failed with. I'm worried about him, nearly as much as Gabriel but even with the power that I have, of which new facets appear practically daily, I'm at a loss as to what to do.

I will find him though. Even if it takes me the rest of my life I will do it. I owe him just as much as I owed Ryan and Gabriel. His part in trying to save me couldn't be ignored and I only wish he was here now so that I could tell him to his face.

I'm supposed to go back to Earth soon. Father wanted me to go back sooner but I fought against it. After everything we'd been through, a demonic marriage the least of it, there is no way I am leaving without Ryan. While he might not hold a special bond with me the way Gabriel and Graham both did, he did hold something more important and special.

He held my heart.

I wouldn't go anywhere in this life without him beside me. All he had to do was wake up and I'd show him exactly what I meant.

Experiencing what we did with Lucifer taught me so much. Things I will take with me forever, even when my human life is over. I have seen the dark side of life now, how one single event can change the course of forever and turn you into something you never believed you could be. It's what you do when you notice the change that matters.

Lucifer at one time loved Heaven, his father and family so much that he hadn't wanted to see it split apart when the world was created. He had somehow been able to see how humans would turn it dark and twisted so he had fought tooth and nail against it even though it meant going against the very family he loved to do so. When he was cast out, he could have easily come back had he just realized the right way of handling things. Instead he let the darkness build inside of him until he became someone completely unrecognizable, even to himself. It's sad really because the smile I witnessed on his face on the occasions I'd been around him is proof that the light still resided at least a little inside of him.

It may have been sick and twisted in its meaning but it didn't make it any less beautiful. Even though he had been about to kill me and essentially wipe the world out, I mourned his passing just as his brothers did. I believe it's a part of the greatest lesson of all that I've learned.

Goodness will always win over Evil, no matter how strongly that evil attempts to break you and more than that, you are never truly in darkness. Sometimes all you need to do is turn on the light.

Graham

I wanted nothing more than to get out of here. Days seemed to run into each other until I no longer knew what day of the week it was or even if months or years had passed. All I knew is that my bright idea to free Serenity had failed and now I'm the one that is being tortured in captivity.

For what felt like forever I have been chained to this chair alone with only the three times a day visit from him, complete with an overload of memories to keep me company. It happened the same way every day. He would come in, a grin on his face that was so evil it made my skin crawl and then he would proceed to show me moments of my life and the people that I loved until I screamed in agony.

Teasing me with a life I would no longer live. That is what he called it. He wanted to break me as he said that once I was broken, only then would I be viable. What I needed to be viable for he would never say but given how he seemed to enjoy torturing me I could only assume it isn't anything good.

Serenity died. At least that's what he told me before slamming me full of memories of her and I together, in every lifetime. I finally got to see the way she'd been with me in the two lifetimes I had her. Also the way I lived those lifetimes without her.

I learned that I killed Ryan's biological father, something that while I should have felt happy about I found myself torn up over. I have never hurt another living being before and seeing myself going through the motions and doing just that hurt on a level I've never experienced.

He informed me that I hadn't actually finished the man off. That it was impossible to do so given that he was in fact a demon who had only possessed the body of a human. There was a man out there in the world that had suffered at my hand though, possessed or not and living with that is not something I am sure I'm capable of doing.

I want out of here. I want to go home. I want someone to realize that I wasn't alright and find me but with the way time continued to move on it was becoming less and less likely that I'd ever be discovered.

I thought of my mother, hoping that wherever she had ended up she was alright though I wasn't naïve. I knew that given the way he destroyed my house after he'd captured me that the odds were that she was lost to me. A loss I refused to feel in an effort to retain at least some level of sanity. Hearing about Serenity's final moments had been bad enough, dumping my mom's inevitable end on top of it would really push me over the edge.

I often wondered where Gabriel is and if he's aware that I'm gone. If there is some form of a bond between host and angel and he'd eventually come for me, bringing the power of Heaven down on the man that spent hours happily torturing my soul. I wish I learned more about his abilities before this happened because maybe then I'd be able to hope for it and be able to hold out just a little bit longer.

There were times that the fear got the better of me so badly that I pleaded with my captor to just end it all. Death almost seemed like a better alternative then what I am left with now. He never did it of course but the urge is there, especially when he haunted me with the death of the only girl I'd ever loved and the mother that had loved me unconditionally, no matter how much pain I actually caused her.

I just never did. I couldn't give the smiling bastard the satisfaction of surrendering.

He is here again. Which means I'm about to be flooded with even more memories. As he places his hands on both sides of my head and pushes the memories my way at an alarming speed, I do the only thing I can do, I scream.

"Someone help me!"

To Be Continued...

251

Acknowledgements

I have to start by thanking my parents, Otto and Rowena, for being my biggest supporters' right from the very moment they brought me home from the hospital. This book would never had gotten to the point it is now if they hadn't been the parents they are. My love and admiration for you both knows no boundaries.

My four real life angels, who put up with a lot of frozen dinners, ordered out pizza and hearing 'just one second, I've gotta get this line down' more times than I can count while I was locked away writing. Thank you to all four of you for showing me real unconditional love.

To the mothers of special needs children all over the globe. As a parent of three myself, it does not go unnoticed. Your love, constant strength, support and determination in making the world a better place for your kids is inspiring. Continue fighting the good fight.

The two craziest guys I've ever known, Aaron & Joey. It is because of you both and your ever present and never ending support and love of me that the story is written at all. So yes guys, that means you can give yourselves a gigantic pat on the back. You most definitely deserve it.

My girls in the HMC. The countless hours spent with you possibly drooling (I'll never tell!) over photographs are ones I would gladly spend over again. Thank you for all of your support in me and this project. So Jennifer Ankles-Kendrick, Jill Fritz , Faith Walsh, Lisa Morris, Savanna Decker, Jenn Lierman, Linda Rabinowitz and Jennifer Hicks, this one's for you ladies. Much love to you all.

For everyone taking the chance and picking up this book. Thank you for spending your time with the story and characters that are so dear to my heart they're almost like family. I appreciate each and every one of you and the time you took out of your busy schedules more than you will ever know.

About The Author

Holding On To Heaven is Melyssa's big debut. What started as an almost obsessive fascination with Heaven, Hell, Angels and Demons slowly blossomed into a love story for the ages. It helps when the person writing the story is well known as a hopeless romantic. She is currently working on her sophomore effort titled No Surrender, the second story in the Love United Series.

Melyssa is a mother of four from Toronto, Ontario, Canada. Previously spending her daylight hours freelance editing for friends and family, she happily traded in her gig for a rewarding career writing young adult supernatural novels. The best part being that in working from home, she gets to spend more time with her own set of real life angels, and maybe a demon or two as well.

When she's not writing, you can find her buried under the covers with her portable DVD player, watching marathons of Supernatural and Veronica Mars. When those aren't available, she can be found curled up in a corner with her e-reader and a plethora of books, falling in love with characters written so well she deems them her book boyfriends and girlfriends. If you want to find her, check Facebook or Twitter as she may just have an addiction to both. If those don't work you can always keep up with her progress on her personal site where she more than loves blogging about her various endeavors.